Longman Study Texts

The Cone-Gatherers

Robin Jenkins

The Cone-Gatherers

edited by
Malcolm Fain

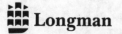 **Longman**

LONGMAN GROUP UK LIMITED
Longman House
Burnt Mill, Harlow, Essex CM20 2JE, England
and associated companies throughout the world.

First published by Macdonald, London 1955
This edition © Longman Group Limited 1987
Copyright © Robin Jenkins, 1955, 1980, 1987

ISBN 0 582 34323 2

Set in 10/12pt Baskerville, Linotron 202

Produced by Longman Group (F.E.) Limited
Printed in Hong Kong

Contents

Introduction

Robin Jenkins's fourth novel, *The Cone-Gatherers*, was first published in 1955 when rationing had just ended and memories of the Second World War were still vivid. Its republication in 1980, and again in this edition, brings it before a readership for whom the war is an experience confined to books, newsreels and conversations with parents or grandparents. It is also worth considering the major changes in general attitudes, legislation and social behaviour which have occurred in the last twenty-five years and which have a bearing on events in the novel, for example, more democratic behaviour on the part of the aristocracy and the growth of the trades unions. Set against this background, the achievement of the novel is considerable. It has lost none of its impact with the fading of memories of war, even though most of the characters in the novel are quite crucially affected by it. This timeless, universal appeal coupled with the power and beauty of the language in which it is expressed are largely responsible for the success and importance of the novel. However, you should not be put off by the book's fundamental seriousness. It is punctuated by flashes of delightful humour and has the essential quality of being 'a good read' – the tension, pace and skill of the story-telling make it quite simply 'un-put-down-able'.

This novel is often compared with a fable or parable, which are simply terms to describe short, apparently simple, stories which point a moral. In a fable human beings are often presented as animals, such as those of Aesop (Greek sixth century BC), La Fontaine (French seventeenth century), Kipling's *Just So Stories* (1902) and even George Orwell's *Animal Farm* (1945). The cone-gatherers themselves, Neil and Calum, work in such proximity to nature and animal- and bird-life that they almost take on animal characteristics – hence the use of the term 'fable'. The novel is also relatively short and the story line apparently simple. Two brothers,

Calum and Neil, are sent by a forester called Tulloch to work on a large Scottish estate, managed in her husband's absence by Lady Runcie-Campbell. Black, the estate forester, is on transfer as part of National Service, and Duror, the game-keeper, is therefore in charge. He resents the intrusion of the brothers into what he regards as his domain and he pursues a vendetta against them. The crux of the story is that Duror concentrates his hatred on Calum, the younger of the two brothers, who is a disfigured hunchback.

Fables or parables use a simple story line so that characters can represent particular qualities, thus giving the story two meanings. In George Orwell's *Animal Farm*, for example, the primary meaning is an animal story such as would appeal to children, whereas the secondary or below-the-surface meaning concerns a political satire on the Russian Revolution with other intermediary levels of meaning connected with human nature. Stories with secondary meanings are called allegories, from the Greek word *allegoria*, which literally means 'speaking otherwise'. The most famous allegory in English is Bunyan's *Pilgrim's Progress* (1678), which represents the average man's journey through the trials and difficulties of life on his way to heaven, or, in allegorical terms, Christian's journey from the City of Destruction through the Slough of Despond, the Valley of Humiliation, the Valley of the Shadow of Death, Doubting Castle and so on until he reaches the Celestial City. *The Cone-Gatherers* is not an allegory in this sense but it undoubtedly has allegorical overtones and uses symbols which have a deeper significance beyond their face value. It is not therefore surprising that *Pilgrim's Progress* is mentioned on page 117 and that Roderick's abortive 'pilgrimage' to meet the cone-gatherers is specifically compared to Christian's journey, making it all the more exciting and frightening to a sensitive fourteen-year-old with a highly developed imagination. We shall consider Jenkins's use of symbol and allusion again later in this introduction, but it is now time to investigate the three groups of characters on whom the action of the story depends:

the cone-gatherers, Neil and Calum; the Runcie-Campbells;
and Duror and his family.

Cone-gathering

The novel is set during the Second World War and, despite
the relative remoteness of the Scottish estate from the front
line, its peace is shattered by the flight of aeroplanes overhead
and the passage of warships along the loch. War is of course
a great destroyer and consumer of raw materials, of which
timber for use in construction work and munitions cases is one.
The forest is therefore soon to be felled, but in order to replace
it as soon as possible a period of grace has been allowed during
which the cones, principally spruce, larch and pine, can be
collected to be planted as seed. Such is the importance of the
task and the limited time available for it that in bad weather
conditions Neil is to be found searching fallen seed cases from
beech trees for fertile seed (page 134). It is hard, dangerous
work demanding physical agility and a good head for heights.
The cone-gatherers are exposed to all weathers and, were it
not for the fact that the brothers are quite content in each
other's company, would also be extremely lonely. They were
'the men most easily spared' from other forestry work at
Ardmore and, although the work is congenial to Calum, the
assignment is deeply resented by Neil (page 7). However, Neil
and Calum have little choice in where they work and have
some cause to be grateful to Mr Tulloch, their employer. War
prevents timber from being imported and the Runcie-
Campbells have graciously made their stock available. Thus
representatives from the two extremes of the social scale, the
poor and weak and the rich and powerful, are brought into
troublesome proximity by the fulfilment of basic needs in the
face of war.

Cone-gathering is therefore a force for creation and preser-
vation of an important part of the natural world and is set in

sharp contrast with Duror's responsibilities as gamekeeper, which largely concern the control – that is, the slaughter – of vermin in the form of rabbits and deer. The cones themselves become symbols of life and Calum is always seen carefully safeguarding his (pages 125 and 126) whereas Neil in a violent spasm of anger and frustration throws them from him (page 7). At the end of the novel, when life is extinguished, cones are 'spilt' as well as blood (page 181). The 'sweet resinous cones' (page 1) carry an aroma which lingers on the air, and this impresses even Sheila, who is not particularly well disposed towards the cone-gatherers, after her mother expels them from the beach hut. 'They've left a nice perfume behind them' (page 131). It is only in Duror's most warped and insane imagination that the fertile tree seed becomes confused with the slanderous lies he fabricates about Calum having exposed himself in the wood (page 158).

Calum and Neil

Calum and Neil are the title characters, the cone-gatherers of the story; they are also its protagonists. 'Protagonist' is another Greek word, meaning, literally, 'first combatant' or first actor in a play. Nowadays it is used to mean the principal actor or character and often the hero. Thus the story follows the daily lives of the brothers very closely and is normally told through their eyes. Occasionally the action centres on Duror or the Runcie-Campbells, as for example in Chapters 3 and 4, but even here the cone-gatherers are central to the action because they have become a focus for Duror's obsessive hatred and because they fall within Lady Runcie-Campbell's sphere of responsibility whilst they are working on the estate. Even when the reader is not actually with the brothers, he knows where they are and has a fairly good idea of what they are doing.

Although cone-gathering is presented as a virtuous occupation, it does not seem to affect both brothers equally, and it is significant in this context that Calum is 'a much faster gatherer than his brother' (pages 1–2) and also a much more skilful and confident climber (page 5). In fact the brothers are deliberately set in sharp contrast and this helps to explain why Duror conceives such a hatred of one, whilst evidently disliking them both. The brothers are different in physical appearance: Neil, the older one, is tall and thin and troubled by rheumatism; Calum is a disfigured hunchback but with a handsome face – 'the face and curls of Lord Byron' (page 100).

More important than physical appearance, their characters, thoughts, feelings and preoccupations are equally different. Although Calum is the younger brother, he is thirty-one years of age (page 7), and therefore his child-like attitude to animals and complete dependence upon Neil would seem to suggest that in worldly matters he is to some extent retarded. However, in anything to do with nature or the natural world, he is distinctly superior, partly because he has animal characteristics. 'Part-bird then, part-man, he suffered in the ineluctable [inescapable] predicament of necessary pain and death' (pages 2–3). In the tree-top 'he was as indigenous [native, and hence at home] as squirrel or bird' (page 1). 'He shared the suffering of the rabbit' (page 6) and, like the animals, seems to act according to instinct rather than reason. Although he cannot explain why trapped animals should be killed and put out of their misery, he knows it is right. Talk to him is 'bondage' (page 5) because it is a human means of communication, which animals manage very well without. It is also probably one of the reasons why he 'was always unhappy in the pub' (page 54), preferring the society of animals to that of humans. Calum's favourite leisure activity is carving animals out of wood and even Duror senses in this 'the kinship between the carver and the creature whose likeness he was carving' (page 12).

Calum's proximity to and identification with nature does, however, draw attention to 'the terrifying mystery, why creatures he loved should kill one another' (page 3). For all his instinctive sympathy with wild creatures Calum's love for them prevents him from understanding their habit, sometimes but not always necessary, of killing one another. Man is scarcely superior to animals in this respect, particularly in view of the events of the Second World War, and this urge to kill can never be entirely explained. Thus Duror's pursuit of Calum can also be only partly understood, and one of the haunting qualities of the novel is this element of mystery in what motivates Duror to such extreme actions.

The cone-gatherers are respected figures in the community; it is not only Mr Tulloch, the forester, who goes out of his way to help them, the inhabitants of the nearby village of Lendrick are friendly and respectful (page 10) and show them special favours when they go into the village for their Saturday visit (Chapter 7). Roderick defends them in the face of his mother's insensitive treatment of them; Mrs Morton is reluctant to believe Duror's lies about Calum; Doctor Matheson encourages Duror to take a more charitable attitude towards them – 'the wee chap's reputation in the village is pretty high' (page 101) – and even Sheila, who as a good baronet's daughter is very conscious of her own superiority, admires their climbing ability (page 3). All this helps to build the reader's sympathy for the two brothers, and this is a standard technique. It is almost a prerequisite for a tragic hero or heroine that other characters in the drama should admire and respect him or her. What distinguishes our own protagonists is of course their regard for one another, making them even more deserving of sympathy. The reader is impressed by their devotion to each other and by their capacity for self-sacrifice. Neil had sacrificed the chance of marriage to look after his brother, and the memory of it often 'turned his heart melancholy' (page 4); Calum in his turn helps his brother down from the tree and endures the bruises without complaint.

Neil is very different from his brother. Whereas Calum is humble and modest enough not to mind living in the cramped conditions of the improvised hut in the forest, Neil is bitter and jealous of the big house with fifty rooms. His desire to protect his brother from the inevitable slaughter of the deer during the drive contributes to his resentment of Lady Runcie-Campbell's ability to give them orders as if they were servants. It is one thing to be aware of social injustice but quite another to fight against it, and, in Neil's case, his sense of the world at war makes him more forceful than he would normally have been: 'it was necessary now for him to fight back against every injustice inflicted on him, and especially on his brother' (page 82). Although Neil's motives are admirable, his actions sometimes are not – for example, lying to Mr Tulloch about the rain penetrating their hut and in particular his refusal to help Roderick when he gets stuck in the tree. This desire for revenge, the wish to hurt others as a way of compensating for hurt suffered, although unchristian, is very human, and to do him justice, Neil does recognise his own faults and in a small way attempts to make up for them by offering to stay until the end of the week. Perhaps this is why he escapes Duror's gunshot; he is contaminated by the evil in the world, whereas his brother contrives to smile in the face of it, even in death.

Neil therefore is worldly-wise, and likes human society as is shown in the scenes in the pub and the café. He even manages to feel sympathy for his oppressor, Duror, in his great loneliness – 'he felt the sympathy he could never withhold when he saw any human being alone in a vast place, on a hillside say, or here in a wood' (page 54). He is aware of the vulnerability of human nature in a natural world which he sees as 'essentially hostile' (page 55), unlike his brother who, even when he becomes 'a deer hunted by remorseless men' (page 69) offers forgiveness to all. Ultimately, Neil is redeemed by his great love for his brother and his recognition of the saintly qualities which lie beneath that disfigured and contradictory exterior:

'And I ken too that though you're simple, you're better than any of them. Is to be always happy a crime? Is it daft never

to be angry or jealous or full of spite? You're better and
wiser than any of them.'

In the final terrible moments of the novel Neil tries to reach
his brother 'with moans and yelps of lamentation like an
animal' (page 181), reminding the reader for the last time of
Calum's affinity with the animal world and suggesting that we
are all animals beneath a human skin, particularly at times of
crisis.

The Runcie-Campbells

At the opposite end of the social hierarchy from the cone-
gatherers are the Runcie-Campbells, guardians of the social
order (and particularly of their elevated position within it) and
of the estate which provides the setting for the novel. Sir Colin
never actually appears as he is serving in the army, but what
he would say in the current situation, or what he has so often
said in the past are often quoted by his wife. Sir Colin is a
baronet, which, although the lowest hereditary title, nevertheless confers considerable wealth and power. Lady Runcie-
Campbell is the daughter of a judge and has inherited a
'passion for justice' (page 41). However, she also has an
'almost mystical sense of responsibility as a representative of
the ruling class' (page 41) and this is often in conflict with her
desire to lead a truly Christian life. It is highly ironic that she
should think nothing of turning the cone-gatherers out into the
storm with the repeated expression 'For God's sake' (page 129)
even if they were there without permission. Such conflicts in
Lady Runcie-Campbell's mind inevitably lead to indecision,
and it is at such times that she turns to Duror for advice, not
perceiving until it is too late that he is chronically sick and in
no position to advise anyone.

Perhaps more interesting than Lady Runcie-Campbell
herself are her two children, Roderick aged fourteen and Sheila

aged twelve. Like the cone-gatherers, they are sharply contrasted; Roderick is 'weak in body and complicated in mind' but his sister is 'beautiful, healthy, courageous, and as assured as any lady' (page 30). We first meet Roderick earnestly but totally unsuccessfully playing cricket with his uncle, Captain Forgan, a kindly figure with a humorous turn of phrase, who is on short leave from active service. As Roderick befriends the cone-gatherers, he is brought into greater conflict with his mother. Like Calum he tends to follow his instincts – for example, in wanting to offer the cone-gatherers a lift home or shelter from the storm – but in speaking out against the kind of social injustice which humiliates them he appears, to his mother at any rate, to be denying the assumed superiority of his class: 'The maintenance of society on a civilised basis depends upon us' (page 141). At the beginning of the novel the Runcie-Campbells appear all-powerful and impregnable in 'the mansion behind its private fence of giant silver firs' (page 1) but by the end only Sheila and the irrepressible Monty remain relatively unaffected by events. Roderick, inspired by the example of the cone-gatherers, climbs to the top of a tall tree and is unable to descend; Calum has to be sacrificed at the top of his tree before Roderick can be brought to safety.

Duror

The third group of characters consists of Duror, the game-keeper, his invalid wife, Peggy, and his mother-in-law Mrs Lochie. It is Duror who supplies the impetus for most of the events of the novel. Without him there would certainly have been a deer drive, but it is by no means certain that Lady Runcie-Campbell would have forced the cone-gatherers to participate and it would obviously have lacked its disturbing conclusion. In short, Duror is the most important character in the novel after the cone-gatherers themselves; he is also the most puzzling. Even his name is significant with its associations with the French *dur* and Latin *durus* meaning 'hard' and even closer relevance of the Scottish dialect word *dour* meaning 'severe' and 'stern', but also by extension 'obstinate' and 'sullen'. Duror has all of these characteristics, which are symbolised by his powerful and upright physique even after his breakdown at the end of the deer drive: 'Duror felt tired, weak, hungry, and sick; yet he would not lean against the gate. He stood erect, giving the impression of aloofly but impartially considering the question' (page 78). If Calum's physical disfigurement can conceal a healthy mind, the converse is true of Duror; a healthy body conceals a diseased mind. Duror's stiff and inflexible nature means that once overcome by obsession, no one can save him or divert him from it. To everyone except Effie Morton, the housekeeper, who is fond of him, and very occasionally Mrs Lochie, he is Duror. Even Lady Runcie-Campbell forgets that his Christian name is John (page 147).

Duror has already been in conflict with the cone-gatherers before the novel actually opens; the first mention of him on page 5 has him threatening the brothers with his gun: 'His rage had been quiet but intimidating.' Already there is a sense of suppressed anger and hatred presently under control beneath the gamekeeper's dour exterior but which might erupt at the least provocation. Duror is like the oak in the parable of the oak and the reed, immensely strong but prone to crack in a storm, unlike the reed, which bends and which consequently survives. In one sense Duror symbolises violent death because of his occupation, which is to destroy vermin; necessary and legitimate work, part of 'the ineluctable predicament of necessary pain and death' (pages 2–3) discussed earlier. Nature, both human and animal, is at war with itself, and, as Doctor Matheson shrewdly remarks, 'poor Duror for all his pretence of self-possession and invulnerability had been fighting his own war for years' (page 17). This is a reference to Duror's domestic quarrels with Mrs Lochie, his mother-in-law, who nurses Peggy, his invalid wife. When Neil asks his brother what is wrong with him and attributes his fear to the war, he says, ' "There seems to be death in the air" ' (page 4). He is not aware at the time that, although they are thousands of miles away from the battlefields of war, Duror has his gun trained on Calum and is indulging in the fantasy of doing away with what he sees as 'one of nature's freaks' (page 9).

As if to throw Duror into more obvious conflict with Calum's Christian attitudes, Duror is an atheist. He does not believe in the existence of God or in an afterlife, he does not even say grace. He has lost the old love and affection he once felt for his wife and, now repelled by her obesity, spends as little time with her as possible. He is nagged and tormented by Mrs Lochie, and when he tries to seek some comfort from the companionship of his dogs, they sense that something is seriously wrong and are not sure what he will do next. What is wrong is that Duror, alone of all the characters in the novel, has become the victim of an obsessive hatred of the cone-gatherers. Working in close proximity in the wood they are almost like three brothers, and as early as the end of the first chapter Duror contemplates a 'hideous but liberating fratricide' which will restore sole occupancy to him (page 13). Duror is in the grip of 'a force more powerful than common sense or pride. He could not name it, but it dragged him irresistibly down towards that hut.' The reader immediately speculates as to what this 'force' (page 12) can be. Some possibilities are evil, prejudice, intolerance, frustration, jealousy or madness. Duror's condition is variously described as sickness and insanity and the deterioration is rapid. Part of Robin Jenkins's skill in this novel is his lack of specificity about the precise nature of the evil or insanity which drives Duror to persecute the brothers. There is undoubtedly evil and hatred in the world, particularly obviously during a World War, and Duror becomes a symbol for much of it. In dramatic terms, however, Duror is still a figure of sympathy and his motives must be seen to be credible.

This is perhaps the most fascinating question raised by the

story; what is responsible for Duror's behaviour towards the cone-gatherers? The answer is to be found as much in Duror's own make-up as in any act by the cone-gatherers themselves; they are very much the innocent victims of his aggression. It is helpful to list the reasons given in the novel, some of which are suggested by Mr Tulloch when he asks himself the very similar question: 'Why had Duror taken a spite against Calum?' (page 159).

1   We are told that 'Since childhood Duror had been repelled by anything living that had an imperfection or deformity or lack' (page 10). Physically strong and well-built himself, he appears to be revolted by physical disfigurement or disability in others. He avoids his wife's company for the same reason. This in itself is an unnatural and mysterious affliction which Duror has borne patiently for twenty years and which is brought to a head by the arrival of the hunchback.

2   Duror is by nature and by occupation something of a loner and he has always in the past found comfort in his solitary patrols though the wood. However, 'his stronghold and sanctuary' has now been 'invaded and defiled; its cleansing and reviving virtues were gone' (page 9). In the past he has always been able to 'fortify his sanity and hope' (page 9) in the forest when his wife's self-pity and his mother-in-law's nagging have become unbearable. Now the presence of the cone-gatherers in *his wood* pushes him towards insanity and hopelessness. We learn from Doctor Matheson that Duror is a fastidious man, and it is therefore to some extent understandable that he should be revolted by the inevitable accumulation of refuse and ordure near the cone-gatherers' primitive hut.

3   Duror is a bitter and disappointed man. He has tried three times to get into the army but has been rejected every time because he is too old. He is nagged daily by his wife's mother who lives with him, and his wife became paralysed by disease three years after their marriage and has been bedridden ever

since. Unable to make love to his wife, he is therefore suffering to an extent from sexual frustration and Doctor Matheson offers three remedies for this. However, they are not taken up by Duror whom we have already seen rejecting Mrs Morton's friendship. It is a mistake, however, to attribute Duror's 'quiet inconceivable hatred' (page 52) entirely to his lack of sexual fulfilment. It certainly does not explain his particular vendetta against Calum, especially when Neil is in fact responsible for the decision not to help Roderick, and, as the very experienced Doctor Matheson says: 'with your physical strength and natural sanity, you could endure such symptoms for a hundred years' (page 103).

4 However, as we have seen, Duror does not retain his 'natural sanity'. Unable to share his lonely obsession with anyone, it feeds upon itself and gradually becomes more extreme and irrational until even the discovery of the broken doll in the hut is used as evidence of depravity. Mr Tulloch suggests that 'it could be that the dislike was simply inexplicable' (page 159), and there is undoubtedly an element of mystery about it, in spite of the motives listed above. It is after all impossible to give a fully adequate explanation of the existence of evil in the world, of why nation should war against nation or of why an individual should go mad.

The minor characters

In addition to these three main groups of characters, other individuals have lesser, but by no means insignificant, rôles to play. They often provide a welcome relief to the almost unbearable tension and conflict which exists between the main characters, whilst at the same time making perceptive and unprejudiced comments about them. Dr Matheson is the clearest example of this. From the privacy of his consulting rooms, and even in his car whilst offering Duror a lift, the doctor is in an excellent position to offer comment on Duror's psychological and physical state. A talkative but good-natured man, the doctor's only weakness is his taste for Scotch whisky and venison. Although his diagnosis of Duror's condition is accurate and although he tries hard to save him, in the end he is powerless to help, knowing that he cannot cure someone whose mind is diseased.

Erchie or Old Graham, the handyman, is another interesting if minor figure. At sixty-nine years of age he is none too pleased to be dragooned into taking part in the deer drive, particularly as he had been shot on a previous occasion. There is therefore no love lost between him and the baronet but he is devoted to young Roderick, hence his impassioned plea to Neil to save him. It is in the final chapter that Old Graham has his moment of glory; he is sent by Lady Runcie-Campbell to fetch the cone-gatherers to save young Roderick. Just as the Porter's scene provides comic relief before the revelation of King Duncan's murder in *Macbeth*, so Old Graham's grumbling, self-pitying and not particularly rapid 'gallop' has a similar effect here. The mission makes the old man feel more self-important than normal and some of his remarks touch on central themes in the novel whilst being highly amusing at the same time – for example, his parting shot to Neil, '"in a world that's at war we can't expect sanity from every man we meet in a wood." The next man he met in the wood was Duror' (page 174), and his comic exaggeration of class distinction, 'Young Roderick would be safely descended, revived on chicken broth, cossetted in pink cotton wool, and snug in a bed with six hot-water bottles' (page 170).

Mrs Effie Morton, the cook-housekeeper to the Runcie-Campbells, is a rather sketchily drawn character invariably at her baking with her hands covered with flour. She is important for the values she represents: attracted by Duror but loyal and charitable towards Peggy, fond of children and reluctant to believe ill of the cone-gatherers. She is a generous, warm-hearted woman and in rejecting her friendship, 'another way, clear, like a sunlit ride in a thick wood' (page 40), Duror takes the dark, embittered road towards inevitable self-destruction.

The Cone-Gatherers *as tragedy*

A tragedy is more than just a play or story with a fatal ending; as defined by Aristotle in his *Poetics* it concerns the change in fortune of the hero from happiness to misery, caused by some fatal flaw of character or error of judgement. The heroes and heroines were invariably persons of rank or influence and their falls were often predicted and invariably characterised by a sense of hopeless inevitability. Hope existed after the tragedy but not during it. Thus we can see that with the exception of the fact that the two central characters are fairly well down the social scale – a humble gamekeeper and an even more humble cone-gatherer – the novel has many of the elements of a conventional tragedy. The reader's attention is drawn to this parallel quite specifically, 'Duror's tragedy was now to be played in public: it must therefore have a crisis, and an end' (page 34) and 'the next step in the drama' (page 35).

Earlier in this introduction we referred to the novel's 'un-put-down-able' quality and attributed this largely to the skill of the storytelling. This is characterised by concentration on a small number of characters in one place during the events of only a few days. This closely follows the rules of Greek tragedy which required adherence to the concept of the so-called Unities of Action, Time and Space: a play should have one unified plot which takes place during twenty-four hours in one setting. These very strict rules were not taken seriously by playwrights in this country but it is interesting that the parallel should be so close in a novel, which would normally cover a broader canvas with many different characters and settings.

Some recurrent themes

The Cone-Gatherers can be seen to achieve its effects by unity of plot, time and setting in the manner of a classical tragedy, but it also achieves them by concentrating on several themes. These themes are sometimes called 'leitmotifs', which was a term coined to describe the musical themes in Wagner's operas. The most important ones are: class conflict in the social order; the nature and presence of evil; the human and the animal world; the influence of war; loneliness and perhaps, at the symbolic or allegorical level, Christian values as represented by the crucifixion of Jesus Christ.

Class conflict

In one sense the whole novel concerns the place of the individual in the social order, and references to social position are legion. The irony of the Lendrick policeman's remark to the cone-gatherers puts the point nicely: '"so it's hobnobbing with the gentry you are, is it?"' (page 85). The seclusion and lack of facilities in the cone-gatherers' hut and their subsequent eviction from the beach hut hardly suggest social familiarity! In many ways the deer drive presents a turning point in the novel, and it is hard to think of a more graphic representation of class distinction; the lower orders stumbling through the undergrowth against their will and at some personal danger in order to give the gentry the pleasure of the kill with the minimum of inconvenience. Lady Runcie-Campbell believes in the system of privilege, perhaps for her husband's sake, and tries to enforce it. She even tries to convince herself, one suspects unsuccessfully, that it is the Christian way. 'Surely an order of society in which so honourable a man as Duror knew his subordinate place and kept it without grievance or loss of dignity, must be not only healthy and wise, but also sanctioned by God?' (page 91). Roderick of course represents the next, and rather more democratic, generation and is taunted and scolded by his mother for his attempts to build bridges between the classes. Class distinction affects all walks of life; even in the war 'there were different medals for privates and officers, although they fought in the same battles' (page 180). Robin Jenkins leaves the reader to come to his own conclusions about class structure and is fairly even-handed in his treatment of the rich and the poor. Both have their advantages and disadvantages and neither group is particularly to be envied, for with privilege comes responsibility; elevation brings isolation. What is to be regretted is the great gulf between them, so movingly described at the end of Chapter 12: 'Between her [Lady Runcie-Campbell] and the sharny-toed brier-ragged heather-nibbling boys had been no kinship: just as now there was none, she in her many-roomed mansion perplexed by duty, they in a sunny hollow in her wood, throwing scraps of bread to her birds.'

The influence of war

The Runcie-Campbells' estate may be remote from the Western Front but the war is never far from the minds of the characters in the story. Calum does not really understand it, or indeed violence of any sort, so he tends to be protected from its worst excesses by his brother. Duror's inability to participate, to perform an active, manly and patriotic rôle, contributes to his sense of frustration. Unable to turn his hatred against the national enemy, he focuses it exclusively on the unfortunate hunchback. Neil's sense of injustice is sharpened, and even Lady Runcie-Campbell, by her enforced separation from her husband, has been made to experience to a very limited extent the plight of others less fortùnate than herself. '"This war with its dreadful separations has shown me at least what she [Peggy] has missed all these years. Something has come between us and the things we love, the things on which

our faith depends: flowers and dogs and trees and friends"'
(page 43). The war has therefore sharpened everyone's percep-
tions and has made them question their own values and beliefs.
From a historical point of view it is also a time when the
country becomes indebted to ordinary men and women on a
massive scale, something which causes the absent baronet
some disquiet. '"After this war, the lower orders are going
to be frightfully presumptuous"' (page 130).

The nature and presence of evil

At the allegorical level, evil is represented in the story by
Duror's obsessive hatred which leads to insanity, and it is this
which pollutes the wood, not the cone-gatherers. The first
sentence of the novel is important in describing the wood in
terms reminiscent of the Garden of Eden: 'It was a good tree
by the sea-loch, with many cones and much sunshine; it was
homely too, with rests among its topmost branches as comfortable as chairs' (page 1). This sentence is a good example of
the concentration of meaning and economy of style in the
writing, telling the reader in a very brief space that there is
warmth, light and water which produces a fertile soil and
productive environment but that the wood is also home for the
cone-gatherers. At the beginning of Chapter 5 they 'were safely
in another good tree by the lochside' (page 52), and the
repetition of 'good' together with the association of trees with
'the Bible remembered from childhood' (page 11) contrasts
clearly with the evil introduced by and associated with Duror
'as a presence like air, infecting everyone' (page 94). Effie
Morton is a clear example; on page 35 she is described as with
'no apprehensions of evil', whereas by page 115 she is warning
Roderick, '"Always be careful .... There's evil about."'
Roderick comes up against the presence of evil when he sees
Duror lurking beneath the cypresses outside the cone-
gatherers' hut. Once again there is a hint of a biblical parallel

in the description of the hut, which resembles the stable in which Christ was born: 'Roderick knew that the struggle between good and evil never rested: in the world, and in every human being, it went on. The war was an enormous example' (page 119). On this occasion the brooding figure of Duror represents a clear victory for the forces of evil as Roderick becomes more and more frightened, eventually crawling home in tears leaving his 'cake of friendship' (page 118) to be eaten by ants. However, this is not always the case. After Corney's good-natured apology for his joke which may unintentionally have given offence to the cone-gatherers (Chapter 9), everyone becomes genuinely more friendly towards one another and it is Duror who leaves in disappointment.

If Duror represents evil, it is not difficult to see virtue, and particularly Christian virtue, as represented by the cone-gatherers, and this is the conclusion that Roderick comes to as he waits outside the hut, from which light radiates like a halo. There are a number of references in the novel which liken Calum to Christ, and some have already been mentioned. Others are Lady Runcie-Campbell's recognition that 'the perfect exemplar of uniqueness was Christ Himself' (page 49) and Mr Tulloch's defence of the cone-gatherers to Lady Runcie-Campbell, 'I find no fault in them' (page 77), which closely resembles Pilate's judgement during the trial of Jesus Christ. The novel can therefore be read as an allegory of the life of Christ in which Calum is crucified to save mankind, (Roderick), thereby destroying the forces of evil, (Duror), and providing hope and salvation for the future.

The human and animal world

Mention has already been made of this particularly in the section on Calum, who is so closely in tune with animals that he is described as part-animal himself. It is, however, worth considering the relationship between the world of nature and the world of man as portrayed in the novel: the natural or animal world is often seen to be superior to that of man. At the close of Chapter 4, after Duror's interview with Lady Runcie-Campbell and brief exchange with Effie Morton, Duror leaves with his dogs, who 'so innocent of lust or hate or cunning, followed him like guardians' (page 51). Each of these unattractive qualities has been demonstrated by the humans in this chapter, and Duror's dogs are therefore nobler and able to protect their master. Even Sheila's pet dog Monty, who as a short-legged terrier is at the other end of the canine social scale, sees through Old Graham's exaggerated haste when he carries out Lady Runcie-Campbell's orders.

Loneliness

Solitariness and separation from society are themes which feature in several of Robin Jenkins's novels. It is a state which induces pity from outsiders but which does not necessarily induce self-pity on the part of the separated. Thus Neil feels sympathy for Duror but is himself resigned to his lonely, separated life spent mainly in his brother's company. Duror's loneliness largely accounts for the reader's sympathy for him, and when he comes in after his solitary vigil with his dogs, the image is of a terrified child suddenly separated from its mother (page 29). Notice too how loneliness is commonly seen as the forerunner of madness: '"It seems to me they've both lived in loneliness so long that they're strange in the mind"' (page 177).

The language of the novel

We have seen that much of the impact of the novel is achieved by the strength of the characterisation and the unity of theme. Attention has also been drawn to the skill of the storytelling, the pace of the drama and the management of suspense. The uncertainty of Duror's mental state and the anticipation of the outcome of the story, strongly hinted in the first chapter, carry the reader irresistibly forward. The language is for the most part typical of the 'fairy-tale' to which the story is compared on page 146, apparently simple and economical but concealing complexities of meaning below the surface.

Two aspects deserve particular attention and the first is the quality of the descriptive writing. There are countless examples of descriptive passages which impress by their diction – the selection of vocabulary and choice of detail. See, for example, the first paragraphs of Chapters 3 and 5.

The other aspect is imagery and its capacity to illuminate meaning. One image, that of the tree, is central enough to justify analysis in some detail. The tree is essentially a life-giving force, hence the collection of cones for seed. One particular elm tree outside Duror's house represents 'the burden of endurance' (page 18), and by touching it or even just looking at it̄he has kept in touch with the self-renewing forces of nature. This has some foundation in fact, since it is claimed by some people that by embracing the trunk of a large tree one can sense the rise of the sap through it. However, the tree image is also used to describe the destructive force of Duror's hatred, 'the overspreading tree of revulsion within him' (page 9), 'And is its fruit madness?' (page 26). Trees are also associated with God and hence religious faith because they reach towards heaven (page 11). Thus within one image we have the suggestion of the productive and destructive forces within nature; the problem of why animals and humans prey on each other. This might be solved by the Christian faith, if unlike Duror you are fortunate enough to believe in the sacrifice of Jesus Christ on the tree of the Cross.

Robin Jenkins – a literary and biographical note

Published fiction

Go Gaily Sings the Lark, Glasgow, Maclellan, 1951.

Happy for the Child, London, Lehmann, 1953.

The Thistle and the Grail, London, Macdonald, 1954; Paul Harris, Edinburgh, 1983.

The Cone-Gatherers, London, Macdonald, 1955; Paul Harris, Edinburgh, 1980; Taplinger, New York, 1981; Penguin, 1983.

Guests of War, London, Macdonald, 1956.

The Missionaries, London, Macdonald, 1957.

The Changeling, London, Macdonald, 1958.

Love Is a Fervent Fire, London, Macdonald, 1959.

Some Kind of Grace, London, Macdonald, 1960.

Dust on the Paw, London, Macdonald, and New York, Putnam, 1961.

The Tiger of Gold, London, Macdonald, 1962.

A Love of Innocence, London, Cape, 1963.

The Sardana Dancers, London, Cape, 1964.

A Very Scotch Affair, London, Gollancz, 1968.

The Holy Tree, London, Gollancz, 1969.

The Expatriates, London, Gollancz, 1971.

A Toast to the Lord, London, Gollancz, 1972.

A Far Cry from Bowmore and Other Stories, London, Gollancz, 1973.

A Figure of Fun, London, Gollancz, 1974.

A Would-Be Saint, London, Gollancz, 1978; New York, Taplinger, 1980.

Fergus Lamont, Edinburgh, Canongate 1979; New York, Taplinger, 1980.
The Awakening of George Darroch, Edinburgh, Paul Harris, 1985.

Robin Jenkins's bibliography is an impressive one but, if you have enjoyed *The Cone-Gatherers* and wish to read more Jenkins, you may not find it easy to trace his other novels. Apart from those reprinted by Paul Harris of Edinburgh in the Scottish Fiction Reprint Library, only the most recent novels remain in print. Paul Harris must be commended for recognising the universal qualities of *The Cone-Gatherers* and for bringing it before a wider readership.

Paul Harris has also reprinted *The Thistle and the Grail*, which is equally highly recommended. It charts the progress of the Drumsagart Thistle football team from bottom of the league for three seasons to finalists in the Scottish Junior Cup, but it is probably more remarkable for its picture of Scottish society than for its sporting descriptions. As in *The Cone-Gatherers*, Jenkins stresses the interdependence of all classes within society; in the final scene of the novel Rutherford, the club manager, meets Crutch, an old and poor cripple at the graveside of his old friend Tinto (they had both slipped away from the victory celebrations to share the good news with a loyal, but now departed, fan). When Crutch prefers to hobble home alone, it is not mere embarrassment which is the cause, rather 'that ultimate, irremediable loneliness of every human being, which ought to bring regret or sorrow but which also ought to bring profoundest sympathy'. There is more than an echo of Duror in this, particularly in Lady Runcie-Campbell's last sight of him as he goes off to commit suicide. Other hall-marks of Jenkins's style are there too, notably the deft handling of suspense, which is such a feature of *The Cone-Gatherers*. In one scene the men of Drumsagart cluster around a public telephone box in pouring rain to await news of an away game, an apt demonstration of the novelist's focus on the community rather than on the field of play.

Robin Jenkins was born in Cambuslang in the suburbs of Glasgow in 1912 and went to Hamilton Academy and Glasgow University. He took a degree in English and taught at Dunoon Grammar School for some years before continuing his career abroad at Ghazi College, Kabul (1957–59), the British Institute, Barcelona (1959–61) and the Gaya School, British North Borneo (now Sabah and part of Malaysia) (1963–68). During the Second World War Robin Jenkins worked in forestry, and this explains what might seem to the modern reader an unusual, if highly effective, setting for *The Cone-Gatherers*. His recent novel, *Fergus Lamont*, also set in Scotland, is a skilful attempt at that very difficult form, the first-person narrative. It provides a more fully developed analysis of what Jenkins sees as the self-destructive element in the Scottish character: '. . . a clash between two traditions in Scotland, that of love or learning and truth, and that of Calvinistic narrow-minded vindictiveness'. One example of this conflict had been enacted twenty-four years earlier in *The Cone-Gatherers*, more brutally but underlaid by the same class and religious differences.

Robin Jenkins describes himself as 'orthodox and traditional in my view of what the novel ought to do; that is, create credible characters, in situations that move and in some way illuminate . . . . I am naive enough to believe that the future of literature must lie in a more hopeful view of humanity.' This fundamentally serious attitude to the rôle of the novel is equally apparent in his novels which take place outside Scotland. These fall into two groups: *Some Kind of Grace*, *Dust on the Paw* and *The Tiger of Gold*, which take place in 'Nurania', a fictional version of Afghanistan, and *The Holy Tree*, *The Expatriates* and *A Figure of Fun* set in 'Kalamantan' or Malaya. In the 1960s, Robin Jenkins was struck by the irony of the fact that his most successful novel, *Dust on the Paw*, contained some forty characters but not one single Scot. Perhaps republications in the 1980s have done something to redress that anomaly.

Even in novels with tropical settings, characters are often beset by dilemmas similar to those of their Scottish counterparts. Harold Moffat in *Dust on the Paw* is torn between Christian ideals of racial equality and his own emotional prejudices, just as Lady Runcie-Campbell finds it difficult to reconcile what is required of her as a Christian with what is required of her as a baronet's wife. Even in *The Holly Tree*, which satirises the irrelevance of Western education in a primitive community, there is some similarity in the loneliness of Michael Eking and that of Duror. In Eking's case it is imposed by scholarly ambition, in Duror's by hatred but they both come to a violent end. Thus *The Cone-Gatherers* can be seen to explore many of the themes which have preoccupied Robin Jenkins throughout his writing career: the betrayal of innocence, the existence of evil, the class struggle, the problems of religious faith, the pity and the peril of loneliness and the salvation of love. In this way it is central to Robin Jenkins's work and prompts a deeper understanding of the other novels but it is equally able to stand alone, guaranteeing a rewarding experience to the thoughtful and sensitive reader.

The Cone-Gatherers

To
JOHN CURRIE
who gathered many cones

Chapter One

It was a good tree by the sea-loch, with many cones and much sunshine; it was homely too, with rests among its topmost branches as comfortable as chairs.

For hours the two men had worked in silence there, a hundred feet from the earth, closer, it seemed, to the blue sky round which they had watched the sun slip. Misted in the morning, the loch had gone through many shades of blue and now was mauve, like the low hills on its far side. Seals that had been playing tag in and out of the seaweed under the surface had disappeared round the point, like children gone home for tea. A destroyer had steamed seawards, with a sailor singing cheerfully. More sudden and swifter than hawks, and roaring louder than waterfalls, aeroplanes had shot down from the sky over the wood, whose autumnal colours they seemed to have copied for camouflage. In the silence that had followed gunshots had cracked far off in the wood.

From the tall larch could be glimpsed, across the various-tinted crowns of the trees, the chimneys of the mansion behind its private fence of giant silver firs. Neil, the elder of the brothers, had often paused, his hand stretched out from its ragged sleeve to pluck the sweet resinous cones, and gazed at the great house with a calm yet bitter intentness and antici-pation, as if, having put a spell on it, he was waiting for it to change. He never said what he expected or why he watched; nor did his brother ever ask.

For Calum the tree-top was interest enough; in it he was as indigenous as squirrel or bird. His black curly hair was speckled with orange needles; his torn jacket was stained green, as was his left knee visible through a hole rubbed in his trousers. Chaffinches fluttered round him, ignoring his brother; now and then one would alight on his head or shoulder. He kept chuckling to them, and his sunburnt face was alert and beautiful with trust. Yet he was a much faster gatherer than

1

his brother, and reached far out to where the brittle branches drooped and creaked under his weight. Neil would sometimes glance across to call out: 'Careful.' It was the only word spoken in the past two hours.

The time came when, thrilling as a pipe lament across the water, daylight announced it must go: there was a last blaze of light, an uncanny clarity, a splendour and puissance; and then the abdication began. Single stars appeared, glittering in a sky pale and austere. Dusk like a breathing drifted in among the trees and crept over the loch. Slowly the mottled yellow of the chestnuts, the bronze of beech, the saffron of birches, all the magnificent sombre harmonies of decay, became indistinguishable. Owls hooted. A fox barked.

It was past time to climb down and go home. The path to the earth was unfamiliar; in the dark it might be dangerous. Once safely down, they would have to find their way like ghosts to their hut in the heart of the wood. Yet Neil did not give the word to go down. It was not zeal to fill the bags that made him linger, for he had given up gathering. He just sat, motionless and silent; and his brother, accustomed to these trances, waited in sympathy: he was sure that even at midnight he could climb down any tree, and help Neil to climb down too. He did not know what Neil was thinking, and never asked; even if told he would not understand. It was enough that they were together.

For about half an hour they sat there, no longer working. The scent of the tree seemed to strengthen with the darkness, until Calum fancied he was resting in the heart of an enormous flower. As he breathed in the fragrance, he stroked the branches, and to his gentle hands they were as soft as petals. More owls cried. Listening, as if he was an owl himself, he saw in imagination the birds huddled on branches far lower than this one on which he sat. He became an owl himself, he rose and fanned his wings, flew close to the ground, and then swooped, to rise again with vole or shrew squeaking in his talons. Part-bird then, part-man, he suffered in the ineluctable

predicament of necessary pain and death. The owl could not
be blamed; it lived according to its nature; but its victim must
be pitied. This was the terrifying mystery, why creatures he
loved should kill one another. He had been told that all over
the world in the war now being fought men, women, and children were being slaughtered in thousands; cities were being
burnt down. He could not understand it, and so he tried, with
success, to forget it.

'Well, we'd better make for down,' said Neil at last, with
a heavy sigh.

'I could sit up here all night, Neil,' his brother assured him
eagerly.

Neil was angry, though he did not raise his voice. 'Are you
a monkey to want to spend all your life in a tree?'

'No, Neil.'

'What would you eat up here? The cones?'

Calum laughed. 'I don't think so, Neil. They're not good.'

'Don't tell me you've tried them?'

This time Calum's laughter was a confession.

Neil would not see it as a joke.

'No wonder they come and stare up at you, as if you were
a monkey,' he said.

Calum knew he was referring to the boy and girl who lived
in the big house. They had only come once, and he had not
minded their admiration.

Neil was silent for nearly a minute.

'But why shouldn't we be called monkeys?' he muttered.
'Don't we spend most of our lives in trees? And don't we live
in a box fit for monkeys?'

Calum became sad: he liked their tiny hut.

'Yonder's a house with fifty rooms,' went on Neil, 'every one
of them three times the size of our hut, and nearly all of them
empty.'

'But we couldn't live in the big house, Neil.'

'Why couldn't we? We're human beings just like them. We
need space to live and breathe in.'

3

'We get lots of space in the trees, Neil, and on the hills.'

'Like birds and animals, you mean?'

'We're just simple folk, Neil. I want us just to be simple folk.'

Neil yielded to the appeal in his brother's voice, and also to the uselessness of complaint.

'I ken you do, Calum,' he said. 'And I ken too that, though you're simple, you're better than any of them. Is to be always happy a crime? Is it daft never to be angry or jealous or full of spite? You're better and wiser than any of them.'

Calum smiled, scarcely knowing what the words meant.

'But it wouldn't have hurt them to let us stay in the summer-house,' cried Neil, with another burst of passion, 'for all the time we'll be here. No, we would soil it for them; and as soon as the war's over it's to be knocked down anyway. It just wouldn't do for us to be using what the grand folk once used.'

He paused, and sighed again.

'What's the matter with me these days, Calum?' he asked. 'Is it I'm getting too old? Am I frightened at something? It just comes over me. Sometimes I think it must be the war. There seems to be death in the air.'

Calum shivered: he knew and feared death.

'This wood,' said Neil, 'it's to be cut down in the spring.'

'I ken that,' whimpered Calum.

'There's no sense in being sorry for trees,' said his brother, 'when there are more men than trees being struck down. You can make use of a tree, but what use is a dead man? Trees can be replaced in time. Aren't we ourselves picking the cones for seed? Can you replace dead men?'

He knew that the answer was: yes, the dead men would be replaced. After a war the population of the world increased. But none would be replaced by him. To look after his brother, he had never got married, though once he had come very near it: that memory often revived to turn his heart melancholy.

'We'd better get down,' he muttered. 'You lead the way, Calum, as usual.'

'Sure, I'll lead the way, Neil.'

Delighted to be out of this bondage of talk, Calum set his bag of cones firmly round his shoulders, and with consummate confidence and grace began the descent through the inner night of the great tree. Not once, all the long way down, was he at a loss. He seemed to find holds by instinct, and patiently guided his brother's feet on to them. Alone, Neil would have been in trouble; he was as dependent on his brother as if he was blind; and Calum made no attempt to make his superiority as climber compensate for his inferiority as talker. Every time he caught his brother's foot and set it on a safe branch it was an act of love. Once, when Neil slid down quicker than he meant and stamped on Calum's fingers, the latter uttered no complaint but smiled in the dark and sucked the bruise.

It was different as soon as they were on the ground. Neil immediately strode out, and Calum, hurrying to keep close behind, often stumbled. Gone were the balance and sureness he had shown in the tree. If there was a hollow or a stone or a stick, he would trip over it. He never grumbled at such mishaps, but scrambled up at once, anxious only not to be a hindrance to his brother.

When they reached the beginning of the ride that divided a cluster of Norway spruces, Neil threw over his shoulder the usual warning: to leave the snares alone, whether there were rabbits in them half throttled or hungry or frantic; and Calum gave the usual sad guilty promise.

During their very first day in the wood they had got into trouble with the gamekeeper. Calum had released two rabbits from snares. Neil had been angry and had prophesied trouble. It had come next evening when Duror, the big keeper, had been waiting for them outside their hut. His rage had been quiet but intimidating. Neil had said little in reply, but had faced up to the gun raised once or twice to emphasise threats. Calum, demoralised as always by hatred, had cowered against the hut, hiding his face.

Duror had sworn that he would seize the first chance to

5

hound them out of the wood; they were in it, he said, sore against his wish. Neil therefore had made Calum swear by an oath which he didn't understand but which to Neil was the most sacred on earth: by their dead mother, he had to swear never again to interfere with the snares. He could not remember his mother, who had died soon after he was born.

Now this evening, as he trotted down the ride, he prayed by a bright star above that there would be no rabbits squealing in pain. If there were, he could not help them; he would have to rush past, tears in his eyes, fingers in his ears.

Several rabbits were caught, all dead except one; it pounded on the grass and made choking noises. Neil had passed it without noticing. Calum moaned in dismay at this dilemma of either displeasing his brother or forsaking a hurt creature. He remembered his solemn promise; he remembered too the cold hatred of the gamekeeper; he knew that the penalty for interfering might be expulsion from this wood where he loved to work; but above all he shared the suffering of the rabbit.

When he bent down to rescue it, he had not decided in terms of right and wrong, humanity and cruelty; he had merely yielded to instinct. Accordingly he was baffled when, with one hand firmly but tenderly gripping its ears, he felt with the other to find where the wire noose held it, and discovered that both front paws were not only caught but were also broken. If he freed it, it would not be able to run; it would have to push itself along on its belly, at the mercy of its many enemies. No creature on earth would help it; other rabbits would attack it because it was crippled.

As he knelt, sobbing in his quandary, the rabbit's squeals brought Neil rushing back.

'Are you daft right enough?' shouted Neil, dragging him to his feet. His voice, with its anger, sounded forlorn amidst the tall dark trees. 'Didn't you promise to leave them alone?'

'It's just one, Neil. Its legs are broken.'

'And what if they are? Are you such a child you're going to cry because a rabbit's legs are broken in a snare? Will you never grow up, Calum? You're a man of thirty-one, not a child of ten.'

'It's in pain, Neil.'

'Haven't I told you, hundreds of times, there's a war? Men and women and children too, at this very minute, are having their legs blown away and their faces burnt off them.'

Calum whimpered.

'I ken you don't like to hear about such things, Calum. Nobody does, but they are happening, and surely they're more to worry about than a rabbit.'

'Put it out of its pain, Neil.'

'Am I to kill it?' In spite of him, his question was a gibe.

Calum had not the subtlety to explain why death, dealt in pity, was preferable to suffering and loneliness and ultimately death from fox's teeth or keeper's boot.

'Why don't you kill it yourself?' persisted Neil.

'I couldn't, Neil.'

Not only love for his brother silenced Neil then: he knew that what Calum represented, pity so meek as to be paralysed by the suffering that provoked it, ought to be regretted perhaps, but never despised.

Nevertheless he remained thrawn.

'I don't like to do it any more than you do, Calum,' he said. 'It's not my nature to seek to hurt any creature alive.'

'I ken that fine, Neil.'

'We'll just have to leave it for the keeper. He'll kill it soon enough. It's not our business anyway. If he finds we've been interfering again he'll tell the lady on us and she'll have us sent out of the wood. Not that that would worry me much. I don't like it here as much as you seem to. I'd far rather be back at Ardmore, cutting the bracken or clearing the drains.'

'But Mr. Tulloch wants us to work here, Neil. He says the cones are needed.'

'The cones!' In anger Neil snatched from his bag a fistful of cones and flung them viciously into the trees. They rattled against the branches and fell to the ground. He hated these cones, which kept them prisoners in this wood just as the snare held the rabbit. Mr. Tulloch, the forester at Ardmore, where they worked, had asked them as the men most easily spared to take on this six or seven weeks' spell of gathering larch and pine and spruce cones. The seed was necessary, as the usual imports were cut off by the war. Lady Runcie-Campbell had given permission as a patriotic duty. She managed the estate in the absence of Sir Colin, who was in the army. If they offended her so that she insisted on their being removed, Mr. Tulloch, for all his kindness, might be so annoyed he would sack them altogether, and they would have to set out again in search of work, shelter, and friendliness. For five years they had been happy at Ardmore, planting trees on remote hills, living in their own cosy bothy, and bothering no-one.

Defeated by the cones, Neil took another handful and flung them, this time feebly.

'It's not the cones' fault,' he muttered. 'I'm daft to blame them. I don't ken whose fault it is. Come on, we'd better get to the hut.'

Calum clutched him.

'What about the rabbit, Neil?' he wailed.

Neil shook off the beseeching grasp.

'Never mind it,' he cried, as he strode away. 'Leave it. It'll die soon enough. Do you want to ruin us just because of a rabbit? Haven't I told you a thousand times there's a war in the world? Where will the likes of us ever find anybody as good and fair as Mr. Tulloch's been? He'll not want to sack us, but there are men above him who'll be furious if they hear we've offended the lady who belongs to this wood.'

While his brother was moving away shouting, Calum was kneeling by the rabbit. He had seen it done before: grip the ears firmly, stretch the neck, and strike with the side of the hand: so simple was death. But as he touched the long ears, and felt them warm and pulsating with a life not his own, he realised he could not do the rabbit this peculiar kindness; he must leave it to the callous hand or boot of the gamekeeper.

He rose and ran stumbling and whimpering after his brother.

Hidden among the spruces at the edge of the ride, near enough to catch the smell of larch off the cones and to be struck by some of those thrown, stood Duror the gamekeeper, in an icy sweat of hatred, with his gun aimed all the time at the feebleminded hunchback grovelling over the rabbit. To pull the trigger, requiring far less force than to break a rabbit's neck, and then to hear simultaneously the clean report of the gun and the last obscene squeal of the killed dwarf would have been for him, he thought, release too, from the noose of disgust and despair drawn, these past few days, so much tighter.

He had waited for over an hour there to see them pass. Every minute had been a purgatory of humiliation: it was as if he was in their service, forced to wait upon them as upon his masters. Yet he hated and despised them far more powerfully than ever he had liked and respected Sir Colin and Lady Runcie-Campbell. While waiting, he had imagined them in the darkness missing their footing in the tall tree and coming crashing down through the sea of branches to lie dead on the ground. So passionate had been his visualising of that scene, he seemed himself to be standing on the floor of a fantastic sea, with an owl and a herd of roe-deer flitting by quiet as fish, while the yellow ferns and bronzen brackens at his feet gleamed like seaweed, and the spruce trees swayed above him like submarine monsters.

He could have named, item by item, leaf and fruit and branch, the overspreading tree of revulsion in him; but he could not tell the force which made it grow, any more than he could have explained the life in himself, or in the dying rabbit, or in any of the trees about him.

This wood had always been his stronghold and sanctuary; there were many places secret to him where he had been able to fortify his sanity and hope. But now the wood was invaded and defiled; its cleansing and reviving virtues were gone. Into it had crept this hunchback, himself one of nature's freaks, whose abject acceptance of nature, like the whining prostrations of a heathen in front of an idol, had made acceptance no longer possible for Duror himself. He was humpbacked, with one shoulder higher than the other; he had no neck, and on the misshapen lump of his body sat a face so beautiful and guileless as to be a diabolical joke. He was now in the wood, protected, not to be driven out or shot at or trapped or trampled on; and with him was his brother, tall, thin, grey-haired, with an appearance of harsh meditation obviously false in a man who read no books and could only spell through a newspaper word by word. They had been brought into the wood: a greasy shed, hardly bigger than a rabbit-hutch, had been knocked together in a couple of hours, and set up in one of Duror's haunts, a clearing amongst cypresses, where, in early summer, hyacinths had bloomed in thousands. Already, after only a week, the ground round about was filthy with their refuse and ordure. They were to be allowed to pollute every tree in the wood except the silver firs near the big house.

Duror was alone in his obsession. No one else found their presence obnoxious; everybody accepted the forester's description of them as shy, honest, hard-working, respectable men. Lady Runcie-Campbell, without seeing them, judging by what she had been told, had said she was sorry for them, and she had issued an order to all her employees that they were to be treated with sympathy. Her fourteen-year-old son Roderick looked on them as heroes because they climbed into the very crests of the trees; even Miss Sheila, sophisticated beyond her twelve years, had gone to admire their climbing. It was true that the children of Lendrick, the village five miles away, where the brothers visited every Saturday, shouted names after them in the street; but they did not shout with the wholehearted cruelty that children could, and their elders, the shopping housewives and the dark-jerseyed fishermen outside the hotel, reproved them instantly and sharply.

Since childhood Duror had been repelled by anything living that had an imperfection or deformity or lack: a cat with three legs had roused pity in others, in him an ungovernable disgust. Other boys had stripped the wings off flies, he had been compelled to squash the desecrated remnants: often he had been struck for what was considered interference or conceited pity. Nobody had guessed he had been under a compulsion inexplicable then, and now in manhood, after the silent tribulation of the past twenty years, an accumulated horror, which the arrival of these cone-gatherers seemed at last about to let loose.

When he was sure they were too far in front to hear him he came out from the pines. For a minute or two he stood beside the rabbit, pitying it not for its terror or pain or nearness to death, but for having so recently been the victim of the hunchback's drivelling sorrow. Anyone seeing him there, so silent and intent, might have thought he was praying, or at any rate making some kind of preparation in his mind for the taking of life. When he did kneel, on one knee, to break the rabbit's neck with one blow, it was like an act of sacrifice, so swift, so efficient, and somehow so purposeful. When he arose his fist was clenched, and in the darkness he opened it and held it open, empty, for a few seconds.

He went along the ride, climbed the fence, and followed the path that led by the side of a stream to the hut. Weeping ashes there gleamed paler than the rushing water. Beside the great cedar of Lebanon, the vastest tree in the wood, he paused for a minute or two, listening to what ought to have been the silence of the night accentuated rather than blemished by such noises as water's gurgle, trees' rustle, and a far-off seagull's screaming. But at that high point on the path, beside this gigantic tree whose branches reached as high as the stars, and beyond into the darker haunted night of the Bible remembered from childhood, the light from the cone-gatherers' hut could be seen. Therefore what Duror heard was a roaring within him, as if that tree of hatred and revulsion was being tossed by a gale. He was shaken physically by that onslaught and had to rest against the cedar, with his gaze upon that small gleam in the clearing below on the other side of the burn. He knew it would be more sensible and more worthy of himself to turn and go home: here there could be only further degradation and shame, with possible disaster; but in him was a force more powerful than common sense or pride. He could not name it, but it dragged him irresistibly down towards that hut.

Amidst the bottommost branches of a cypress, curving out like hard green tusks, he stood and once again abandoned himself to that meaningless vigil.

The hut was lit by oil-lamp. He smelled paraffin as well as woodsmoke. He knew they picked up old cones to kindle the fire, and on Sunday they had worked for hours sawing up blown timber for firewood: they had been given permission to do so. The only window was not in the wall facing him, so that he could not see inside; but he had been in their hut so often, they were in his imagination so vividly, and he was so close every sound they made could be interpreted; therefore it was easy for him to picture them as they went about making their meal. They peeled their potatoes the night before, and left them in a pot of cold water. They did not wash before they started to cook or eat. They did not change their clothes. They had no table; an upturned box did instead, with a newspaper for a cloth; and each sat on his own bed. They seldom spoke. All evening they would be dumb, the taller brooding over a days-old paper, the dwarf carving some animal out of wood: at present he was making a squirrel. Seeing it half finished that afternoon, holding it shudderingly in his hands, Duror had against his will, against indeed the whole frenzied thrust of his being, sensed the kinship between the carver and the creature whose likeness he was carving. When complete, the squirrel would be not only recognisable, it would be almost alive. To Duror it had been the final defeat that such ability should be in a half-man, a freak, an imbecile. He had read that the Germans were putting idiots and cripples to death in gas chambers. Outwardly, as everybody expected, he condemned such barbarity; inwardly, thinking of idiocy and crippledness not as abstractions but as embodied in the crouchbacked cone-gatherer, he had profoundly approved.

At last he roused himself and moved away. Yet, though he was going home, he felt was leaving behind him in that hut something unresolved, which would never cease to torment him. It was almost as if there were not two brothers, but three; he himself was the third. Once he halted and looked back. His fists tightened on his gun. He saw himself returning, kicking open the door, shouting at them his disgust, and then blasting them both to everlasting perdition. He felt an icy hand on his brow as he imagined that hideous but liberating fratricide. Surely they would lie there unheeded under the cypresses. Surely they were of no more consequence than the frogs which in mating time, with the smaller male on his mate's back, crossed the public road and were crushed in their thousands under the wheels of the army trucks. Surely their deaths like the frogs' could not be called murder.

As he went on his way again to reach the road, he thought how incomprehensible and unjust it was that in Europe, in Africa, and in China, many tall, strong, healthy, brave, intelligent men were killing one another, while in that dirty little hut those two sub-humans lived in peace, as if under God's protection. He could not understand that, and he was sure nobody could.

Chapter Two

Duror had walked about a quarter of a mile along the road when a motor car, with masked headlights, overtook and passed him, hooting peevishly. It drew up a short way in front, with two apologetic and welcoming toots of its horn. When he came nearer he recognised it as Dr. Matheson's car, and wished he had waited in the wood a half-hour longer.

The old man grinned at him.

'Thought I recognised your stalwart figure, Duror,' he chuckled. 'You're not frightened, though, strolling along like that in the dark. Country folk these days ought to be supplied with luminous behinds. Been out on the prowl for poachers?'

'Yes, doctor.'

The doctor smacked his lips. 'Damned if I blame them,' he said, 'with meat as scarce as it is. You know I'm partial to a tender haunch of venison myself. Get in. I'll take you as far as the gate.'

Duror hesitated: he was in no mood to suffer the doctor's inquisitive inanities.

'Put your gun at the back. Hope it's not loaded. I hate the things. If you'd your dogs with you, damned if I would have stopped. Can't abide the brutes in a car. My wife used to have one, a brown spaniel; it would keep licking the back of my neck. She said it was only showing its affection. Queer affection, eh, to tickle me into the front of a bus. Get in, man. What are you waiting for?'

Duror climbed in, placing his gun beside the doctor's bag on the back seat.

Soon they were moving on again.

'Is Black still at Laggan?' asked the doctor.

'Aye.'

Black was the estate forester. He had been loaned by his mistress to the Timber Control Authorities, who were felling a wood at Laggan. He had had to accept the transfer as a national service. In the spring he would return to superintend the cutting down of his own wood.

The doctor was smiling slyly.

'So you're the monarch of the woods?' he asked.

Duror said nothing.

'A nice fellow, Tom Black,' said the doctor, 'but a shade too severe and upright for comfortable Christian intercourse. I understand he believes that every leaf that falls belongs to his master.'

'So it does.'

'In theory, certainly. But you and I know, as men of the world, that a wide breathing-space must be allowed between theory and practice; otherwise ordinary mortals like us would be suffocated.'

Duror made no comment.

'Shoot any deer these days?'

'Now and again.'

The doctor, sniffing hard, was not only in fancy relishing venison; he was also indicating that, in Black's absence, deer might safely be killed and shared with a friend.

'Wolf it all up at the big house, I suppose?'

'Most of it goes to hospitals.'

The doctor was surprised; he was even shocked; he whistled. 'Is that so? Take care of the sick, and let the healthy pine.' Uneasiness entered his laughter as Duror glanced at him. 'A joke, Duror,' he added, 'clean against all professional ethics. But all the same it is damned scunnersome, spam, spam, spam, at every meal. One of the pleasures I thought I could look forward to in my old age was that of the palate. They tell me even as a baby in my pram I chose the choicest cherry. Why not? Fine eating's a civilised pastime, and fine drinking too, of course. God, how scarce good whisky's become. It's not to be had for love nor money.'

'I'd have thought a man in your position, doctor, would have a better chance than most any folk.'

'Meaning what?' The doctor was involuntarily peevish: the

15

quest for whisky and palatable food was real, bitter, and ceaseless.

'Well, you carry life and death in your bag.'

'Ho,' grunted the old man.

'And you attend butchers and grocers and farmers and publicans.'

'Are you insinuating I use my professional position to extort favours from my patients?'

Duror smiled at that haughty senile indignation.

The doctor saw that indignation was a foolish tactic. He began to cackle.

'Damn your impudence, Duror,' he said. 'You're a sleekit one all right. You don't say much, but you think plenty. Well, however I fare in other directions, and I'm admitting nothing, I never see any venison. I've seen it on the hoof all right racing across the hillsides, but it's a hell of a long time since I smelled it on my plate. How's Peggy keeping these days?'

It was an astute question. Peggy was Duror's wife: for the past twenty years she had lain in bed and grown monstrously obese; her legs were paralysed.

Duror's voice was as stripped of emotion as a winter tree.

'As well as can be expected,' he said.

'Like myself, still eating more than's good for her, I suppose? Well, God help us, we've to take our pleasures where we can; and skimpy pleasures they are today. Your Peggy's had a raw deal from life, Duror.'

'Aye.'

The doctor, with professional interest, glanced aside at the lean, smooth, handsome, tight-lipped face. For all its composure he suspected a sort of fanaticism lurking in it. God knew how many inhibitions, repressions, and complexes were twisting and coiling there, like the snakes of damnation. God ought to know, for the human mind and its vicissitudes were more His business than a country doctor's. Physically Duror was as strong as a bear: a fastidious man too, not any whore would suffice. Well, there used in the palmy days before the war

to be a fine selection of maids to choose from in the big house.
There were few now: Mars had claimed his nymphs, and paid
them well.

'And Mrs. Lochie?'

'She never complains.'

The doctor was surprised by a sudden pang of pity for his
companion. In that conventional answer was concealed the
kind of stoicism and irony that he admired. Mrs. Lochie was
Duror's mother-in-law, who kept house for him and nursed his
wife. Behind his back she slandered him to everybody, even,
it was said, to passing pedlars. What she said to his face in
private could be conjectured. Yes, thought the doctor, poor
Duror for all his pretence of self-possession and invulnerability
had been fighting his own war for years: there must be deep
wounds, though they did not show; and there could not be
victory.

Unaccountably the doctor laughed: annoyed with himself,
he had to lie.

'Excuse me, Duror,' he said. 'Something old Maggie
McHugh of Fernbrae said. I've just been having a look at old
Rab's leg; he broke it three weeks ago taking a kick at a thrawn
cow. She's a coarse old tinker, yon one, but refreshing. Anyway,
I find her refreshing. What she was for doing to Hitler.' He
laughed again. 'Well, here we are at the manorial gates.'

He stopped the car, and Duror, picking up his gun, got out.

'Thanks, doctor,' he said, touching his cap.

'Don't mention it. This a Home Guard night?'

'No.'

'Well, if you should happen to shoot any deer, be sure to
tell it I was asking for it.'

'I'll do that, doctor.'

'And, Duror – ' The doctor, wishing out of compassion and
duty to say something helpful and comforting, found there was
nothing he could think of.

Duror waited.

'We've just got to make the best of things, Duror. I know

that's a bloody trite thing to say, and not much help. Good night.'

'Good night, doctor,' replied Duror, smiling, 'and thanks again for the lift.'

As he watched the car move away his smile faded: a profound bleakness took its place.

'Greedy old pig,' he murmured. 'So it's only venison you lack?'

At his usual easy assured pace he walked through the gateway. Passing the gate-house, he remembered young John Farquarson whom he had once seen lying outside it in his pram, and who now was soldiering in Africa. The envy that he felt, corrosive and agonising, was again reduced outwardly to a faint smile. Thus for the past twenty years he had disciplined himself to hide suffering. By everyone, except Mrs. Lochie, he was known as a man of restraint, reticence, and gravity; she alone had caught glimpses of him with the iron mask of determination off for a rest. This overwhelming aversion for the insignificant cone-gatherers had taken him unawares; with it had come the imbecile frenzy to drive them out of the wood, the even more imbecile hope that their expulsion would avert the crisis darkening in his mind, and consequently the feeling of dependence upon them. For a long time he had dreaded this loss of control, this pleasing of itself by his tormented mind; now it was happening.

A large elm tree stood outside his house. Many times, just by staring at it, in winter even, his mind had been soothed, his faith in his ability to endure to the end sustained. Here was a work of nature, living in the way ordained, resisting the buffets of tempests and repairing with its own silent strength the damage suffered: at all times simple, adequate, pre-eminently in its proper place. It had become a habit with him, leaving the house in the morning, returning to it at night, to touch the tree: not to caress it, or press it, or let his hand linger; just lightly to touch it, with no word spoken and no thought formed. Now the bond was broken. He could not bear to look at the tall tree: he was betraying it; he no longer was willing to share with it the burden of endurance.

Like a man to whom time was plentiful, and numerous resources still available, he set his gun neatly in the rack in the porch and hung his cap on its peg. It seemed to be that obvious and commonplace act, the hanging of the old tweed cap on brass peg in the oak panelling of the porch, that deranged his mind so that abruptly it became reluctant or even unable to accept that he was now at home, in his own house, amidst carpets, pictures, and furniture all familiar in themselves and in their tidiness. He saw all these, just as he heard the Scottish dance music from the living-room, and felt the warmth after the chilly evening; yet it was as if, after his long vigil under the cypress tree, he had at last entered the cone-gatherers' hut. Hesitating there in the hallway, he felt himself breaking apart: doomed and resigned he was in the house; still yearning after hope, he was in that miserable hut.

He allowed himself no such gestures as putting hand to brow or closing his eyes. Why should he no longer simulate pleasure at being home? What salvation was he seeking in this hut under the cypress?

'Is that you, John?' called his mother-in-law sharply from the living-room.

'Aye, it's me,' he answered, and went in.

She was seated knitting beside the wireless set. The door to Peggy's bedroom was wide open to let her too listen to the cheerful music.

Mrs. Lochie was a stout white-haired woman, with an expression of dour resoluteness that she wore always, whether peeling potatoes or feeding hens or as at present knitting a white bedjacket. It was her intimation that never would she allow her daughter's misfortune to conquer her, but that also never would she forgive whoever was responsible for that misfortune. Even in sleep her features did not relax, as if God too was a suspect, not to be trusted.

'You're late,' she said, as she rose and put down her knitting. It was an accusation. 'She's been anxious about you. I'll set out your tea.'

'Thanks,' he said, and stood still.

'Aren't you going in?' she asked. 'That's her shouting for you.' She came close to him and whispered. 'Do you think I don't ken what an effort it is for you?'

There was no pity in her question, only condemnation; and his very glance towards the bedroom where his wife, with plaintive giggles, kept calling his name proved her right.

'It's a pity, isn't it,' whispered Mrs. Lochie, with a smile, 'she doesn't die and leave you in peace?'

He did not deny her insinuation, nor did he try to explain to her that love itself perhaps could become paralysed.

'Take care, though,' she muttered, as she went away, 'you don't let her see it.'

With a shudder he walked over and stood in the doorway of the bedroom.

Peggy was propped up on pillows, and was busy chewing. The sweetness of her youth still haunting amidst the great wobbling masses of pallid fat that composed her face added to her grotesqueness a pathos that often had visitors bursting into unexpected tears. She loved children but they were terrified by her; she would for hours dandle a pillow as if it was a baby. Her hair was still wonderfully black and glossy, so that she insisted on wearing it down about her shoulders, bound with red ribbons. White though was her favourite colour. Her nightdresses, with lace at neck and sleeves, were always white and fresh and carefully ironed. When she had been well, in the first two years of their marriage, she had loved to race with him hand-in-hand over moor and field, through whins and briers, up knolls and hills to the clouds: any old skirt and jumper had done then.

Though not capable of conveying it well, either by word or expression, she was pleased and relieved to see him home. Her voice was squeaky with an inveterate petulance, although sometimes, disconcerting everybody who heard it, her old gay laughter could suddenly burst forth, followed by tears of wonder and regret.

He stood by the door.

'Am I to get a kiss?' she asked.

'I've still to wash, Peggy. I've been in the wood, handling rabbits.'

'I don't care. Amn't I a gamekeeper's wife? I used to like the smell of rabbits. I want a kiss.'

Her wheedling voice reminded him of the hunchback's. There wouldn't, he thought, be room in the hut for so large a bed. Here too everything was white and immaculate, whereas yonder everything was dull, soiled, and scummy. Yet he could see, almost as plainly as he saw his wife in heart-rending coquettish silly tears, the hunchback carving happily at his wooden squirrel.

'It was another fine afternoon,' he said.

'Fine for some folk,' she whimpered.

'Didn't you manage to get out into the garden?'

'You know it's too much for my mother to manage by herself. I just had to lie here and watch the tops of the trees.' Then her voice brightened. 'Do you know what I was thinking about, John?'

'No, Peggy.'

'I was thinking of a day at Fyneside long ago. It was autumn then too. I think autumn's the bonniest season. You put rowan berries in my hair.'

'The rowans are just about past,' he said.

'For me they're past forever,' she cried. 'I used to love the time when the berries were ripe and red.'

He saw the appeal in her streaming eyes, but he could not respond to it; once it had sent him away with his own eyes wet.

'Red as blood,' she sobbed.

Her mother called from the kitchen: 'Will I put out your tea, John?'

'In a minute, Mrs. Lochie,' he shouted back. 'I'd like to

wash first. I'll have to go, Peggy. I'll come in later, after I've had my tea.'

Upstairs in the bathroom he was again haunted by that feeling of being in the cone-gatherers' hut. Such amenities as toilet soap, a clean towel, and hot water, recalled the bareness and primitiveness there. The flushing of the cistern sent him crouching in the darkness of the cypress. When he stared into the mirror and saw his own face, he was for an instant confused, disappointed, and afraid. He could not say what he had expected or hoped to see.

The table was set for him in the little kitchen. The morning, newspaper, which usually arrived in the late afternoon, lay beside his heaped plate of eggs, bacon, and beans. Mrs. Lochie was glancing over the table to see that nothing was missing. He never grumbled if anything was, but she always took it as a trick lost.

He thanked her and sat down. He said no grace.

'Any news at six?' he asked, nodding in the direction of the wireless set.

They listened for a few moments to the sadness of 'The Rowan Tree' played in waltz time. He remembered, with a strange jarring of his mind, his wife's talk of rowans. For an instant he seemed to see a way clear: the tree within was illuminated to its darkest depths. Next moment darkness returned, deeper than ever.

'It was about Stalingrad,' she said.

'Has it fallen yet?'

'No. It's in the paper.'

He glanced at the headlines. 'Aye, so it is.'

Lately she had taken thus to lingering in the kitchen while he ate. Neither of them enjoyed it.

'Peggy's getting difficult,' she said.

It was spoken as if she'd been saving it up for months; yet she'd already said it that morning.

She laid her hand on her heart. 'I'm finding it beyond my strength to lift and lay her when you're not in.'

'There's Mrs. Hendry,' he murmured.

Mrs. Hendry was the wife of the gardener; she lived next door.

'She's not a young woman any longer, and she's never been strong. I don't like to ask her.'

'There's Mrs. Black.'

She was the wife of the forester, as devout as he.

'She's strong enough,' he said.

'But is she willing?'

'I would say so.' He thought she was jealous of Mrs. Black, who was very patient, kind, and capable; besides, Peggy liked her.

'Every time she's asked,' blurted out Mrs. Lochie, 'she comes running, but there's always a sermon to listen to. My lassie was never wicked. You should ken that, John Duror.'

He nodded.

She sniffled grimly. 'Peggy was not just happy herself,' she said. 'She made other folk happy too.'

He had been one of the other folk.

'What pleasure is it for me then,' she asked fiercely, 'to listen to Mary Black making out that what happened to Peggy was a punishment.'

'You've misunderstood her.'

'I ken it's your opinion, John, that I'm just a stupid stubborn old woman; but I'm still able to understand what the likes of Mary Black has to say to me. A punishment inflicted by God, she says. And when I ask her to explain what she means, what does she say then? She just shakes her head and smiles and says it's not for her, or for me, or for anybody, to question God or find fault with what He thinks fit to do. But I told her I'd question God to His very face; I'd ask Him what right had even He to punish the innocent.'

He had kept on eating. Not even this impiety was original. God had been defied, threatened, denounced, reviled, so many times before.

'Why argue with her?' he asked. 'You only vex yourself. Forby, she means well enough.'

She pretended to be astonished.

'How can she mean well enough,' she demanded, 'when she suggests your wife deserved a punishment worse than any given to bloodstained murderers.'

'Does she not also say there's to be a reward?'

'If the punishment is suffered gratefully?'

'Aye.'

'After death?'

He nodded.

'Do you believe that, John?'

'No.'

She glanced away from him. 'Even if I did,' she muttered, 'even if I had a guarantee in my hand this very minute, saying that Peggy in heaven would have it all made up to her, I still wouldn't be satisfied. It seems to me a shameful thing, to torment the living unjustly and think to remedy it by pampering the dead.'

'This pampering is supposed to last forever.'

She spat out disgust. 'I have my own religion,' she said proudly. 'I don't think the Lord's a wean, to be cruel one minute and all sugary kindness the next.'

He wanted the conversation to end, but he could not resist asking, not for the first time: 'Is there an explanation, in your religion?'

Once she had retorted by saying that not Peggy's sins were being punished, but his. It had seemed to him a subtle and convincing theology, but she had immediately retracted it: she would not insult God by crediting Him with less decency and intelligence than the creatures He had made.

'You ken,' she answered, still proudly, 'I have never found that explanation.'

Then they heard Peggy shouting. Instead of the dance music a man's solemn voice issued from the radio: he was talking about the war. Peggy wanted something more cheerful. Would her mother come and switch to another programme?

His mother-in-law hurried away. He went on with his meal, but suddenly he realised that he was envying the tranquillity and peace of mind in the cone-gatherers' hut. He paused with his fork at his mouth: that he should envy so misbegotten and godforsaken an imbecile as the hunchback was surely the ultimate horror, madness itself? To hate the hunchback, and therefore to wish to cleanse the wood of his defiling presence, was reasonable; but to wish to change places with him, to covet his hump, his deformed body, his idiot's mind, and his face with its hellish beauty, was, in fact, already to have begun the exchange. Was this why the hut fascinated him so much?

A comedian was now joking on the wireless. The studio audience howled with laughter. He heard Peggy joining in.

Mrs. Lochie returned to the kitchen.

'Did you remember to feed the dogs?' he asked.

'I remembered.'

'Thanks. I'm sorry I was late.'

'Are you really sorry, John? You're late nearly every night now. This is the third time this week.'

He thought, afterwards, he would go up the garden to the dogs' house. Silence and peace of mind were there too; he wished he could share them. The handsome wise-eyed animals would be eager to welcome him in, but he would not be able to enter. All he would succeed in doing would be to destroy their contentment: they would whine and lick his hands and sorrow because they could not help him.

'You think the world of those dogs,' she said accusingly.

'I need them for my work.'

'You talk to them oftener than you talk to your wife.'

It was true: the bond between him and the dogs still held.

'You sit up in that shed for hours with them,' she said. 'Fine I ken why. It's so that you don't have to sit with your wife.'

'I told Peggy I'd be in later.'

'For five minutes.'

He did not speak.

'It's what will happen to her when I'm gone that worries me,' she said. 'Who will toil after her as I have done? Nobody in this wide empty world.'

He let her enjoy her sobs.

'I can only hope she's taken before I am,' she went on, 'though she is thirty years younger. If I went it would be an institution for incurables for her. I'm not blind. I see the way things are shaping.'

Do you really, he thought, see this tree growing and spreading in my mind? And is its fruit madness?

'Was there any message for me from the big house?' he asked.

'Aye. It seems the mistress's brother has arrived for a day or two's leave before he goes overseas. She sounded excited. He's younger than she is. Anyway, she wants a deer hunt arranged for him tomorrow.'

'But I've got no men for a deer drive.'

'That's none of my business. You'd better explain it to her when you see her. She wants you to be early: half-past nine. Are you finished here? Have you had enough?'

'Aye, plenty, thanks.' He rose up.

She began to gather the plates and cutlery. Out of the window he caught sight of stars glittering above the dark tops of trees.

'You'll be going in to talk to Peggy?'

The comedian was still cracking jokes, and the laughter of his audience surged like waves. Peggy would tell him about the jokes he had missed.

'Later,' he said. 'I want to have a look at Prince's paw. He got a thorn in it yesterday.'

'I ken a heart with thorns in it.'

For a moment he almost gave way and shouted, with fists outstretched towards those stars, that in his heart and brain were thorns bitterer than those that bled the brow of Christ. Instead, he merely nodded.

'I'll not be long,' he murmured. 'I'm frightened the paw might fester.'

Quick though he had been in his restraint, she had caught another glimpse of his torment. It shocked her and yet it satisfied her too: she saw it, clear as the sun in the sky, as divine retribution.

'A heart can fester too, John,' she said, as he opened the door and went out.

Going up the path to visit the dogs, he loitered and tried to light his pipe. It was such a night as ought to have enticed his head and shoulders amongst the stars. But he could not even enjoy his pipe. When he had it at last lit, after striking eight matches, he found that as usual he had been expecting too much from it; it seemed merely a device to exercise his agitation rather than to allay it.

The air was keen with frost. Tomorrow would be another warm sunny day, ideal for a deer drive. An idea suddenly occurred to him, simple, obvious, likely to be approved by his mistress, yet to him a conscious surrender to evil. It would be easy for him to persuade Lady Runcie-Campbell to telephone Mr. Tulloch to ask for the services of his men as beaters for the drive. The forester would not dare refuse. The cone-gatherers would have to obey; and surely the dwarf, who slobbered over a rabbit's broken legs, must be driven by the sight of butchered deer into a drivelling obscenity. Lady Runcie-Campbell, in spite of her pity, would be disgusted. She would readily give him permission to dismiss them from the wood. That dismissal might be his own liberation.

All the time that he was ministering to his three golden Labrador dogs, he was perfecting his scheme to ensnare the cone-gatherers: preparing what he would say to Lady Runcie-Campbell to overcome her scruples; planning the positions he would give them during the deer drive; and considering what would be the best setting in which to give them the order to go for ever from the wood.

The dogs were uneasy. Although he spoke to them with

27

more than customary friendliness, and handled them with unwonted gentleness, they still mistrusted him. They nuzzled into his hands, they thrust themselves against his legs, they gazed up at him with affection; but there was always a detectable droop of appeasement, as if they sensed what was in his mind and were afraid that it might at any moment goad him into maltreating them. He was more and more aware of their apprehension, and saw himself, in furious revenge, rising and snatching a switch from the wall and thrashing them till their noses and eyes dripped faithful blood: they would suffer his maddest cruelty without retaliation. But as he saw himself thus berserk he sat on the box and continued to pat the cringing dogs and speak consolingly to them.

Several times his mother-in-law shouted to him from the back door that Peggy was asking where he was and when he was coming to see her. He did not answer, and left the shed only when his wife's light had gone out.

He was going into his own bedroom when Mrs. Lochie opened the door of hers. She was in her nightgown.

'So you've come in at last,' she whispered.

He closed his eyes.

'I thought you'd like to ken your wife sobbed herself to sleep. I thought if you knew that it might help to soothe you over yourself. I ken you find sleep hard to come by.'

He smiled, with his eyes still closed. Several times, desperate in his sleeplessness, he had left the house and wandered in the wood long after midnight.

'I think,' she whispered, 'you'll never sleep again this side of the grave.'

He opened his eyes and looked at her.

'And on the other side?' he asked, in a voice so mild it disconcerted her.

'If you have deserved mercy, John, you'll get it,' she answered.

Then she closed her door, but not before he had heard her sobbing.

'It's too late,' he muttered, as he went into his room and stood with his hand on the bed-rail. 'It's too late.' He did not clearly know what it meant, but he recognised the sense of loss that began to possess him, until he felt as terrified and desolate as an infant separated from his mother in a great crowd.

Chapter Three

Next morning was so splendid that as he walked through the policies towards the mansion house despair itself was lulled. The sky was vast and bright; the withered leaves underfoot were iridescent with melting frost; the very air glittered. As if in contrition for last night's mistrust in the dim shed, his dogs showed him how to enjoy such sunshine as they ran here and there, giving holiday sniffs and yelps, and barking up at squirrels as tawny as themselves darting along red pine branches. It was a morning that seemed to beguile the mind with recollections of a time of innocence before evil and unhappiness were born.

Peggy and her mother had been asleep, and the stars still shining, when he had slipped out. He had taken no breakfast and hadn't shaved.

He walked under the squirrels, gun under his arm, smiling.

When he came near the house he heard cries and the crack of ball against bat. They must be playing cricket on the lawn. Young Roderick would have coaxed his uncle to play with him. The boy was useless at games, as far as Duror could judge; his awkwardness, physical and mental, prevented him from being proficient no matter how zealously he persevered. Duror had watched him once kicking a football for an hour; at the finish he had been clumsier and keener than at the beginning. Perhaps because he was like his father outwardly, with startled deer's eyes and hare's teeth, he was his mother's favourite, although his sister Sheila, two years younger, was beautiful, healthy, courageous, and as assured as any lady. Roderick from birth had been weak in body and complicated in mind. He had had to be removed from school, and now was tutored at home. He had never liked Duror, and when little had not hesitated to say so. His mother more than one had had to apologise for him.

Duror was early. He stood behind a thick holly to watch the

players on the lawn; his dogs sat at his feet. Roderick batted; his uncle bowled; and Sheila was supposed to field, assisted by her dog, a small short-legged terrier called Monty. Roderick was very earnest as he faced up to the ball, swiped out at it, missed, and shouted an explanation for his miss. He immediately ran behind the wicket to retrieve the ball and throw it back to his uncle so that the whole thing could be repeated as soon as possible. Once he struck the ball, and began to race between the wickets as if those runs would mean the winning of a Test Match. His uncle called to him laughingly that there was no need for such hurry. Roderick paused to glance towards where the ball had flown. He was obviously displeased to see that Monty had it in his mouth and was playing a game of come-and-get-it-if-you-can with Sheila. Roderick shouted to his sister that she was spoiling the game; but his uncle, still laughing, came down the pitch and put an arm round his neck. He was a tall almost bald man of about thirty-five, in peacetime a lawyer from Edinburgh, where his father, Lord Forgan, had been a judge. Duror knew him as a quiet, pleasant, considerate man, with his only vanity a moustache as black and glossy as a snail.

Duror came out from behind the holly and walked respectfully along the path by the side of the lawn. His dogs too recognised the presence of superiors; when Monty came scampering along to sniff and yap insolently at them they endured it with glances up at their master as if to make sure he was noticing their forbearance.

Captain Forgan waved his hand; then, as if that gesture had not been cordial enough, he came striding across the lawn.

'Good morning, Duror,' he cried.

'Good morning, sir.'

Forgan smiled up at the sky and held out his hands as if to catch some of the benison dropping from it. His face, ruddy but hardly military from open-air life in army camps, beamed with gratitude as if he thought this spell of magnificent weather was being provided in his honour.

'This is a real honey of a morning, Duror,' he said, 'and no mistake. Air like champagne.' He breathed it in deeply and gratefully. Although he was smiling he was serious: in two or three weeks he would be in an African desert.

'Well, is there going to be a deer drive?' he asked.

'I think we'll be able to arrange something, sir.'

'Good man. I knew I could rely on you.' He bent down to pat the dogs. 'Handsome creatures,' he said, with zest. 'Why do we talk about a dog's life, Duror? What right have we to feel superior to these chaps?' He glanced up at their master with a smile. 'They have no wars, Duror.'

'No, sir.'

Forgan rose up and laughed. It was a comprehensive laughter, at the fine scenery, at his sentimental envy of dogs, at the forlorn wickets on the lawn, at Roderick with bat at rest like a sentinel, and at himself in well-creased khaki trousers.

'We were playing cricket,' he said.

'Yes, sir.'

Forgan gazed all round. 'It's really a beautiful place,' he murmured. 'I'm glad I could come. It'll be very pleasant to have these memories so fresh. You know, Duror, I envy you your life here.'

Duror did not smile back.

'If you'll pardon me for saying it, sir,' he said, 'I'd prefer to be going with you.'

The captain was taken by surprise; his smile turned foolish, and he did not know what to say. These days he tried to think like a soldier, and often reached no conclusion.

'I'm too old, sir,' said Duror. 'They won't have me. I've tried three times.'

Forgan thought he had hurt the keeper's pride as patriot.

'No, no, Duror,' he cried, shaking his head. 'When I said I envied you I wasn't meaning that you were lucky to escape the big and bloody war.' He laughed. 'Not in the slightest. I was just carried away by the beauty of the morning. We all know you're more than willing to do your bit. You're a stalwart of the Home Guard here, aren't you?'

Duror would not be appeased.

'I'll try again, sir. Perhaps they'll be glad enough to have me yet.'

The captain twisted his snail-black moustache with rueful whimsicality.

'You mean, when all the young cock sparrows have been shot off the tree?' he asked.

'I hope not, sir. May I be allowed to wish you a good journey and a safe return?'

'You are allowed, Duror; you are allowed, as the kids say, with knobs on. But I see Master Roderick glowering at me like a sergeant-major. Jove, he wanted us to start before the frost was off the grass. How glorious to be young! When d'you think the drive will start?'

'About two o'clock, sir. After I've seen her ladyship, I'll let you know where I think the best place will be.'

'Thanks, Duror. It's all in your hands, as far as I'm concerned. Just show me where to stand. I hope I get a kill.' He smiled wryly. 'It's a funny thing, Duror, we moan about the vast amount of killing going on in the world, and here I am thirsting for more.'

'Deer are vermin, sir. They must be kept down.'

'I suppose so.' He hesitated, and cast a glance at Duror which seemed to the gamekeeper to be a prelude to a rebuke about his unshavenness; there had already been several of these glances. But he was wrong.

'And Mrs. Duror? How's she keeping?'

Duror smiled. 'Not too well, sir.' He flicked his chin. 'I'm afraid we had a disturbed night. I see I've forgotten to shave.'

Embarrassed, Forgan looked away: he had never seen Mrs. Duror, but had heard about her from his sister. He remembered he had said he envied Duror. He remembered too unshavenness was a military offence.

'Don't worry about that, Duror,' he said. 'Well, I'll get back to my cricket.'

'Thank you, sir.'

Touching his cap, Duror walked on. His dogs followed, glad to escape from the tyranny of Monty.

As he made for the servants' entrance at the back of the house, he realised that by lying to the captain about Peggy he had in some way involved him; and in a few minutes, by persuading Lady Runcie-Campbell to conscript the cone-gatherers, he would involve her too. His tragedy was now to be played in public: it must therefore have a crisis, and an end.

Out of sight round the corner of the house, he paused. They were talking about him on the lawn. Roderick had said something shrill and petulant.

'Be quiet, Roddy,' cried his sister. 'He'll hear you.'

'I suggest we get on with this manly game of cricket,' called their uncle.

'Oh, all right, I'm sorry,' said Roderick.

'That's more like you, old chap,' said his uncle. 'Now I think it's my turn to bat.'

'But I'm not out yet,' protested the boy.

Smiling, Duror walked along to the door, tied up his dogs, and entered.

Mrs. Morton, the cook-housekeeper, was alone in the kitchen, preparing the silver tray for the family's morning coffee. She was a widow of about his own age, cheerful, shrewd, pink-faced, bonny and buxom. She was one of the few regular visitors to his wife. His mother-in-law had recently insinuated that the housekeeper's interest was in him, not in Peggy. He had dismissed the insinuation, but later had found himself wondering whether he wished it was true. To a man she liked, she could no doubt bring joy and oblivion; but, though neither religious nor prudish, she had a sense of fairness and a quick reliable judgment. He knew she was attracted by him, but she was genuinely sorry for Peggy and would not readily betray her.

This morning, as she welcomed him into the sunny kitchen, he thought that surely the next step in the drama should be his involvement of her.

She had no apprehensions of evil. Round her plump neck, indeed, like a talisman protecting her, was a gold locket on a chain: it contained the picture of her twenty-year-old son Alec, who was in the Merchant Navy.

'You're just in time for a cup of tea,' she said.

'Thanks, Effie.' He sat down, smiling at her deft ministrations, like a proud husband. 'I'm due in the office at ten.'

She glanced at the clock on the dresser.

'Plenty of time,' she said. 'And how's Peggy?'

Still smiling, he milked and sugared his tea, and stirred it.

'Peggy?' he murmured. 'There's no change in *her*.'

She offered him a plate heaped with scones freshly baked. He took one, and contrived to make the offering and his acceptance seem significant.

'You're my favourite baker, Effie,' he said.

She laughed but turned pinker.

'Och, I'm sure Mrs. Lochie's as good as ever I could be.'

'At baking?'

'Aye, John, at baking. What else?'

For a few seconds he did not answer. Apparently composed himself, he noticed she was a little flustered.

'When I said there was no change in Peggy,' he said, 'I was really hinting there *was* a change in somebody else.'

'I guessed as much.'

'Maybe I ought to say no more, Effie. You see, you come into it.'

'Me, John?'

As he nodded, it never occurred to her that he was lying. She had always thought that suffering had brought to him distinction of body and mind. With his black hair now thickly powdered with white at the sides, and his lean brown meditative face, he seemed to her a more distinguished man than Sir Colin himself. Never had she heard him say an indecent or false word. Several times she had found herself, deep in her own mind, regretting that his ordeal seemed to have purged him of passions. She had also indulged in the supposition of Peggy's death and his freedom to remarry: if he asked her, she did not think she would refuse.

'Aye, you Effie,' he said. 'But maybe I should change the subject. There's something else I want to ask you.'

'But I'd like to know how I come into it, John, whatever it is.'

He laughed. 'Och, why not? You're a sensible woman, Effie, and not likely to let silly tittle-tattle upset you. Somebody has got it into her head you and I are too fond of each other.'

She seemed more agitated than indignant.

'Mrs. Lochie, do you mean?' she asked.

He nodded. 'I don't think she's really got a spite against us, Effie. It's God she blames, but where's the satisfaction in slandering him?'

'I was aware she slandered you, but I didn't think she'd started on me.'

'Don't blame her, Effie.'

'I'm certainly not going to be sorry for her either, if she spreads dirty slanders.'

He chuckled. 'So it's a dirty slander, Effie, to say that you and I are fond of each other?'

She was blushing; her throat was aflame, and perhaps her breasts.

He leaned towards her.

'I didn't think that was what she meant,' she said hoarsely.

'It wasn't, Effie,' he whispered. 'She made it plain enough what she meant. She accused us of being in bed together; but she put it more coarsely than that.'

'My God!' she cried, and made to rise.

He put his hand on her breast and gently pushed her down.

'She's an old woman, Effie, crazy with anxiety. She sees I have difficulty whiles in showing affection for Peggy; which is the truth, I'm sorry to say. She thinks then I must be showing it to somebody else. It doesn't occur to her I might be empty of affection altogether.'

She stared at the table.

'I hope that's not true, John,' she said, still hoarse.

He wondered if he could risk kissing or embracing her. Were her scruples sufficiently annulled by desire for revenge, or by lust, or even by genuine affection for him? To his own destruction, and the cone-gatherers', ought he to add hers?

He sat still.

'I think we should drop this subject in the meantime, Effie,' he said, at last. 'I see I've just got a minute or two left to ask your advice about a different matter altogether.'

'It would be a mistake,' she said, in such a low voice he could scarcely hear, 'to let affection die in you altogether.'

He stretched out his hand and laid it on hers.

'Given the circumstances, Effie,' he whispered, 'I could blossom again like a gean-tree.'

With a shudder, she withdrew her hand.

'What was it you wanted to ask me?' she murmured.

'Oh aye. You're a Lendrick woman, Effie, and you know all that goes on there.'

'I like to take an interest in folks' affairs.'

'Which is to your credit, surely. Maybe you know we've got a couple of men from Ardmore Forest working in our wood here.'

'I heard about it. They're gathering cones.'

'That's right. Cones are really seed, tree seed. Before the war this country got its supplies from abroad, from Norway and Canada and Corsica, I believe, among other places. You'll appreciate better than most that our ships have more important cargoes to fetch these days. Yet if we're to replace the multitude of trees being felled for the war, we must have seed. It's the same with human beings: after a big war they've got to be replaced as well; but in their case the seed's easily come by.'

'I don't think this is what you wanted to talk to me about, John.'

'No, Effie. To tell you the truth, I'm as tongue-tied as a tree with everybody else; with you I talk, it seems, too much.'

'I didn't mean that. I was thinking of the time.'

'These two men from Ardmore, Effie. I wonder if you can tell me anything about them.'

'Ardmore's a good eight miles out of Lendrick,' she said, 'though most of the men there come in on Saturdays. But I know the two you mean.'

'Brothers,' he murmured, 'one a hunchback, the other tall and dour.'

She nodded. 'Their name's McPhie. They're well enough known in Lendrick.'

'I thought they would be.'

Something in his tone made her glance up.

'There's nothing known to their discredit, if that's what you mean, John. It's true the small one's not as God meant a man to be; but that's God's business, not ours.'

'Maybe it is our business, Effie.'

'What do you mean?' She glanced at the clock. 'I hope you're watching your time.'

'How long have they been at Ardmore?'

'I couldn't say for certain. About four or five years.'

'They're quartered in the wood yonder in a hut as small as a rabbit-hutch, and as filthy.'

'Is that their fault? Simple men like them, John, aren't asked where they'd like to live. But what's all the mystery about? What have they done?'

'I'll tell you. But it's what they might do that worries me.'

She waited for him to explain. He paused, searching for words that would bind her and him and the imbecile dwarf together in common defilement.

'The hunchback's not right in the head,' he said.

'He's a bit simple.'

'More than that, Effie. Indecency's not simple. The papers

are often full of what such misbegotten beasts have done.' He smiled, marvelling at the steadiness of his hand holding the tea cup; within him was a roaring, like a storm through a tree. 'I'm referring, of course, to assaults on wee lassies. There was one reported just the other week.' He began to describe it, calmly, in the coarsest terms he knew.

She stopped him. 'I understand well enough,' she said. 'I'm not a child. But it's a serious charge to make against any man, stooped or straight, daft or wise.'

'I'm making no charge, as yet. But I've got to remember that if anything of the kind was to happen here the responsibility would be mine. There's Miss Sheila sometimes walks in the wood alone; and of course the mistress.'

'You hinted they'd already done something. What?'

He stood up, with a smile at the clock, now at a minute to the hour.

'I saw that imbecile exposing himself,' he said; 'and worse.' He described it briefly, enjoying her fascinated embarrassment. A lie, he saw, could cause as much distortion as the truth.

'Where was this?' she asked.

'In the wood.'

'And nobody saw it but you?'

'There was a thrush, I think.'

She would not smile. 'I'm sorry to hear it,' she said, 'and surprised too. He's been in and out of Lendrick dozens of times and there's never been the slightest hint of anything like that. I thought that sort of abnormality liked an audience.'

'Seed,' he murmured, with quiet intense disgust; and then he smiled.

The clock struck ten.

'It's a minute or so fast,' she said. 'They've been kicked about that pair, from what I've heard. Nobody can say life's been generous to them. A thing like this if it got about would destroy them completely. The wee one would be dragged off to jail or the asylum, and the big one would break his heart. There's affection between them.'

'Likely enough, Effie. Even the murderer on the scaffold has a mother weeping for him.'

She came close, panting.

'Don't become embittered, John,' she said.

Lightly he put his hand on her head, and then snatched it away again.

'Will you help me to stay sweet, Effie?' he murmured.

She closed her eyes, as if not to see her own surrender; she nodded.

'Thanks, Effie,' he said, but he did not, as she evidently expected, embrace her. He walked over to the door. 'That's a promise I'd better give you time to consider.'

'I've considered it, John, many a time.'

For a moment, realising that her feeling for him was genuine, he saw another way, clear, like a sunlit ride in a thick wood.

'You're in danger too, John,' she whispered, 'of being destroyed completely. I couldn't stand by and watch that happen, if there was anything I could do to stop it.'

'I do need help, Effie,' he said, and then, as he closed the door and set off respectfully through the large rich house, he thought, Did she think he could be saved by her offering him her fifty-year-old body in a dark room, with gasps of conscience mixed with any sounds of satisfaction?

Chapter Four

Lady Runcie-Campbell was in the office at the front of the house writing letters. When he knocked, she bade him enter in her clear courteous musical voice.

A stranger, hearing her, would have anticipated some kind of loveliness in so charming a speaker; he might not, however, have expected to find such outstanding beauty of face and form married to such earnestness of spirit; and he would assuredly have been both startled and impressed.

Duror, who knew her well, had been afraid that in her presence he might be shamed or inspired into abandoning his scheme against the cone-gatherers. In spite of her clothes, expensive though simple, of her valuable adornments such as earrings, brooches, and rings, and of her sometimes almost mystical sense of responsibility as a representative of the ruling class, she had an ability to exalt people out of their humdrum selves. Indeed, Duror often associated religion not with the smell of pinewood pews or of damp Bibles, but rather with her perfume, so elusive to describe. Her father the judge had bequeathed to her a passion for justice, profound and intelligent; and a determination to see right done, even at the expense of rank or pride. Her husband Sir Colin was orthodox, instinctively preferring the way of a world that for many generations had allowed his family to enjoy position and wealth. Therefore he had grumbled at his wife's conscientiousness, and was fond of pointing out, with affection but without sympathy, the contradiction between her emulation of Christ and her eminence as a baronet's wife.

She would have given the cone-gatherers the use of the beach hut, if Duror had not dissuaded her; and she had not forgotten to ask him afterwards what their hut was like. He had had to lie.

Now when he was going to lie again, this time knowing it would implicate her in his chosen evil, he felt that he was about to commit before her eyes an obscene gesture, such as he had falsely accused the dwarf of making. In the sunny scented room therefore, where the happy voices of the cricket players on the lawn could be heard, he suddenly saw himself standing up to the neck in a black filth, like a stags' wallowing pool deep in the wood. High above the trees shone the sun, and everywhere birds sang; but this filth, as he watched, crept up until it entered his mouth, covered his ears, blinded his eyes, and so annihilated him. So would he perish, he knew; and somewhere in the vision, as a presence, exciting him so that his heart beat fast, but never visible, was a hand outstretched to help him out of that mire, if he wished to be helped.

He saw her hand with its glittering rings held out to invite him to sit down.

'Good morning, Duror,' she said, with a smile. 'Isn't it just splendid?'

'Yes, my lady.'

She looked at him frankly and sympathetically: it was obvious she attributed his subdued tone to sorrow over his wife. If at the same time she noticed with surprise that he hadn't shaved, it did not diminish her sympathy, as it would have her husband's.

'How is Mrs. Duror?' she asked gently.

'Not too well, I'm sorry to say, my lady. This spell of fine weather has upset her. She asked me to thank you for the flowers.'

She was so slim, golden-haired, and vital, that her solicitude for Peggy gripped him like a fierce cramp in his belly.

She noticed how pale he had turned, how ill he looked.

'I often think of your poor wife, Duror,' she said.

She glanced at her husband's portrait in uniform on the desk in front of her.

Duror could not see the photograph from where he sat, but he could see clearly enough in his imagination the original, as gawky as she was beautiful, as glum as she was gay, and as matter-of-fact as she was compassionate.

'This war,' she went on quickly, 'with its dreadful separations has shown me at least what she has missed all these years. Something has come between us and the things we love, the things on which our faith depends: flowers and dogs and trees and friends. She's been cut off so much longer.'

She glanced again at Sir Colin as if expecting to find him glummer than ever at this condescension. She was not mistaken. With a sigh she turned to business.

'Mrs. Lochie would explain what I wanted to see you about?' she asked.

'Yes, my lady. I've been out having a look through the wood.'

'You think we can manage all right?'

'I think so, my lady.'

'Good. Captain Forgan seems to have set his heart on it. He has a belief that nothing impresses the scenery on one's mind like taking part in a deer shoot, especially if you get a kill.'

'I understand what the captain means, my lady.'

She laughed. 'I'm not sure I do, Duror. Often it's a long cold wait for nothing. And if you're lucky and shoot a deer, well, I suppose it is sentimental of me to think that a living deer is much handsomer than a dead one.'

He remembered that her son, as an infant of four, also a sentimentalist, had seen him with a dead roe deer, and for years afterwards had disliked him. Perhaps she too was remembering that.

'They're classified as vermin, my lady,' he said.

'Oh no.' She laughed and gestured. 'I won't have it, Duror. Whatever any government says, I refuse to call deer vermin. They're far too beautiful.'

'They're enemies, my lady.'

'Yes, call them that. Not all our enemies are ugly, cruel, savage, and beastly; some are beautiful and gentle.'

He noticed how her hands involuntarily clasped, and her eyes avoided the portrait.

'There's a herd in the wood just now, my lady,' he said, 'between Runacraig and Lettermore Burn. It should be a fairly easy stretch to drive, which is important, for we'll be short of drivers. How many guns will there be, my lady?'

She became brisk.

'I was thinking of that before you came,' she said. 'Not many, I'm afraid. It's not like the old days.'

'We might not need many, my lady. We'll drive towards Runacraig. Three or four guns in the drive there should have a good chance.'

'Well, there's Captain Forgan for one. Oh yes, Duror, here's a problem for you to solve. Captain Forgan has one opinion, I have another. I'm going to abide by your decision.'

He smiled. 'I'll do my best, my lady.'

'It's simply this: Master Roderick wants to be one of the guns. Now I know he's handled one before: he's shot a few rabbits. But naturally at his age he's somewhat nervous. Is it safe to let him loose on a deer drive? What do you think, Duror, as the expert? I may say that Master Roderick will accept the decision as coming from me.'

Was this, he thought, another opportunity? Say that it would be safe enough and hope for an accident? If the boy stumbled in excitement and shot himself, she would be inconsolable, for all her goodness and beauty. Why not therefore add this shade to the encompassing darkness?

He could not afterwards say why he replied as he did.

'If you'll pardon me putting it in this way, my lady,' he said: 'if he was my son, I'd say no, not just yet.'

For a moment he thought of that incommunicable phantom, his son; and he felt the treachery of regret.

'Then that's settled,' she said firmly. 'If Master Roderick wishes to be there, it'll have to be as a spectator, like his sister. I'll take a gun myself. Mr. Baird has promised to come.' (As the grieve in charge of the home farm he could scarcely have refused.) 'And Mr. Adamson of Ledaig is always keen; though of course,' she added smiling, 'Master Roderick is sure to tell me that if Mr. Adamson can be trusted with a gun, so surely can he.'

Will Adamson, over seventy, had once put a pellet into old Graham the estate handyman.

'That gives us four,' she said. 'Five, counting yourself.'

'I think, my lady, I ought to go with the drive. If I can, I'll try to head the deer towards where the captain will be posted.'

She was pleased. 'Thank you, Duror.'

Now, he thought, comes the lie; the obscene gesture; the spitting upon her lovely generous face.

'The beaters are the trouble,' he said.

'Yes, I know. Whom have we got? I suppose Graham, though he does complain so and gets stuck in brambles. Young Harry, who's usually very useful: I mean, he can be depended upon to make a merry noise. Then Betty the landgirl, whom Mr. Baird has said can be spared. Mr. Adamson's going to supply a man, but apparently he's rather deaf and has a poor sense of direction. That makes four of a sort. Hardly enough.'

'No, my lady. When the spaces are too wide between the beaters the deer get too good a chance to double back, and then all our labour's been in vain.'

'Yes, I know. But what are we to do? I suppose we could borrow men from neighbouring farms, but ought we to? After all, it is war time, and our drive is for pleasure.'

'I've got a suggestion, my lady, that might help.'

'What is it, Duror?'

'I was wondering if we could have the use of the two men who are in the wood gathering cones. I'm sure Mr. Tulloch wouldn't mind if we borrowed them for a couple of hours.'

She was delighted. 'The very thing, Duror! Why couldn't I have thought of that? Of course Mr. Tulloch will oblige. He's an admirable person, and he spoke very highly of these men.'

She had her hand on the telephone ready to pick it up when a doubt occurred to her; she frowned.

'Isn't one of them a kind of cripple?' she asked.

45

'I wouldn't call him that, my lady. He's a hunchback, but he's as agile as any monkey.'

'Yes. So Roderick says. He has an immense admiration for him. I can't for the life of me tell why. Climbing trees, I suppose, is a fairly common accomplishment, and, though useful, is scarcely worthy of reverence.' She noticed his surprise at her use of that last word. 'Yes, reverence,' she repeated, laughing. 'He became embarrassed when I questioned him. It's really very odd. I understand this hunchback has rather a striking face?'

Duror nodded. 'Yes, my lady.'

'And fine black curls,' she added.

As she laughed at this odd but praiseworthy interest of her children in so insignificant a person, Duror wondered if this was a good time to repeat the lie he had told to Mrs. Morton.

He hesitated too long.

'However,' she said, still laughing, 'I suppose I'd better telephone Mr. Tulloch.'

While she was speaking to the exchange, and then waiting to be put through to Ardmore, Duror saw all that he was doing with a strange clear neutrality: his ignoring of Peggy, his lying to Mrs. Morton, and above all his resolution to torment the cone-gatherers and destroy them, if he could. Seated in this chair, with his cap respectfully on his knee, and his hands laid upon it so calmly, without a twitch, he thought it incredible that all that villainy should be schemed by him; but then, he did not wish to be there, the part of his life associated with this bright room and this beautiful woman was over, and if he was where he wished to be, close to the hut in the darkness, under the cypress tree, he would not only understand and approve of what he had done, but would find in it his only possible consolation and release.

Lady Runcie-Campbell at last was talking to the forester.

'No, no, there's been no trouble, Mr. Tulloch. On the contrary. Your men are being as discreet as squirrels. I haven't set eyes on them myself, but I intend to soon, as my son assures me their climbing is really wizard. No, what I want to consult you about is this: we're hoping to have a deer drive this afternoon in honour of my brother who's been posted overseas. The trouble is, we're desperately short of beaters, and I thought you might consider lending us your two men for the afternoon. We'll pay them, of course.'

She paused, and listened to what, from her expression, must have been fervent assurances.

'Thank you so much, Mr. Tulloch. Oh yes, I think so. I'll ask him just to make sure.'

She turned from the telephone to ask Duror if he knew where the cone-gatherers were working. He nodded.

'Yes, it's all right,' she went on. 'He knows where to find them. It's very obliging of you, Mr. Tulloch.' Then she listened with amused pout. 'A quid pro quo, is that it? Pardon the Latin. I'm having to coach the children myself these days, as their tutor is on a visit to England.' She laughed again at some remark of Tulloch's. 'Well, I'll think about it. You know my objection: I just don't want them too near the house, over-looking the windows. Yes, I know I did, but squirrels are inquisitive creatures. No, of course not. Well, I promise I'll give it further consideration. One good turn deserves another, and besides, it's flattering to be told my silver firs are so hand-some and eligible. Good-bye, Mr. Tulloch, and thanks ever so much.'

She smiled as she was thanked in return, and then she set the receiver down.

'A very sound person, I think,' she said. 'Well, Duror, I take it you got the gist of that. We're to have our beaters. That gives us six altogether; which will have to do.'

'Yes, my lady. Would it be suitable to start the drive from the dead ash tree at the burn at two o'clock? The guns could be in their places along the ride by then.'

'Very good, Duror. Perhaps two is rather soon after lunch. Let's make it half-past. If you see to the beaters, I'll see to the guns.'

'Thank you, my lady.' He rose. 'With your permission, I'll go now and tell these men gathering the cones.'

'Yes, please do that, Duror.'

She was interrupted by the ringing of the telephone. She picked it up.

'Lady Runcie-Campbell speaking. Oh, it's you, Mr. Tulloch.' She began to frown, and signalled to Duror not to go. 'How extraordinary. Yes, I knew there was something peculiar about him, but I thought it was restricted to his physical appearance. I wasn't aware he also suffered from abnormal squeamishness. Is it some outlandish religious objection? You think so? Surely not. I look upon myself as a reasonably conscientious Christian, and I have shot deer before now, and will again. Is he utterly consistent? I mean, would he set traps for rats? Does he eat meat? Surely then, his objection is really rather frivolous? How old is he? Over thirty! Good heavens, I thought he could hardly be more than twenty with such callow views. My own son, who's not quite fourteen, wishes to be one of the guns at this deer drive, but I've refused simply because he's not experienced enough. Certainly I wouldn't wish to force anyone into acting against his principles, but I'm afraid I can't recognise principle in this case. Would I encourage my own son to take part in what was wrong? I understand you have some conscientious objectors working at your forest. He's not one of these, is he? Well, has he been influenced by them at all? I see. That makes it all the more peculiar. Do you mind if I consult my gamekeeper for a second?'

Duror noticed that in spite of the confidence in her voice the hand holding the telephone trembled. She seemed either insulted or dismayed. He guessed that within her was a struggle between her Christian sympathy for the weak-minded hunchback and her pride as a patrician, to whom hunting on her own estate was as sacred as singing in church.

Her voice now had that harsh edge which always denoted that she was about, for duty's sake, to assert her authority.

'What do you make of this absurdity, Duror?' she asked. 'He tells me that one of these men, the deformed one, has some kind of scruple about taking part in deer drives. Apparently he's excused them in the forest.'

'What is his objection, my lady?'

'You might well ask, Duror. Something dismally vague.'

'They say he's next door to being an imbecile, my lady.'

'That *would* be an explanation. What do you advise, Duror? Ought we to humour the fellow?'

It astonished Duror that she, so genuinely good, should be helping him in his plan of evil.

'I think, my lady, he owes you something. He's earning his living in your wood.'

'Yes, I suppose that's true. I wouldn't like,' she added, her voice a little shrill, 'to be unfair.'

'There are all kinds of shirkers, my lady. Did Mr. Tulloch say these conscientious objectors had been at him?'

'Apparently they have not. It seems they take part in deer drives. Our friend is unique.'

She uttered that last remark cuttingly, but remembered a moment after that the perfect exemplar of uniqueness was Christ Himself. She could not endure that rebuke, and snatched up the telephone.

'Mr. Tulloch?' she said haughtily. 'I'm so sorry to have kept you waiting. It seems we require every help we can get, otherwise the drive is sure to fail. Therefore I'd like your permission to approach your men. We shall do our best to protect their sensibilities. Is that all right then? Thank you. Good morning.'

She put down the telephone firmly.

'He agreed all right,' she said, 'but he did not sound at all pleased.'

Duror had discreetly sat down again while she was telephoning. Now he rose.

'I'll talk to them, my lady,' he said. 'I'm quite sure I can persuade them.'

49

'Yes, please do, Duror.'

When he was at the door, she called sharply: 'Duror!'

'Yes, my lady.'

She was staring at her clasped hands. He was sure she had moved the portrait so that she could not see it.

Her voice was still harsh. 'Are we being unfair to this poor wretch?' she asked. 'After all, he *is* deformed, and a simpleton.'

'He's an active man, my lady, and he's sensible enough to earn a pay.'

'Yes, yes,' she said testily. 'But he does seem to be abnormal. Heaven knows what may go on in his mind.'

He waited as she made up her mind.

'I tell you what,' she said, 'if you are convinced his reluctance is genuine, for whatever reason, just leave him in his tree to gather his cones. His brother alone will have to do.'

'I doubt, my lady, if they'll separate.'

'But good heavens, they're not children.'

'I know, my lady, but they're always together; even in a tree where there's sometimes little room.'

'In that case, Duror,' she cried, 'they'll just have to come. We cannot have them dictating to us in every way.'

'No, my lady.'

'Be sure and tell them you have my and Mr. Tulloch's authority.'

'Yes, my lady.'

'Oh, and by the way, Duror,' she said, with an attempt to restore the pleasantness and music to her voice, 'tell your wife I'll be dropping in to see her soon.'

'Thank you, my lady. I'll be sure to tell her. She'll appreciate it very much.'

Then he shut the door quietly, walked calmly along the corridor hung with stags' heads and cases of stuffed birds and fish, and entered the kitchen. To Mrs. Morton's obvious annoyance Jean the maid was there, pert and talkative. He chatted for a minute or two, and then went to the door. Mrs. Morton accompanied him.

In the sunshine his dogs showed their red pleased tongues.

Mrs. Morton asked him in a whisper if he had told the mistress about the hunchback.

'No,' he said.

She smiled nervously. 'Maybe you should have, John.'

'I've got to be sure, Effie. As you said yourself, such a charge would break the man. His life's not worth tuppence ha'penny, I fancy, but to him it's precious.'

'It's generous of you to say that, John, especially when you've got such worries of your own.'

'What worries, Effie?' he asked, with a laugh.

He thought, from her quick breathings and furtive peeps at the sky, that she wished to make some assignation but still found shame in the way.

He touched his cap and left her in her predicament. The dogs, so innocent of lust or hate or cunning, followed him like guardians.

Chapter Five

They were safely in another good tree by the lochside. So brightly shone the sun, amongst the orange branches and on the blue water, it dazzled their eyes and made every cone glitter, so that they seemed to be plucking nuts of sunshine.

In Neil, so canny about admitting happiness, all the hindrances had vanished one by one, like the early mists over the loch. Now in the warmth and splendour he sang softly the sad Gaelic song that had been his mother's favourite: it was about a girl who, though without tocher or dowry, still did not lack sweethearts. He sang it in Gaelic, although his knowledge of that ancestral language was grown meagre and vague.

Among those hindrances to happiness had been the big gamekeeper. He could not forget Duror's quiet inconceivable hatred; and all last night he had felt that his and Calum's argument over the trapped rabbit would in some way be sensed by the gamekeeper, strengthening his vow to have them driven from the wood. In the morning sunlight, however, that fear of their desperate pity being detectable in the dead fur and glazed eyes seemed ridiculous. Duror would come to the ride, pick up the rabbit, and put it into his bag, without even thinking of them. Indeed, according to what Mr. Tulloch had said, the gamekeeper had enough to worry him in that his wife had been an invalid for many years. If they kept out of his way, they would not be troubled by him; and how much more out of the way could they be than at the top of this ninety-foot larch?

Another hindrance had been the ·constant sight of the mansion house chimneys, reminding him of their hut, which to him remained a symbol of humiliation. But this morning he remembered what Mr. Tulloch had said about the lady: she was rich and high in rank, but she was also generous and just; and her son, the thin boy in the red cap, had waved to them and shouted in a friendly voice. Those people represented the power of the world, and so long as he was humble it would be benignant. He and Calum would be humble. In spite of his bitterness, humility and acquiescence in public had always been his instinctive defence: so far it had been successful enough.

The greatest and most persistent obstacle to his happiness was, of course, the fear of what would become of his brother if he were to die. Though he was a healthy man, except for his rheumatism in wet weather, he could meet with any of a number of likely accidents: a fall from a tree, for instance; a wound from axe or rutter, followed by lockjaw; pneumonia after a day's soaking on the hill; even an adder bite. Once, when suffering from a suppurating finger caused by a splinter from a fence stob, he had been chaffed by Mr. Tulloch for looking so solemn and frightened over what, by manly standards, was a trivial injury. He had confided in the forester, who had listened with a smile of sympathy, and had assured him there was no need to worry about Calum, who would always find a place at Ardmore. Neil had learned that even kindness made promises it could not fulfil; but he had been grateful to Mr. Tulloch, and afterwards his heart had been lighter. In the larch tree this morning, when he had examined that promise anew, he found it fresh and sound.

Therefore he was able to sing and look forward to Saturday's visit to Lendrick. They would go by the red bus which came all the way from Glasgow. The afternoon would be spent in shopping: groceries would have to be ordered, so that the van next week could leave them by the roadside; their rations of cigarettes and sweets would have to be got from old Mrs. McTavish; and Calum needed a new shirt. If the herring drifters were in, perhaps they would stroll along after the shopping to visit the *Aphrodite*, whose captain and crew were their friends. Then they would have tea in the café overlooking the harbour, and would exchange news with Ardmore workmates who would have cycled in by that time. Afterwards they might go into the hotel bar for half an hour or so. After the loneliness of the wood, Neil would enjoy sitting in a corner and smiling out at the noise and bustle of the crowd. His pint of beer in his hand would be the token of his membership of the community. When anything funny was said he would have permission to laugh as heartily as anybody else. Calum was always unhappy in the pub; but that could not be helped.

In the tree here was Calum's happiness. Here were his friends the finches, safe from the hawk scouting above. The ground of snares and stumbles was far below. In the loch the seals were playing, with audible splashes. In a nearby Douglas fir cushat doves were crooning. Above all, his brother beside him was singing. So much present joy was there for him he did not have to look forward. He did not wonder, as Neil sometimes did, whether the cones he was gathering would be fertile; nor did he see the great trees born from this seed in his hands being toppled down in fifty years' time to make ammunition boxes for that generation's war. He was as improvident as the finches to whom he had fed more than half of his morning slice of bread.

Yet it was he who first saw the gamekeeper approaching through the sunshine and shadow of the wood, with his three glossy dogs running silently in front. In agitation he stretched over to touch Neil, and point.

Neil paused in his singing and picking to watch Duror. The latter, he thought, must be on a patrol of the wood, looking for deer or foxes or weasels to shoot. Even if he saw their ladder against the tree, and from it learned where they were, he would still pass by. While they were gathering cones, they were none of his business: his own mistress had given them permission.

'It's all right,' he murmured to Calum. 'He's got nothing to do with us. He'll pass by.'

Indeed, as he watched the gamekeeper now in and now out of sight on the dappled ground among the trees, he felt the sympathy he could never withhold when he saw any human being alone in a vast place, on a hillside say, or here in a wood.

Unlike his brother, he saw nature as essentially hostile; and its resources to take away a man's confidence were immense. He felt sure, for instance, that the gamekeeper treading on the withered leaves must be thinking of his sick wife.

In a clearing Duror halted, laid down his gun, took his binoculars out of their case, and trained them on the top of the larch.

Neil knew that they must be clearly visible; it seemed to him typical of nature that the foliage was gone which would have hidden them. It took an effort to go on picking cones. He told Calum to keep on picking too. He objected to this spying on them, but would not show it even by stopping work.

Calum could not concentrate on the cones. He became like an animal in danger with no way of escape. He began to whimper, and tilting over in a panicky attempt to hide from that distant scrutiny he let some cones dribble out of his bag.

'What's the matter with you?' asked Neil. 'Aye, I ken he's looking at us. But where's the harm in that? He's just doing his work, like you and me. Maybe he's not looking at us at all. Maybe it's that hawk we saw that he's looking at. Didn't I tell you, that if we keep out of his way, he can't harm us? Well, we're out of his way up here.'

Calum was not reassured; he still whimpered and cowered, like a dog in the presence of someone who has been cruel to it.

Neil's own fear suddenly increased. He became angry.

'What are you moaning for?' he demanded. 'I ken he doesn't like us, but we don't like him either. This wood doesn't belong to him; it belongs to the lady and she's given us permission to climb the trees and pick the cones. You heard Mr. Tulloch say it. As long as we don't saw branches off and injure the trees, nobody would interfere with us, he said. Have we ever sawn any branches off?'

He repeated that last question in a passion of resentment, for on most trees the best harvest of cones was on the tips of branches too far out from the trunk to be reached. If sawing was permitted, then those branches, so small as hardly to be noticed, could be dropped to the ground where it would be easy and safe to strip them of every cone. The trees' wounds would soon heal, the yield of cones would be doubled, and the strain on arms, legs, and back would be greatly relieved.

'The trees are more precious than we are,' he added bitterly.

Duror was returning the binoculars to their case. That done, with the buckle properly fastened, he picked up his gun, called on the dogs, and with leisurely stride made straight for the larch.

'Oh, he's coming, Neil,' cried Calum.

'What of it?'

'Maybe he'll shoot at us!'

'If you can't talk sense, Calum, don't talk at all. Why should he shoot at us? Do you think he takes us for crows? He kens fine who we are. Whether he likes us or not, we're men, and you can't shoot men as if they were crows.' He remembered that in the war being fought far from there, men were being shot in greater numbers and with bitterer hatred than ever crows were. 'He's just making for the loch,' he muttered.

Again they caught a glimpse of the gamekeeper. He was still heading towards them, but by no means with the hurrying stagger of a man with violence in his mind. He walked calmly, taking time to duck under low branches and lift tendrils of brier out of his way.

It was likely enough, thought Neil, or it should be, that a man walking by himself in a great wood, catching sight of other human beings, should want to exchange a word or two with them. Duror then would advance to the foot of the tree and shout up something about the fine weather or about the war. He, Neil, would shout down a reply. Then Duror would go on his way. In this world of trees it was necessary for human beings to maintain contact. In the ocean survivors of a torpedoed ship did not refuse to be rescued by enemies.

'If he stops to talk,' said Neil, 'you're not to be frightened. I'll answer him.'

Calum nodded; he had crept as close to his brother as he could.

Duror came under the tree and halted. They could not see him clearly because of the screen of branches. He spoke quietly to his dogs. Then, to Neil's astonishment and Calum's terror, he began to climb the ladder.

'It's all right,' whispered Neil. 'I tell you it's all right. We've got nothing to be afraid of.'

He thought it must be all right. There could be no other explanation of this visit than curiosity. Seeing the ladder, Duror had wanted to climb up. In so grave a man, such a boyish impulse was perhaps odd; but in a way it was also reassuring. This larch was their present address; here was the formidable gamekeeper paying them a friendly visit; the ladder against the tree would seem like a door open. Doubtlessly he had left his gun on the ground.

They heard the scrapes and thumps of his nailed boots on the rungs and then on the branches. A branch cracked suddenly. He exclaimed as if in anger, and paused for a full minute. When he resumed he climbed even more slowly than before. Soon he stopped again. He was still a long way below.

They waited, but he did not start to climb again. For three or four minutes they waited. Still he remained motionless and silent. One of the dogs barked unhappily.

They thought he must have climbed as high as he wished, and now was admiring the view of the loch. After all, the tree was not private just because they happened to be in it; the ladder, too, belonged to the estate. At the same time Neil felt curiously embarrassed and could not think to start gathering cones again. Calum kept shivering.

They were far from guessing the truth, that Duror had ceased to climb because of fear; that, weak and dizzy and full of shame, he was clinging with ignominious tightness; that the dread of the descent was making him sick; and that he had almost forgotten his purpose in ascending to them.

At last Neil had to end the suspense.

'Hello, Mr. Duror,' he called. 'It's a grand day, isn't it?'

No reply came.

Neil tried again.

'Do you want to talk to us about something?' he shouted.

This time, after another long delay, there was a reply. They were surprised by the mildness of his voice. It was so faint too they had to strain to hear it.

'I've got a message for you,' he said.

'A message? Is it from Mr. Tulloch?'

There was a pause. 'Aye, from him.'

'Have we to go back home, to Ardmore?' cried Neil hopefully.

'You know these woods belong to Lady Runcie-Campbell?'

'We know that.'

'She wants you as beaters in a deer drive this afternoon.'

Neil was shocked.

'But we're here to gather cones,' he yelled. 'She can't order us about. She's not our mistress.'

'She telephoned Tulloch. He said you've to work for her this afternoon.'

'How could he? Didn't he tell us we'd to gather every cone we could? Didn't he ask us to work as much overtime as we liked? What's the good of all that if we're to be taken away for deer drives.' Neil's voice grew hoarse with indignation. 'My brother's never asked to take part in deer hunts,' he shouted. 'Mr. Tulloch knows that. I don't believe he knows anything about this. It's just a trick to get us to work for the lady.'

Duror was silent. His triumph was become a handful of withered leaves. When he had seen the ladder, he had thought how gratifying it would be to deliver the deadly message to them in the eyrie where they fancied themselves safe. He had not anticipated this lightheadedness, this heaving of the stationary tree, this treachery of nature, this sickening of his very will to hate. He had never dreamed that he would not be able to do once only what the hunchback did several times a day. It seemed to him that he must therefore be far more ill and decayed than he had thought. He was like a tree still straight, still showing green leaves; but underground death was creeping along the roots.

As he clung, he tried to remember whether as a boy or youth he had had a good head for climbing; but his memories too were giddy and he could not sort them out.

'If my brother is excused deer drives in the forest,' Neil was shouting, 'why should he be made to take part in one here? I'm sure Mr. Tulloch never gave any such order. It's a trick, that's what it is.'

When no answer came, he went on in a passion of anger.

'Who does the lady think she is, that she orders us about like dogs? But if we were dogs, she'd treat us better than she does. Aren't the kennels at the big house bigger than our hut?'

He had never seen the kennels at the big house, and he knew the lady had nothing to do with the size of their hut. Mr. Tulloch was responsible for that. All the lady had done was to stipulate that it be built far away from her own house. His faith in his employer snapped. He believed the order to take part in the deer drive had been given. If they disobeyed it they would be sacked and would have to leave Ardmore for ever. Yet how could Calum take part in the drive? Not only might he break a leg in his stumbles and falls, but he might easily be driven out of his mind if there were cries, shots, and the squeals and bleeding of a deer.

Duror had been bracing himself for the descent.

'You've to be at the lilypond behind the garden at two,' he said.

'No,' shouted Neil, 'no, no. We'll not be there. We don't know where it is anyway. We're strangers here, and I wish we had never come.'

Duror no longer heeded. He was slowly climbing down.

'Go and tell the lady,' yelled Neil, 'that we're free men, we're not at her beck and call. It was beneath her to give us the beach hut to live in although it's to be pulled down after the war. Does she think she can treat us like dirt one day, and the next order us about?'

Duror had reached the ladder, but his confidence did not revive. As soon as he touched earth he staggered and had to sink down on his knees, unable to stand up against the weight of a burden of misery as crushing as the tree itself. There was an insect hurrying on its own business in the grass, inches from his hand which could kill it with the lightest touch; he felt, without self-pity, that this insignificant transitory creature was happier than he and infinitely more at home.

His gun was close by; he thought that, salvation being impossible, it offered at least an end. Then his dogs, urged forward by affection and loyalty against the curb of discipline, shyly approached, nudged him, licked his wrists, and whimpered in sympathy. It was enough for them to sense that he was ill; they did not analyse the nature of that illness, or pass judgment, or give advice; so much so that he was able to find within him sufficient strength and gratitude to murmur their names.

Up in the tree Neil was knocking his head in despair against the trunk.

'I don't know what to do,' he muttered. 'I just don't know.'

He was sure Mr. Tulloch had betrayed them: rather than displease the wealthy lady he had sacrificed them because they were humble and poor and homeless. Yet there could be no satisfaction in accusing him; he had always been their friend.

Calum's own fears were removed by love. He tugged at his brother's jacket.

'Never mind, Neil,' he whispered. 'I'll do it. I'll drive the deer.'

Neil kept his face hidden.

'You know you can't, Calum,' he said. 'You know how clumsy you are. You'd catch on every thorn, you'd break your leg or your neck, you'd blind yourself among briers.'

'I'll do my best,' promised Calum eagerly.

'And what if there were deer shot? What would you do then?'

Calum frowned. 'I would shut my eyes,' he said.

Neil was silent: he had imagined the worst, now he tried to imagine the best. If Calum could be given a fairly clear stretch, he might struggle through with only a few scratches and bruises; and there might be no deer killed at all.

But as he gazed down and saw the gamekeeper slowly walk away through the wood he did not shout after him that they would be at the lilypond at two o'clock.

Chapter Six

On the edge of the pond, near the stone Cupid with mossy hair and corroded nose, sat Harry the gardener apprentice playing cheerful tunes on his mouth organ. Beside him, chewing gum and breaking into song occasionally, was Betty the landgirl. They were dressed for the deer drive, he in a tunic of camouflage colours, and she in her official khaki. Over her head, however, she had wrapped a red-white-and-blue scarf.

It was so peaceful by the pond that, in the midst of the music, could be heard such sounds as the drone of a late bee, the plop of a frog, and the rasp of Erchie Graham's nails along his midge-tormented scalp.

Always irascible, the old handyman that afternoon was furious. His proper task should have been to sweep fallen leaves from the paths about the big house. He had looked forward to it, with spits of relish. There would have been no one to superintend him, except a squirrel perhaps or a jenny wren, at which he might have winked. Not a drop of sweat would have been shed, and at his age, sixty-nine, sweat must be hoarded like blood and breath. Now all that bliss had been blasted by this order to take part in the deer drive; the dignity of old age, smoking at leisure in the sunshine in the company of mellow trees, was to be outraged by a sweating roaring helter-skelter race through brambles, briers, and nettles, over marshes and burns, up hills and down precipices, all in pursuit of deer that had never done him any harm and that, as venison, he did not like. Even if the deer were shot at the finish, they were luckier than he: they at least would be put out of the pain of tortured lungs and racked limbs.

'And by God,' he said to Charlie, Adamson's labourer, who sat beside him, 'there's no guarantee I'll not be shot. Your boss once had a damned good try. He put a couple of slugs into me.' He slapped his left rump. 'But for a tree that got in the road, it's doubtful if I ever again would have enjoyed what's every free man's privilege, a seat in comfort.'

Charlie neither agreed nor disagreed: he just puffed at his pipe; he was as deaf as Cupid.

Betty, moved by the tranquillity and loveliness of the scene, asked for something sad. Harry wasn't sure he knew anything.

'Loch Lomond,' suggested Betty, with wide slow meditative chews of her gum.

Harry tried, but could not keep cheerfulness out. The lovers of the song mourned their eternal separation with admirable jauntiness.

Betty was displeased. She even took the gum out to demonstrate, in a Glasgow accent as buoyant as it was raucous, how the sadness of true love ought to be rendered.

Grinning, Harry played sadly.

Graham, scowling at them, informed Charlie he was lucky he was deaf.

Then they were all appalled into silence.

From amongst the rhododendrons came a shout of anguish: 'Peggy! Peggy!' And as they all, except Charlie who kept staring at a frog in the pond, turned in that direction they saw Duror rise up with his hand at his head and stagger about as if he was drunk or had just wakened from a nightmare.

In that nightmare Peggy had been sleeping in the garden. It was spring, for the gean tree in the corner by the elm was in glorious white blossom, and many birds were singing. He had helped her mother to dress her, handling with care and love her legs pale and swollen like monstrous slugs. Then he had wheeled her out into the garden which was more beautiful than he had ever seen it before. She had quickly fallen asleep. A thrush, speckled and alert, had hopped around her as if to protect her from insects. Cold cream had been smeared on her face lest the sun burn her skin, pale as mushroom; the garden was full of that fragrance. Suddenly everything had turned dark. There was a tremendous fluttering and chirping. Thousands of thrushes were flying out of the gean tree straight

63

towards Peggy, until they were round her as multitudinous as midges. When he had made to rush forward to drive them away, he had been unable; and it was in the terror of that paralysis that he had wakened.

Harry waited, with the mouth organ still at his lips. Betty nudged him as a warning to mind his manners. Graham stared at Charlie's frog, as if it was as much his business as a game-keeper with a whale for his wife.

The gum was at rest in Betty's mouth.

'Is there onything the maittcr, Mr. Duror?' she asked.

As he gazed about him the actual scene, with the girl in the bright scarf, the boy with the mouth organ, the two old men smoking, and the pond dotted with lily leaves, became confused in his vision with that imaginary one of his garden invaded by inimical thrushes and his wife pecked to pieces.

Shaking his head like a sick dog, he tried to shake off that hallucination; but though he could tell himself its cause was his lack of sleep over the past months, and lack of food that day, he still could not banish it. Horror of its possible perma-nence was gripping him more and more suffocatingly when he saw slipping through the bushes on the other side of the pond the two cone-gatherers; and he could not be sure whether they were really there in the actual world or had entered the garden. Never had the smaller one looked so like a monkey, as he came shuffling along, his hands close to the ground, his head without a neck turned up towards his brother, and his shoulders humped so grotesquely. Above them in the distance soared the wood, with the sun bright on its many crests of green and bronze and orange; and above those, gigantic cloud-castles with their turrets gleaming. He himself seemed to have shrunken to the tininess of the insect he had watched at the foot of the larch: yet the concept of unattainableness in his mind was as vast and as high as the heavens themselves.

'Here are the cone-men now,' shouted Betty.

She rose, and the rest rose with her. Whatever it was that had disturbed their leader in his doze, here had arrived the men for whom they had been waiting. The deer drive could now proceed.

Betty gave a shiver as she looked at the hunchback.

'God forgie me,' she muttered, 'but he fair gies me the creeps.'

'I saw a picture once,' whispered Harry. 'A jungle picture. There was a man in it had a pet ape; he led it about on a silver chain. It looked just like him.'

'Shut your mouths,' snarled Graham. 'The man's working for his keep.'

Charlie studied the cone-gatherers without bias; he gave them a nod each.

They reported to Duror.

'You're late,' he said.

'We've got no watch,' replied Neil truculently. 'I had to go by the sun. Before I agree to go on this deer drive, Mr. Duror, there's something you'll have to promise.'

Duror said nothing.

'If there's a clear stretch,' went on Neil fiercely, 'my brother's got to have it.' He turned and glared at his fellow-drivers.

'As far as I'm concerned,' said Graham, 'the stretch is his; but, mind you, there's none easy.'

Betty and Harry nodded. Charlie, who did not understand, also nodded; his was a confirming salutation.

'And I would like,' said Neil, 'to be put next to Calum.'

'Fair enough,' grunted Graham, and indicated he was speaking for them all.

Could that dream have had any meaning? thought Duror. Was Peggy dead? Suddenly it was as if the burden of misery was lifted from him. He began to laugh.

'Are you all ready?' he cried, and set off towards the dead ash where the drive would begin.

They hurried after him.

'What the hell's he got to be jolly about?' grumbled Graham. 'And what's the big hurry for?'

Betty and Harry found the quick pace a relief; it exercised their legs after the seat on the stone edge of the pond, and it enabled them to keep ahead of the cone-gatherers. Harry played 'Tipperary' on his mouth organ.

To Graham, Neil confided his worries about Calum.

The old sour-faced handyman glanced at the hunchback, who was smiling like a child.

'I'll tell you one thing,' he said, 'his lack of height will be to his advantage.'

There was no sarcasm in the observation; only much fellow-feeling and considerable envy.

'About the size of a stoat,' he said, 'is the right size for a deer drive through a wood.'

They had now entered the wood, in whose immense unassailable silence Harry's music sounded forlorn and Graham's grumbles seemed as inconsequential as the squeaks of mice. Nevertheless he persevered with them.

Duror's light-footed speed particularly annoyed him.

'Has he no mind I could give him twenty years?' he demanded of the tall trunks he passed. 'It's a wonder he doesn't expect us to catch the damned things by the tails and drag them up to the guns.'

He turned to Neil and Calum.

'Let me give you some advice,' he said grimly. 'When we get near the guns, drop down on your face as if you were praying for your life; and that's exactly what you will be doing, for there's a man yonder with a gun that's as blind as a mole and shouldn't be trusted with a peashooter. He damned near shot the arse off me. I didn't even see the deer. I was too busy finding breath and picking bramble hooks out of my hands. The guns started banging as if I'd wandered into the middle of the war itself. I did what any sensible man would have done. I ran for the nearest tree, but this blind character took me for a deer and banged away at me. Damned if he missed too. Now you would think that that man would never be trusted with a gun again as long as he, or anybody else, lived. You'd think, in a sensible world, nobody would allow him another chance for murder. Well, I'm warning you that he's yonder, at the far end, waiting, with a gun and an itching finger, to let fly at any living thing, deer or man, that bursts out of the wood. There are men getting medals for far less than what we're going to face.'

The dead ash clawed at the sky with branches white as bones. Under it Duror, pale but smiling, issued orders. Somehow he seemed to find it difficult to express himself clearly, or even to pronounce individual words distinctly; he was like a man talking in his sleep. His subordinates were surprised. These vague yet eager mumbles contrasted with his usual cool instructions: just as his bleary anxious unshavenness was so unlike his customary smooth inscrutability. They thought he must be ill; but none cared to ask.

The part of the wood to be beaten for deer sloped all the way from the roadside to the loch. Near the water the ground was gashed by deep gullies, overgrown with wild birches, bracken, and brambles. Harry, imagining himself a commando in the jungle, volunteered for this most perilous section. It was Graham who accepted his offer and packed him off, with the advice that if he met any wolves or tigers there, which was likely, it was better to run up a tree than to jump into the loch. Indeed, it turned out to be Graham who, like a lieutenant, disposed the forces; Duror stood by, smiling, and making an occasional not very relevant remark. Betty at her own request was placed next to Harry; she sauntered off to her station, chewing nonchalantly and letting loose some practice yodels. Her neighbour was Charlie, who was informed by a series of roars fit – so Graham said, in a hoarse parenthesis – to make any sensitive deer drop dead. As they watched him plod away with the deliberation of a man sent to stand upon a particular square foot of the wood, Graham prophesied that even if the drive was successful and deer were quickly shot the rest of the afternoon and most of the evening would have to be spent in searching for Charlie, who would be found miles away in another wood altogether.

Next in line came Calum, Neil, and Graham himself nearest the road. This last was the best stretch really, but only for a man with the devil and the enterprise to break the holy rules of deer-driving. If the going through the wood became too arduous, there was the fence to climb over and the road to sneak along. It was not likely, thought Graham, that the poor wee crooked saftie would be able to take advantage of those circumstances.

Duror took up position with his dogs between Calum and Charlie. At half-past two he fired his gun into the air to start the drive. Out of the trees at the bang shot several wood pigeons, slapping against the branches.

Deer drives can be revealers of personality. A conscript such as Erchie Graham let out at deliberately prolonged intervals snarls and barks and hoots, whose purpose was as much to express his disapproval as to terrify any deer in front of him. Charlie was conscientious, unresentful, and unimaginative. He tried out two or three calls, and decided that the utilitarian 'hoi' was best. He repeated it often. 'Hoi, hoi, hoi,' he would cry, and then would be silent for the same length of time. That was how he began, but later, when exhaustion and confusion had bewildered him, he often forgot to cry, and had to issue as many as ten 'hois' in a row to make up for his dereliction.

Betty had a generous repertoire. She put both hands to her mouth and yelled Glasgow street cries, such as: 'Ripe juicy tomatoes; toys for rags; coal, briquettes.' Then she sang, with an exaggeration of her native gallousness, several sentimental ballads of the day. Once when a sharp stick grazed her knee she flyted like a cheated delf wife; her own performance amused her so much she broke into laughter, which she raised gradually in pitch till it was like what she thought a hyena's would be or a crazy person's. That joke over, she sang or rather screamed to the silent senatorial trees some childhood doggerel:

'Auntie Leezie's currant bun!
We sat on the stairs
And we had such fun
Wi' Auntie Leezie's currant bun.'

Below her, plunging into his gullies and panting up them, Harry was the intrepid commando, dashing single-handed to the rescue: his cries were threats and challenges to the enemy, and encouragement to his captured comrades.

Neil dourly kept his mouth shut: the noise he made crashing through thickets was enough. Calum, however, was enticed by the beauty of the wood and the mystery of the game; he uttered long melodious calls and little chuckles.

It was Calum who first saw the deer.

The drive was nearly over. Only a hundred or so yards away were the waiting guns. Frightened by the noises approaching them from the rear, and apprehensive of the human silence ahead, the five roe deer were halted, their heads high in nervous alertness. When Calum saw them, his cry was of delight and friendship, and then of terrified warning as the dogs too, and Duror, caught sight of them and rushed in pursuit. Silently, with marvellous grace and agility over such rough ground, the deer flew for the doom ahead. Their white behinds were like moving glints of sunlight; without them their tawny hides might not have been seen in the autumnal wood.

Calum no longer was one of the beaters; he too was a deer hunted by remorseless men. Moaning and gasping, he fled after them, with no hope of saving them from slaughter but with the impulse to share it with them. He could not, however, be so swift or sure of foot. He fell and rose again; he avoided one tree only to collide with another close to it; and all the time he felt, as the deer must have, the indifference of all nature; of the trees, of tall withered stalks of willowherb, of the patches of blue sky, of bushes, of piles of cut scrubwood, of birds lurking in branches, and of the sunlight: presences which might have been expected to help or at least sympathise.

The dogs barked fiercely. Duror fired his gun in warning to those waiting in the ride. Neil, seeing his brother rush into the danger, roared to him to come back. All the beaters, except Charlie far in the rear, joined in the commotion; the wood resounded with their exultant shouts. Realising this must be the finish or kill, Graham, recuperating on the road, hopped back over the fence into the wood and bellowed loudest of all.

As Duror bawled to his dogs to stop lest they interfere with the shooting, and as the deer hesitated before making the dash across the ride, Calum was quite close to them as, silent, desperate, and heroic, they sprang forward to die or escape. When the guns banged he did not, as Neil had vehemently warned him to do, fall flat on the ground and put his fingers in his ears. Instead, with wails of lament, he dashed on at demented speed and shot out onto the broad green ride to hear a deer screaming and see it, wounded in the breast and forelegs, scrabbling about on its hindquarters. Captain Forgan was feverishly reloading his gun to fire again. Calum saw no one else, not even the lady or Mr. Tulloch, who was standing by himself about twenty yards away.

Screaming in sympathy, heedless of the danger of being shot, Calum flung himself upon the deer, clasped it round the neck, and tried to comfort it. Terrified more than ever, it dragged him about with it in its mortal agony. Its blood came off onto his face and hands.

While Captain Forgan, young Roderick, and Lady Runcie-Campbell stood petrified by this sight, Duror followed by his dogs came leaping out of the wood. He seemed to be laughing in some kind of berserk joy. There was a knife in his hand. His mistress shouted to him: what it was she did not know herself, and he never heard. Rushing upon the stricken deer and the frantic hunchback, he threw the latter off with furious force, and then, seizing the former's head with one hand cut its throat savagely with the other. Blood spouted. Lady Runcie-Campbell closed her eyes. Captain Forgan shook his head slightly in some kind of denial. Roderick screamed at Duror. Tulloch had gone running over to Calum.

The deer was dead, but Duror did not rise triumphant; he crouched beside it, on his knees, as if he was mourning over it. His hands were red with blood; in one of them he still held the knife.

There were more gunshots and shouts further down the ride.

It was Tulloch who hurried to Duror to verify or disprove the suspicion that had paralysed the others.

He disproved it. Duror was neither dead nor hurt.

Duror muttered something, too much of a mumble to be understood. His eyes were shut. Tulloch bent down to sniff; but he was wrong, there was no smell of whisky, only of the deer's sweat and blood. All the same, he thought, Duror had the appearance of a drunk man, unshaven, slack-mouthed, mumbling, rather glaikit.

Lady Runcie-Campbell came forward, with involuntary grimaces of distaste. She avoided looking at the hunchback, seated now against the bole of a tree, sobbing like a child, his face smeared with blood.

'Has he hurt himself?' she asked of Tulloch.

'I don't think so, my lady. He seems to have collapsed.'

Graham came panting down the ride.

His mistress turned round and saw him.

'Oh, Graham,' she said, 'please be so good as to drag this beast away.'

Graham glanced at deer and keeper. Which beast, your ladyship? he wanted to ask. Instead, he caught the deer by a hind leg and pulled it along the grass, leaving a trail of blood.

She turned back to Duror, now leaning against Tulloch.

'Have we nothing to wipe his face with?' she murmured peevishly.

Her brother was first to offer his handkerchief. With it Tulloch dabbed off the blood.

Duror opened his eyes.

'Peggy?' he asked. 'What's happened to Peggy?'

They all exchanged puzzled glances.

'There's nothing happened to your wife, Duror,' said Lady Runcie-Campbell. 'You seem to have fainted.'

Slowly he understood. His face worked painfully. She thought he looked at least twenty years older than he was. He saw the deer with its throat gashed; he made no sign of recognition, until he caught sight of his hands. From them he looked to where the hunchback was being attended to by his brother.

Duror seemed possessed by a fury to rise up and attack the hunchback. Tulloch and the Captain had to restrain him. They thought he was blaming the hunchback for having turned the drive into this horrid fiasco.

Lady Runcie-Campbell glanced towards the little cone-gatherer with aversion.

'I never thought a deer shoot could be made appear so dreadfully sordid,' she murmured.

She noticed Tulloch glancing at her with a frown.

The rest of the guns came up the ride, announcing with cheerful regret that they had fired but missed. Old Adamson cried that he thought he had winged one but he couldn't be sure. Their cheerfulness died when they saw Duror sitting on the ground. They thought there had been an accident.

Lady Runcie-Campbell felt annoyed: the situation was so grotesque that anything, even decent pity or pardonable amazement, would add to the sordidness. She felt that her own hands and face were all blood. Roderick too was in the thick of this defilement.

'Duror took an ill turn,' she explained sharply. 'I think, Duror,' she said, turning to him, 'the quicker we get you home the better. You'll have to stay in bed for a day or two, and of course you must see a doctor.'

Duror got to his feet, pushing off Tulloch's hand.

'I'm all right, my lady,' he said.

Again he threw a glance of hatred at the little cone-gatherer.

It seemed to them he was still blaming the hunchback for what had happened. They did not know that there by the dead deer he understood for the first time why he hated the hunchback so profoundly and yet was so fascinated by him. For many years his life had been stunted, misshapen, obscene, and hideous; and this misbegotten creature was its personification. Had the face been savage, brutal, ugly, in keeping with the body, there could have been no identification with his own case: then the creature would have been merely itself, as a toad was or a dragonfly larva, horrible but natural; but the face was mild, peaceful, and beautiful.

He knew too his wife was not dead, killed by thrushes' beaks or hunting knife. The misery, so miraculously shed that afternoon by the lilypond, sprang on him again, savage and overpowering as a tiger.

'Never mind, Duror,' said his mistress. 'I quite understand how you feel. The drive has been spoiled, and I agree with you as to the culprit.'

Again she noticed Tulloch glancing at her.

'But that's a different matter from your health,' she went on haughtily. 'You'll have to look after it, you know.'

'I'll live till I'm eighty, my lady,' he said, in an agony of bitterness.

She was taken aback.

'Well, I'm sure we all hope so,' she said at last.

Duror turned to the Captain.

'I'm sorry your drive was spoiled, sir,' he said.

Forgan laughed with nervous good nature. 'Don't worry about that, Duror,' he replied. But it was obvious he would worry about it himself.

His sister noticed. 'I feel pretty displeased about it,' she said. 'I must admit that. You, Duror, really ought to look after yourself more carefully. As for' – she again glanced towards the cone-gatherers – 'certain others, I think the sooner we see the last of them the better. Times are grim enough, heaven knows, without putting up with what's avoidable.'

On Tulloch's long thin bony face appeared a dour huff. She would not argue with him, she decided; if he made himself troublesome, she would go over his head to the District Officer, a man of education, breeding, and discernment.

Duror had turned aside to get on with his job. He ordered Graham to tie the deer by its legs to a long pole brought for the purpose, and carry it down the road to the house.

Graham was incensed. He had wished the beast no harm. He had not even seen it killed. He wouldn't get as much as an ounce of it to eat, and wouldn't eat it anyway if he did get it. Yet here he was being burdened with it all the way to the house, a distance of more than a mile.

'A pole's got two ends,' he observed. 'Am I to take them both?'

Duror looked round. He saw Betty and Harry.

'The boy and the girl can take turn about with the other end,' he said.

'Who,' asked Graham, 'is going to take turn about with my end? Me and Erchie Graham, is that it?'

Duror looked scornfully from him to the deer.

'It's a small beast,' he said. 'I could carry it under my oxter.'

Do it then, said Graham's face; his voice, more discreet, muttered: 'Are you forgetting that I'm above the age when most men are either buried or pensioned off? Anyway,' he added, looking up and down the ride, 'where's Charlie?'

Charlie hadn't yet come out of the wood.

Adamson his master had gone up the ride with Lady Runcie-Campbell and her party.

'Maybe we ought to go and look for him?' suggested Graham.

'Do that if you like,' said Duror, 'so long as you carry the deer back afterwards.'

Then the gamekeeper turned and went up the ride.

Graham put his thumb to his nose and twiddled his fingers after him.

Meanwhile Tulloch had been talking to his cone-gatherers.

'When they asked you to take part in the drive, Neil,' he asked, 'did you explain about Calum?'

'I did, Mr. Tulloch.'

'And yet they still persisted that he should go?'

'Aye.'

'Was it the keeper came to you?'

Neil nodded.

'He seems to have a spite against you. Is there any reason for it?' He saw from Neil's face there was some such reason. 'You'd better tell me, Neil, and be quick about it. I want to speak to the lady about this business. She blames Calum for spoiling the deer hunt.'

'I ken that, and it's not fair.'

'No, it isn't fair, Neil, and I'll tell her so. But first tell me why the keeper's got this grudge against you.'

Bitterly Neil divulged about the rabbits released from the snares.

'How long had they been in the snares?' asked Tulloch quickly.

'A whole night and a day. Maybe longer. It was cruelty.'

'Well,' said Tulloch slowly, 'I suppose the man's short-handed these days. In peacetime he'll have somebody to help him. But it's still against humanity to leave creatures to starve or choke themselves to death. You're sure that's all he's got against you?'

'I'd swear it on my mother's grave.'

Tulloch's voice softened. 'All right, Neil,' he murmured. 'Don't worry. Whatever the upshot of this, I'll see you two don't suffer.'

'There are men above you, Mr. Tulloch. She might appeal to them. She might get you into trouble if you cross her. We wouldn't want that. You've been good to us, and forby you've got a wife and children to think of.'

Tulloch smiled bleakly towards that wife and children. These were hostages which had already thwarted him in his

75

desire to champion his underlings against his superiors. Though he loved them he loved justice too.

'It'll turn out all right,' he said. 'There's nothing to be afraid of. You see, Neil, I think she's genuine. She'll not penalise anybody unfairly.'

Neil shook his head; he did not have so much trust in her. She was wealthy and powerful, they were poor and weak: why should she trouble to be fair to them?

'Just you wait here a few minutes,' said Tulloch. 'I'll come back and let you know how I get on.' He turned to Calum. 'Are you feeling all right now, Calum?'

'Yes,' whispered the hunchback.

Tulloch laid his hand on the deformed back.

'It wasn't your fault, Calum,' he said. 'I saw it all with my own eyes. You weren't to blame.'

'He was,' muttered Neil. 'Why didn't he do what I told him? Why didn't he just drop on his face and stay there?'

Again Tulloch gazed away with that peculiar bleak smile.

'It's not for us, Neil,' he said, 'to say that it's a mistake to break your heart over an injured and dying creature, even if that creature's only a deer. I'll have to hurry though, or I'll miss her. I'll not be long.'

He turned and ran up the ride, while behind him Neil continued to nag at Calum, and Graham, Betty, and Harry called in the wood for Charlie. Tied to the pole, the deer lay bleeding on the grass.

When Tulloch arrived at the big shooting-brake, Lady Runcie-Campbell was about to climb into the driver's seat. Her brother and Roderick were already in the car. Duror stood by the gate, ready to shut it when the car had passed through; his dogs sat beside him.

Adamson and Baird had gone off in the former's rusty rattling old car.

Tulloch suspected that the lady too would have been away had she not felt that courage and decency demanded she wait and tell him what she had already told the others.

Her first words proved him right. She spoke in a high-pitched patrician tone, and her fingers drummed imperiously against the door of the car.

'Mr. Tulloch,' she said, 'I've decided that I want you to remove those two men from the wood. I have no objection to the cone-gathering as such, but please arrange to have two others sent in their place. It will not do any good whatever to argue or plead with me. I have seen all I want of them. It is perhaps a small thing that deer-shooting should have been turned into a shocking demeaning spectacle, permanently it may be; but small thing or not, I object to being subjected to such a humiliation on my own land. They must go, as soon as it can be arranged.'

It was not Tulloch who protested. Her son Roderick cried from the car: 'But that's not fair, mother. You said yourself he didn't want to take part in the deer drive.'

'When I wish to have your advice, Roderick,' she said coldly, 'I shall ask for it.'

His pale toothy rather spoiled face was as stubborn as her beautiful one; and there were other resemblances.

'But it isn't fair,' he insisted. 'He didn't try it; he couldn't help it. If he'd been left to climb the trees, there would have been no trouble.'

'Will you hold your tongue?' she cried.

'You told me yourself,' he muttered intensely, 'never to be quiet if I saw injustice being done.'

She started, and was painfully embarrassed by having that grandiloquent precept, that maternal counsel of perfection, repeated to her there, by him, in the open, in the presence of strangers, of inferiors.

Tulloch intervened. He spoke with quiet sincerity. He knew that right was on his side, and against her such an ally must prevail, provided her pride as the grand lady, the represent-ative of aristocracy, was not insulted.

'I have questioned them, my lady,' he said, 'and I saw what happened; and I find no fault in them.'

She gasped, and looked sharply at him, wondering whether his words were a deliberate quotation aimed against her faith, or whether their resemblance to Pilate's was fortuitous. Her father had been fond of quoting those words.

'If I am to take them away from the wood,' added Tulloch, 'what am I to tell them is the reason? They are simple men, easily discouraged. If they have done wrong, they will accept their punishment; but if they have done no wrong, and are punished, it will take away all their confidence.'

'Is it not enough that I wish them to go?' she asked haughtily.

Tulloch did not answer.

She turned towards Duror. 'What do you think, Duror?' she asked. 'Since Black's away the wood is your province. Surely you agree with me that their presence in it is now, to say the least, distasteful?'

Duror felt tired, weak, hungry, and sick; yet he would not lean against the gate. He stood erect, giving the impression of aloofly but impartially considering the question. The truth was his thoughts were fragmentary and elusive. Yes, he wanted the cone-gatherers out of the wood. Had he not vowed to have them driven out? But the hunchback in some dreadful way had become associated with him, in fact had become necessary to him. If the crooked little imbecile was sent back now to the forest at Ardmore, he would live happily there whilst here in the wood Duror's own torment continued. His going therefore must be a destruction, an agony, a crucifixion. A way to achieve that would be to spread the lie about his indecencies in the wood. But was this a suitable time to let it out, in the presence of the boy, and the brother, and Tulloch, who would deny it and might even be able to disprove it?

'Don't be afraid to speak,' said his mistress, 'even if you do not agree with me. Perhaps I am in a minority of one here. Mr. Tulloch thinks I'm being unjust; Roderick has expressed his opinion most plainly; you hesitate to answer; and Captain Forgan remains neutral.' Though she smiled it was evident she was agitated. 'What do you think, Eric?' she asked her brother. 'It was your deer shoot he spoiled, your memories he polluted. I shall leave the decision to you.'

'No,' he said quietly, shaking his head. 'The decision cannot be mine. If it's any help, though, I may say that I bear the poor fellow no ill will; and my memories are not polluted.'

She threw up her hand in surrender.

'Very well then,' she cried. 'I am outnumbered. Let them stay. But please, for God's sake,' she added with trembling voice as she climbed into the car, 'warn them to keep out of my way; and as for the silver firs near the house, those are forfeit.' She tried to make a joke of this retaliation, and laughed; but they all saw she was deeply troubled.

Tulloch's salute to her, and his gratitude, were genuine. She was wealthy and influential enough to dispense with conscience, or at least to bribe it successfully; but she was too honest in her endeavour to be a Christian. She knew how hard it was for the rich and powerful to enter the kingdom of heaven.

'I'll close the gate after you, my lady,' he said.

'Thank you, Mr. Tulloch. You'd better get in then, Duror.'

The gamekeeper hesitated. 'What about the dogs, my lady?' he muttered. 'Maybe I should walk with them.'

'You will do no such thing. I owe you an apology, Duror. I'm afraid I've been forgetting you're not well.'

'I'm well enough, my lady.'

'You don't look it. Get in. We've had dogs in the car before.'

The Captain repeated the invitation and reached out to help Duror and the dogs in.

As the car passed Tulloch, he was struck most of all by the boy's face; for all its gawkiness it was so like his mother's; and on it was a look of dedication, to what the forester could only guess.

Chapter Seven

On Saturday the beneficent weather continued: frost at dawn, iridescence and gold at noon, and afterwards blue skies, warmth, and astonished singing of birds. That morning, however, Neil chose to work in a Douglas fir tree; the darkness amidst its evergreen branches suited his mood.

Since the deer drive he had been bitter and rebellious. When Mr. Tulloch, with much satisfaction at his own diplomacy and admiration of the lady's sense of fairness, had told them they were to be allowed to stay on in the wood provided they kept out of everybody's way, Neil had listened with eyes on the ground and lips tight: not for Calum's sake even could he at that moment have admitted they owed the lady gratitude. Afterwards, in walking to the hut, he had burst out into a passionate denunciation of the lady and what she stood for. Seizing Calum fiercely, he had dragged him out of the way of a bush whose outermost twigs he might have brushed against in passing, and had shouted that surely he had heard what Mr. Tulloch had said, they were to keep out of the way, they were to provoke nobody, they were to be like insects, not bees or ants which could sting and bite, but tiny flies which could do no harm since there was nothing in creation so feeble as not to be able to molest them. Calum, already bewildered and miserable, had not understood; into his sobs had come entreaty, but this time Neil had not yielded.

Nor had he yielded by Saturday. When Calum accidentally tore off a spray of the Douglas fir and was smelling its fragrance, Neil caught sight of him.

'Is that a cone?' he shouted.

Calum, puzzled, looked at the green spray in his hand.

'I asked you, is that a cone?'

Calum shook his head. He smiled. 'No, Neil, it's just a bit of branch. It came off. I couldn't help it.'

'You're here to collect cones, that's all,' yelled Neil. 'You're to do nothing else. How often have I to tell you that? Didn't you hear Mr. Tulloch himself say it?'

'But I couldn't help it, Neil.'

'The likes of you and me have just got to help it, when our betters tell us. You can't even have an accident and fall from this tree. Do you ken why? Because the lady would get to hear about it, and she'd be annoyed; she'd be annoyed because you'd broken your neck and spilled your blood on her land.'

'I don't think that's what Mr. Tulloch said, Neil.'

'No, but it's what he meant. Didn't he say we'd to keep out of everybody's way? Didn't he say we're just here to gather cones?'

'But that's right, Neil.'

'You're a child, Calum. Though you're past thirty, you're still a child; and you'll always be a child. But I'm a man, and I've got the intelligence and pride of a man. Do you ken what I'm going to do when we get to Lendrick today?'

'No, Neil.'

'I'm going into the bar yonder, and I'm going to get drunk. I've never been drunk before, though I've had many a cause. Why should I stay sober to suffer all their snash?'

Calum could never be sure how serious his brother was in these rages.

'If you get drunk, Neil,' he said, 'the policeman will lock you up.'

Neil swayed towards him, angrily triumphant. 'And what if he did? I'll tell you something: the cell he'd lock me up in would be bigger than our hut, aye, and cleaner.'

Calum went on with his gathering. He did not want to ask what would he do if Neil was locked up; but the question was in his every placating glance, in his plucking of every cone.

Neil noticed the appeal, and though it crushed his heart he would not surrender to it. He could not have explained his obduracy: not only were all past humiliations, real and imagined, accumulated in him like the leaves of forty autumns, but the war itself contributed, though he could hardly have said

81

why or how. He had read often in the newspapers and had heard on the wireless that the war was being fought so that ordinary humble people could live in peace without being bullied and enslaved by brutal men with power; but, living as he did in a lonely, unimportant part of the world, he had never consciously seen himself or Calum as in any way involved. They were not Jews being dragged to the concentration camp. Yet, without his being aware of it, the proud claims of honour and independence and courage made on behalf of his country at war affected him deeply in his own private attitude: it was necessary now for him to fight back against every injustice inflicted on him, and especially on his brother.

On their way back to the hut they came upon a herd of deer, perhaps the same that had been the victims of the drive. One seemed wounded; it limped badly. All were particularly nervous, as if the death of their companion still haunted them.

Calum pulled his brother behind the broad trunk of a Wellingtonia. Then, in a trance of love and reconciliation, he gazed at the deer and uttered little sighs.

For about a minute Neil remained silent and motionless; in him an anger and terror mounted, not against the animals whom he pitied, nor against his brother whom he loved. Suddenly it burst out. Shouting wildly, he scrabbled among the leaves and grass for something to throw, found a stick, and hurled it in the direction of the deer. These had already fled, and the stick, being decayed, disintegrated in the air. As Calum seized his arm, and in a desperate shriek pleaded with him not to harm the deer or even to wish to harm them, Neil punched with his other fist against the soft cork-like bark of the great tree, shouting incoherently. Had it been any other tree his knuckles would have been broken and bloody.

'What is the matter, Neil?' wailed Calum. 'Why did you chase them away?'

'Because they were doing no harm, that's why.'

Calum did not understand.

'I wanted to tell them I was sorry,' he sobbed.

Neil gripped him, and bending glared into his eyes.

'They're just animals,' he cried, 'wild animals. You can't tell them anything.'

Calum nodded eagerly. 'You can, Neil.'

Neil thought of Duror the gamekeeper and the lady who, though human beings, were incommunicable.

'If you like them, you can, Neil,' repeated Calum.

'The lady says she likes them,' muttered Neil, 'and she shoots them for fun.'

Calum cowered under that mystery: he believed the lady liked the deer, and also that she shot them for fun. Yet he could find no solution or solace in hating her for her strange inconsistency.

Neil laughed.

'She prefers them to us,' he said. 'They belong to her, they've got a right to be in her wood, eating her grass. Shooting them is something she can take a pleasure in. Just talking to us would make her grue.'

'I don't ken,' whispered Calum.

'No, Calum, you don't ken. But how could you ken, when I don't ken myself. We're not on her side, and we're not on the deer's. No!' he cried, as he saw the shy sure smile on his brother's face. Again he punched the tree. 'No, Calum, we're not on any side.'

Calum still smiled. 'It's all right, Neil,' he murmured.

'All right?' Neil frowned as he swung round and walked on. 'God help you, Calum. Everybody's at everybody else's throat, and you say it's all right. Maybe,' he added, in a whisper anguished in its disloyalty, 'being soft in the wits has its advantages.'

Lunch on Saturdays was always frugal. By that time the week's provisions were exhausted, but even if there had been plenty of food they would have been too excited to prepare and eat it. Stripped to the waist, they washed the tree griminess off them in the burn that flowed past their hut. Neil would have complained at this having to wash out of doors like animals, had he not remembered that soldiers on the battle-field lacked baths and hot water, and had he not, amidst his truculence, been overwhelmingly moved to tenderness and stoicism by the sight of his brother's misshapen body. There-fore as they crouched on stones in the glittering burn, passing the soap to each other, they chatted about what they would buy in Lendrick that afternoon, and what they would do. Calum was overjoyed that his brother's sullen cantankerous mood seemed at last over; he planned, with chuckles into the chuckling water, to buy Neil a present as a surprise: a new pipe maybe, for Neil's old one was mended with black tape; or even a poke of the mint sweeties that were Neil's favourites.

Dressed in their week-end outfits of blue serge suits, collars and ties, and polished boots, they hurried to the roadside to wait for the bus. As their alarm clock was unreliable, they weren't sure of the time. Calum sat perched, smiling and patient, on a straining-post of the fence; Neil fidgeted and grumbled on the roadway, tugging at his collar and tie, which always for the first hour or so seemed to be choking him.

The bus, which came from Glasgow, a hundred miles away, was late. As they had arrived by the roadside half an hour early, they had to wait such a long time that they began to be afraid they had missed it. There was no other. If they still wished to visit Lendrick they might have to walk. No private car would ever stop to offer them a lift, and since it was Saturday afternoon there would be few lorries. It was not fair, Neil shouted aloud, that for a little enjoyment they should have to suffer so much discomfort: at the big house there were at least three cars.

Then as he stood with clenched fists in the middle of the road round the corner rushed the red bus. Calum bounced off the post. Neil held up his hand. The driver, with a grin, stopped; the conductress, also grinning, pulled open the door; and the passengers looked on in pleasure and sympathy as the two strange shy men climbed in and sat on a seat at the back.

A child, bored by the long journey, made to exclaim in wonder at the sight of Calum, but his mother silenced him and whispered into his ear that it was very rude to remark upon another person's appearance in public. Her son hardly listened, but continued to gaze at Calum in an interest so bright and so willingly committed there could be no mockery in it; so much so that Calum, seeing the boy's smile, smiled back.

As if to prove to Neil that the wood was the only place where unfriendliness flourished and kindness withered, everywhere that afternoon the brothers were received with courtesy, affability, and helpfulness. For instance, when they stepped off the bus at the Lendrick War Memorial, not only the swans in the harbour flapped their wings in welcome, but the big policeman there, outwardly as dour as any stot, touched his helmet in a sunny salute.

'Well, boys,' he said, 'this is surely a strange direction for you to come from.'

Neil explained they were gathering cones in the Lendrickmore estate.

'Oh,' laughed the policeman, 'so it's hobnobbing with the gentry you are, is it?'

Neil frowned, as if his feelings were hurt, so that the policeman quickly added: 'Is it an interesting sort of job at all?'

'Calum likes it,' said Neil. 'But I'm getting a bit stiff to be climbing trees.'

Glad then of his disguising dourness, the policeman glanced at Calum, thought first of his unsuitability as climber and a moment after of his queer sad suitability. Heartily he nodded.

'Just that,' he said. 'But if there's no seed, there's no trees. It's useful work; aye, and dangerous enough. Just you take care.'

It was the same with everybody they met. In the draper's shop which they diffidently entered to buy Calum's new shirt, the man didn't need to have it explained to him why so small a man as Calum required a shirt so wide in the neck. He understood immediately, and attended to them with so much

85

tact, patience, and geniality that they went out laughing and confident into the sunshine, with the parcel under Calum's arm.

In the grocer's shop under-the-counter delicacies were produced for them, and extra rations. Other customers, themselves denied, looked on, smiling, without envy. When they left it was to the accompaniment of cordial nods, smiles, and good wishes. There seemed to Neil to be two sunshines: that shining all round, on the water, in the street, and even on the trees growing round the ancient ruined castle; and that radiating from people's minds. The one warmed his face, the other his heart. As his rancour towards the lady and the gamekeeper disappeared, leaving his mind relieved, cleansed, and buoyant, he knew, with a pang of pride and amazement, that how he felt now Calum must feel nearly all the time. Strolling along the street, therefore, he thought it was not enough that he should keep affectionately close to his brother; he ought to be shouting out to people about this wonderful superiority of Calum, who to look at seemed so pitiful and stunted. Of course he did not shout; the secret lay in his mind sweetening and preserving it.

Only a coastal steamer was at the quay. They went along to look at her. Ships of any kind delighted Neil. He had once confessed to Mr. Tulloch that if he had not had Calum to look after he would have been a sailor. Sea-faring was in his blood, he had said; but when the forester had asked naturally enough if his father had been a seaman he had answered yes, with an abruptness by no means characteristic. The forester had been left with the suspicion that there was a mystery about that paternity: but as he had remarked later to his wife, mystifying her, what did it really matter after all, gulls were wild and white and bonny, and none of them knew their fathers.

Often Neil sat in their bothy on winter nights and told Calum about seas he had never seen. Now, on the quay, staring at the tiny steamer, he imagined it was a huge trans-atlantic vessel of which he was captain: soon, under his guidance, it would leave this little harbour and head for the ocean. Entranced, he saw it after lonely battles with tempestuous waves passing through the Golden Gates into San Francisco.

So absorbed did he become in his reverie, Calum was able to slip away across the street to a shop which sold everything a seaman might need, including pipes. He chose one with a gilt band round it. The shopkeeper searched for a box to put it in, and wrapped the box in brown paper bound with fancy twine; he even wrote on it: For Neil. When Calum came out Neil was anxiously looking for him, but he refused to say what he had been doing. The present was safe in his pocket; he would give it to Neil later as a surprise.

In the café they were escorted to the table they liked in the furthest corner by Joe the proprietor, who would not let them sit down until he had flicked chairs and table clean. Having shouted to Maggie their favourite waitress, he stood for a minute talking to them about their job of gathering cones, and telling them a story about a tree he'd once climbed which had a wasp's byke in it unbeknown to him. While they were all laughing at his remembered panic-stricken flight, Maggie arrived. Abnormal herself with her splayed feet, crimson cheeks, and her perennial good nature, she always seemed to look on it as a privilege more than a duty to attend to Calum; Neil got the advantage of the special favours incidentally. She was never satisfied until they had salt, pepper, vinegar, and two kinds of sauce, thick and thin; their portions of fish and chips were always large and steaming hot; and their cakes and bread were never stale. The first time she had showered these kindnesses upon them they had been uneasy, or at least Neil had been. Afterwards he had not been sure whether he should leave a tip, and how much. He had left a shilling under a plate, but next time they had come in she had insisted on giving it back. Weren't they all friends and neighbours now? she had asked. Hadn't her sister's windows in Greenock been blown in by a bomb?

While they were enjoying their meal and placidly tholing the cacophony from the wireless set, they saw the first of the Ardmore workers arrive in the café. The contrast between his own reception and that given to the three laughing young men made Neil's corner cosier and his chips more succulent: his right to be eating there in comfort, safety, and friendliness now depended on something more valuable than the money he would pay. The newcomers were conscientious objectors.

Neil himself had never any prejudice against them. Indeed, their arrival at Ardmore two years ago had done him and Calum a good turn by accelerating their acceptance into the community. Everybody had united against these outcasts both on and off the hill. Local men, ordered by Mr. Tulloch, had unwillingly instructed them in planting, draining, bracken-cutting, and all the other tasks of forestry; but at break-times, munching their bread and drinking their tea, often with rain pelting down, the two groups had sheltered under different rocks. Neil had taken part in this ostracism, not from choice, but because by conforming he won comradeship for himself. Yet he had watched how slowly and imperceptibly, like a tree's growth, the distrust and contempt had been broken down until now the local men accepted invitations to the pacifists' hut for supper and songs. He had seen too how the incomers had refused to admit the feud or be angered by the animosity. They had remained cheerful, and undefeated. Neil had said nothing, but he had learnt that if a man felt he had done no wrong and kept his head high, he would become respected in the end.

Calum had never taken part in the exclusion. At first his non-cooperation had been resented until it was decided that, as a daftie, he must be excused. The truth was, as Neil knew, Calum was too honest, generous, and truly meek. The young men from the beginning had treated him as if he was an adult human being, with his own views and outlook: instinctively he had returned the compliment. There were some among them with University degrees who were glad to listen to him speaking about birds and animals and flowers.

They were still not welcome here in Lendrick, however; and Neil was. Therefore in the presence of the villagers he did as all the Ardmore men did: he either hurried past them with a nod, or spoke to them as shortly as possible, and behind their backs he condoned the local opinion that they were cowards and scrimshankers. In his heart he knew he was wrong in not speaking up in defence of men whom he worked beside happily for long hours day after day in places of loneliness and beauty. During his lifetime he had suffered so much from neglect that he could not risk being driven from the fold so tight and clamorous but also so warm and secure.

Again Calum was excused; he who spoke to dogs in the street and birds in the sky could speak even to shirkers.

Now in the café the three young men came over to their table and chatted merrily for a few minutes. They gave the news from Ardmore and asked about the cone-gathering. Calum answered them. Neil, mindful of Lendrick eyes watching, nodded or shook his head. Yet, as he heard them say they intended to stay and see the film showing that night, he remembered how not long after they arrived they had come out of the cinema at eleven o'clock on a dark wet winter's night, to find the tyres of their bicycles slashed, so that they had to walk home. Now they still left their bicycles in the same place and no one harmed them. It seemed therefore that hatred could not last but must give way to tolerance. In spite of people the circle of trust widened.

When the brothers left the café and saw the shooting-brake from Lendrickmore big house draw up outside the hotel, Neil found he had no spite against the lady or against the game-keeper, who was coming out of the car with a parcel under his arm.

Calum, on the contrary, was instantly agitated. He did not want to pass them; he pleaded with Neil to turn and go back the other way.

'Why should we?' murmured Neil. 'We've got nothing to be afraid of, or ashamed of either. Come on.'

89

They approached the car, Calum to the inside with his eyes turned away.

'We'll just walk by,' whispered Neil. 'They'll not even notice us.'

He was wrong. Roderick, who was in the car with his sister, saw them and thrust out his head.

'Hello there,' he cried cheerfully.

His mother turned from Duror to see whom her son could be addressing. When she saw, she gasped in astonishment.

Neil's dignity and composure, proper to a sea-captain, crumbled into the abjectness of a peasant. He fumbled at his cap.

'Good evening,' he mumbled, and could not prevent himself adding, 'sir.'

Then he hurried away, not waiting for Calum.

Chapter Eight

Lady Runcie-Campbell burst out laughing; she was still astonished, but she was also fond and proud.

'Well,' she said, 'aren't you the complete democrat? But don't overdo it, please.'

'I wanted to tell them we were sorry,' he said.

Her astonishment sharpened into indignation.

'What!' she cried. 'If this is a joke, Roderick, I don't much admire its taste.'

'It's not a joke,' he said. 'We didn't treat them fairly.'

She frowned. Foreboding chilled her. Too weak physically to be able to attend school like other boys of his class, was he also, as his father when tipsy at midnight had once dolefully declared, faulty in mind? He did not see things or people as a baronet's heir should. Certainly his tutor could not be accused of corrupting him: Mr. Sorn-Wilson was more aristocratic than any duke. Yet there had been a corrupter: her own father now dead; and perhaps there still was one, herself the Christian.

With a sigh she turned again to Duror.

He had been standing respectfully waiting for permission to take his leave.

She found comfort and encouragement in his aloof submissiveness. Surely an order of society in which so honourable a man as Duror knew his subordinate place and kept it without grievance or loss of dignity, must be not only healthy and wise, but also sanctioned by God?

'Of course he knows you're coming, Duror,' she said. 'I telephoned him.'

'It was good of you, my lady.'

'I'll consider my goodness recompensed,' she said, smiling, 'when you come back with a good report.'

'I'm sure I'll be able to do that, my lady.'

'You'd be a hard man to convince you were ill, Duror. I don't ever remember you being ill.'

'I have never been ill, since I had the measles at ten.'

She laughed. 'Touch wood, Duror, touch wood.' She touched it for him. As she did so, she remembered her husband and brother in Africa, where men were killing one another; and she found herself wishing that the ancient superstition had virtue in it. Christ of course would then be banished forever into the darkness.

She shivered.

'Well, Duror,' she said, 'you know we're going to the pictures. We'll pick you up here as soon as the show's over.'

'Very good, my lady.'

'You won't keep us waiting?' She dropped her voice. 'I don't want to keep the children up any later than is necessary.'

He knew she was worried about the boy.

'I'll be here waiting for you, my lady,' he said.

An irrelevant thought occurred to her.

'How will those two get back?' she asked.

He knew whom she meant. 'They'll walk.'

'Walk? Dear me.' She laughed. 'I wouldn't say they look very good walkers, whatever they're like as climbers of trees. They must be very keen surely to visit Lendrick.'

'Likely they'll find it lonely in the wood, my lady.'

'I suppose so.' Admiring Duror for his solicitude, she indulged in a little herself. 'I suppose they're to be pitied really.'

'Why don't we offer them a lift, Mother?' asked Roderick, in the quiet voice she had learned to regard as ominous. 'We've got plenty of room.'

'Don't be absurd,' she said quickly.

'I don't think I'm being absurd. They can sit next to me. I don't mind.'

'Well, I do.' It was Sheila who spoke, rescuing her mother from the predicament of having to rebuke Roderick for naivety, and at the same time trying to preserve his charitable attitude towards his inferiors.

Earnestly he argued with his sister.

'They wouldn't have to be near you, Sheila,' he said. 'You could sit in beside mother. They could sit at the back away from everybody.'

'My dear boy,' said his mother, laughing, 'this is no time for playing Sir Galahad.'

'We've carried dogs in the car,' he said.

'Yes, we have. It's our car, dear boy. We can please ourselves whom or what we carry. You're being too quixotic for words.'

He spoke quietly, in a kind of huff. 'Human beings are more important than dogs.'

'Don't be a prig,' she snapped.

Sheila said firmly, 'Monty's more important to me than they are.'

'That's wrong,' he muttered. 'It's wicked.'

'I don't care if it is wicked,' she retorted. 'What are *you* talking about anyway?' She was about to cast up to him his rudeness to Duror during the cricket game, but she refrained in time.

There was a silence in the car. During it Duror asked for permission to leave.

His mistress gave it reluctantly. Silly and mawkish though this discussion about the cone-gatherers was, still it worried her, and his presence was reassuring. She had enough experience of handling servants to know that among the working-class itself was a hierarchy as jealously observed as that in church or nobility. Duror, for instance, would rightly place himself high above these cone-men.

She called him back. He came at once, quickly, and yet without any appearance of obsequious haste.

'I know it's ridiculous of me even to entertain the thought, Duror,' she said, in a whisper, 'but I'd like your opinion all the same. Ought I to offer these people a lift?'

'No, my lady.'

Roderick said quietly, 'But you've got a spite against them, Duror.'

Duror gazed in at the boy, his superior.

'No, Master Roderick,' he murmured, shaking his head. 'You see, I know that the little one is an evil person.'

There was another silence. Then Sheila gave a gasp, a shudder, and a giggle.

'I must say, he looks it,' she said.

'That's a formidable word you've chosen, Duror,' remarked Lady Runcie-Campbell ruefully.

'I know it is, my lady. I shall explain to your ladyship later why I had to use it.'

'Yes, later.' She meant: For God's sake, not now, whatever it is, in the children's presence. 'You'll be late for your appointment, Duror. I think you'd better go now.'

'Yes, my lady.'

As he walked away, he heard Roderick murmur, 'I don't believe it'; and he smiled at the rawness of the boy who still saw evil as dwelling only in certain men and women, and not as a presence like air, infecting everyone.

Walking along the road by the harbour, he kept smiling as he thought how Lady Runcie-Campbell's displeasure with the cone-gatherers was as rose thorns to the tiger's claws of his aversion. In a few minutes he would be in the surgery, with the stethoscope cold against his bare chest, and in his ears the old doctor's whiskied satisfied grunts. For of course the doctor would hear the beat of a sound heart and the breathing of healthy lungs: not the snarling of the tiger, nor the roaring of storm through the tree of doom now high and ripe in him. 'It may be your heart, you know, Duror,' Lady Runcie-Campbell had said, advising him not to cycle but to travel in her car. He had touched his cap, he had murmured gratefully. She had not seen him suddenly grow enormous and loom over her like a tree falling; she had not heard him shout, in a voice to be heard in the heaven of her faith, that in the wood his wife had changed for an instant into a roe-deer and he had cut her throat and tried to appease his agony in her blood. She had not seen this monster in her so respectful, so self-controlled, so properly subservient gamekeeper. Like the tiger-tamer in his cage, she had again, with inveterate confidence, turned her back.

The doctor's house was the second last villa beyond the pier. At that point, just where the road was about to end in the wilderness of the shore, the first glimpse of the open sea was got, with the far-off twinkle of the lighthouse.

There Duror paused. Whin bushes, profusely golden in summer, stirred rustily in the breeze. Against the darkling sky he saw in the doctor's garden one of the palm trees grown in this mild northern land; and further off, with even stronger temptation of distance, were stars, so remote, and so oblivious of his infinitely petty existence that for a few moments he experienced rest and hope. Sweat broke out over his body. Gazing towards the doctor's lighted window he thought that perhaps the old man might be able to prescribe some powder or pills to induce not sleep only but an awakening into a life where he could again touch the elm tree before he entered his house.

As the hope faded, and the lighthouse's beam strengthened, he recalled his travail under that elm after the deer drive. The shooting-brake had set him and his dogs down outside his house. The sun had been shining and birds singing. Only a few paces across the white shingle was his gate. There were still some flowers on the fuchsia bushes. Suddenly over the whole scene had dropped darkness, in the midst of which the birds had continued to sing, but without purpose, desolately. He could not move; he was as powerless as the elm beside him; and for those two or three minutes he had felt his sap, poisoned, flowing out of him into the dark earth. His dogs had whined up at him in bewilderment, alarm, and love; they had growled at the enemy persecuting him, which they could sense but not see.

By the whins then, empty of hope, he knew there was one thing on earth he did not want ever again to see: the smile of the hunchback. He swung from it as a pony from an adder.

So vivid was his horror of seeing it that he actually shut his eyes there on the darkening road; but there were eyes within him he could not close at will, and these now began to see that smile, and only that smile.

It was the doctor's wife who admitted him. She was a small white-haired woman in black. The sadness of her face was a joke amongst those patients whose ailments were trifling; others, fearful that their pains might be diagnosed as mortal, saw no cause for smiles in her prophetic dejection.

'The doctor's waiting for you in the surgery, Mr. Duror,' she said.

Crossing to the surgery door, she knocked on it and waited till her husband opened it.

He was, on the contrary, as effervescent as if, a minute ago, he had just discovered a panacea. Duror smelled whisky.

'I've brought you some venison, doctor,' he said, 'with Lady Runcie-Campbell's compliments.'

The doctor snatched it and began to dandle it, as if it was new-born baby and he its delighted father.

This, thought Duror, is the man on whom I have to depend for a cure.

Mrs. Matheson was not amused.

'Give it to me,' she said. 'I'll take it to the kitchen.'

He handed it over with mocking tenderness.

'A feudal gift of venison,' he chuckled, smacking his lips. 'It takes one back to the halcyon days of bows and arrows. I wonder,' he added, 'if your mistress, Duror, knows any Russian generals with caviare to spare.'

This remark, as seemed to be its intention, sent off his wife with indignant sighs. He gazed after her with a momentary blank in his glee.

'Mrs. Matheson,' he murmured, 'is an incorrigible Scot. Food is to eat to keep in health to work and praise God. Tatties and saut herring are food. Caviare and venison are gluttony. But in you come.'

He ushered Duror into the surgery, and saw him seated.

'My wife has a sister in Oban,' he said, 'with a son a lieutenant in the Navy. He goes regularly with the convoys to Russia. If I mention caviare, she thinks I'm dropping a hint that she should write to him to fetch me a tin. Whereas, of course, I merely use the word as a symbol. I am well aware these convoys are dangerous and heroic. I hope you're in no hurry, Duror?'

'Not really, doctor.'

'Fine. I hope you don't mind my blethering to you like this? Sometimes I go down to the hotel lounge and say things I rue afterwards. But you're a man of some perception and tact. Did you bike it into the village?'

'No. I came in the car.'

The doctor brought out cigarettes. Duror shook his head. He lit one himself, with unsteady hands.

'She's a fine lady,' he said, 'and still a beauty. Is Sir Colin still in Africa?'

'As far as I know, doctor.'

'Things seem to be going a bit better there now. We're stuck here, Duror, with the women, the children, and the old men. Like yourself, I've offered my services. They were turned down. They also serve who only stand and drink.' He laughed. 'I'd offer you a dram, Duror, but so far you're still my patient. Once the consultation's over we'll become old cronies. How's the girl keeping? Sheila her name is, I believe. She represents the peak of my obstetrical achievement. With the typical confidence of the unborn, she decided to come into this vale of tears before her time. I had to be sent for in a panic. I made an excellent job of her too. She's as bonny and healthy and as stuck-up, I hear, as any baronet's daughter ought to be. Her brother now, he's not been so fortunate: I understand he's unbraw, unhealthy, and diffident. He was an Edinburgh specialist's job too, with fifty guineas at least in the fee. But I can see, Duror, you disapprove of such flippant chatter about your overlord's family.' The doctor switched on a scowling seriousness. 'I'm in a mood for plain speaking, Duror; which

97

is a good thing for you, because otherwise I couldn't offer you any advice worth a pickled toe.'

Duror missed a breath as he sat, apparently relaxed, in his chair. Was it possible that this old vain gluttonous whisky-tippling talkative doctor should have so soon discovered his secret? It seemed as unlikely as if a man should walk into a vast leaf-strewn wood and point to the spot where, years ago, a body had been buried.

The doctor put on a professional brusqueness.

'Lady Runcie-Campbell explained over the telephone,' he said. 'It seems you fainted when you were putting a deer out of its agony. She didn't say just what you were doing.'

'I was cutting its throat.'

'Is that the usual procedure? Or was it just an improvisation in the circumstances?'

'It's often done.'

'There would be blood?'

Duror nodded.

'I take it it wasn't the sight of that? You'll be used to bloodshed.'

Again Duror nodded.

'Lady Runcie-Campbell hinted your heart might be the culprit. Well, if there's anything wrong with your heart, Duror, I'll eat nothing but saps on the next ten Sundays. How old are you?'

'Forty-eight.'

'Have you ever had fits of breathlessness? I don't mean of course when you've been racing up a hill after a hare or stag.'

'No, doctor.'

'Have you ever noticed your lips blue? And don't tell me, only when you've been eating blaeberries. I once got that answer in all solemnity.'

'Never, doctor.'

'All right, Duror, if you'll kindly bare your brawny chest, I'll, as Bruce once said, mak siccar.' He opened the drawer where he kept his stethoscope. 'Was it Bruce though? It was a matter of murder completed, I remember that; murder in a kirk. Are you a staunch kirk hand, Duror?'

Duror was calmly and tidily removing his coat and jacket.

'I put in an occasional appearance,' he said.

'And do you believe what you hear there? I'm not being impertinent, Duror; this is as much a part of my examination as using this. Have you a faith? Do you believe in God?'

'No.'

'Nor do I,' said the doctor, smiling. 'That makes us equal in the eyes, shall I say, of Beelzebub? Now I'll shut up for a minute while I listen in.'

Despite his prattle he carried out the examination thoroughly. He took his time, and now and then grunted, so that Duror wondered if after all a weakness in his heart might be the removable cause.

'Just as I thought,' said the doctor at last. 'You're as sound as an ox. You can get dressed again, Duror.'

As Duror dressed, he remarked, as if casually: 'Have you ever had any dealings, doctor, with a couple of brothers from Ardmore? They work in the forest there. McPhie, I think they're called. One's a deformed hunchback.'

'They're on my panel. But I've never had to attend them professionally. I've seen them in the village, of course. Why?'

'They're working in our wood just now, gathering cones. The small one seems to be an imbecile.'

'Oh, he's not that.'

'At any rate, he's not right in the head.'

'Damned few of us are, Duror.'

'But not many of us commit abominations with ourselves in public, like monkeys.'

The doctor had been putting away his stethoscope. He looked up sharply.

'What do you mean?'

'I think I caught him at it in the wood.'

'You think?'

'Well, I did then.'

'The small one, you mean, with the face and curls of Lord Byron?'

Duror paused, seeing that face and those curls; he felt sweat again breaking out over his body.

'I never saw Lord Byron, doctor.'

'I'm sure you didn't, Duror. He's been dead a hundred years. He was a poet, very handsome. So is your hunchback handsome.'

'Why do you call him *my* hunchback, doctor?'

The doctor laughed. 'Keep your shirt on, Duror,' he said. 'I don't suppose he's yours any more than he's anybody else's. Where did you see him at his abominations?'

'In the wood.'

'Were you alone?'

Duror remembered that he had told Mrs. Morton a thrush had been present.

'Yes,' he said.

'So you've no witness?'

'None.'

'Did he see you? I mean, was he doing it for your benefit?'

Duror frowned.

'Well, Duror, it was either for your benefit or for his own. If for yours, I suppose it was a crime; if for his own, an unpleasant aberration. Did he know you were watching him?'

'I don't think so.'

'I suppose not, for in that case your natural reaction would have been to kick his backside.'

'I would never have soiled my foot,' whispered Duror, betraying a little of his hatred.

The doctor gazed at him, as if puzzled.

'My advice is, Duror,' he said: 'forget you ever saw it. What a man does with himself is his own affair, except if he does away with himself altogether.'

'This is hardly a man, doctor.'

'Be charitable, Duror. His deformity's an accident.'

'I have to remember, doctor, that it would be on my conscience if anything was to happen in the wood. Lady Runcie-Campbell and Sheila often walk in it. There's a young landgirl at the home farm. You're a doctor; you must know better than I do the kind of crime that imbeciles like him commit.'

'I have a fairly wide knowledge of human depravity,' admitted the doctor. 'It used to be a hobby of mine adding to it, until I lost the ability to be surprised. Before we leave the subject, however, I'd like to point out that as far as I know the wee chap's reputation in the village is pretty high. He's got a smile for every limping dog.'

'He's got none for me.'

The ferocity of that answer astonished the doctor; but he made no sign.

'Let's discuss your own case, Duror,' he said. 'I hope you don't mind answering some questions, even though they may seem to you rather inquisitive and impertinent. You're forty-eight you say. What age were you when you got married?'

'Twenty-five.'

'You would be about twenty-eight or thereabouts when your wife was stricken?'

'Yes, doctor.'

'I know this is painful for you, Duror; but I think we ought to get at the truth. You had been married just about three years?'

'Yes.'

'You weren't given much of a chance, were you?' The doctor shook his head. 'What scunners me about these godmongers is the snivelling way they thank their god for lavishing them with blessings, and then, when disaster falls on them, they lack the guts to curse him. In the jungle they show more consistency: there they think their god's angry with them and has to be pacified. There's logic in that. But I apologise, Duror. A man must grapple with misfortune in his own way. You see

101

what I've been leading up to? Since your wife's illness you have never had relations with her.'

Duror sat very still.

'I understand your reluctance,' said the doctor, 'but I assure you this is medical territory. At first it would not be possible, and later it did not seem right. Therefore you've lived like a monk ever since. This has set up stresses and it's now affecting you physically. You said you don't sleep well? I suppose too you feel in some obscure way you are responsible for your wife's misfortune. It's easy enough to diagnose, Duror, but it's a damned sight more difficult to prescribe. A wise man, a member of my own profession as a matter of fact, said hundreds of years ago that it was a pity human beings couldn't propagate as trees do. It seemed to him so much more digni-fied and hygienic. He wasn't so daft, was old Browne. Perhaps trees have minds, for all we know; but they've got the sense to stay in the one place and thole whatever happens. The human mind, on the contrary, ranges from heaven to hell; and usually stays a long time in the latter place. How to bail it out baffles science. Often the key is lost in itself, and there are mind doctors, called psychiatrists, whose job it is to look for that key. They don't always find it. If I was to fling a penny into the loch out there, what chance would there be of ever recovering it? "Canst thou minister to a mind diseased?" No, Duror, I can't. Any advice I can offer has already occurred to you long ago: other women, for one thing; religious accept-ance for another, though that seems to be out, as you don't believe; and of course there's always the old stand-by, the prescription scribbled by primitive man on the sands of time, and still in this twentieth century unequalled: endurance. You've got a burden to carry, it's getting heavier as you get older, nobody will take it from you, even for as short a time as Hercules relieved Atlas of the world. But it could be heavier, your burden: always keep applying that poultice: it could be heavier. You don't sleep well; you have headaches; you feel depressed; and you passed out the other day like a young lassie at the sight of a deer's blood. Why man, with your physical strength and natural sanity, you could endure such symptoms for a hundred years.'

The doctor by this time was over at another cabinet, taking out a bottle of whisky and two glasses.

'Will you join me in a dram, Duror?' he asked.

'Surely, doctor.'

Eagerly the old man poured out the drinks. He handed a glass to Duror.

'What will we drink to, Duror?' he asked. 'To your stoical patience, not only in tholing your affliction, but also in putting up with an old man's longwindedness? To my own youthful dreams of obliterating disease and pain from the earth? Or just to endurance? Aye, to endurance.'

Both drank, the doctor so greedily he spilled some down his chin.

'Stay for a while and talk to me, Duror,' he pleaded. 'Maybe you've thought that if you had a son to share your burden, you could have carried it far more gallantly. Shall I tell you about mine?' Guiltily he glanced towards the door. 'My wife mustn't know I'm talking about him, so if she was to come to the door listening, don't be surprised if I switch onto the succulence of venison properly cooked. I eat my griefs away, Duror, and the amazing thing is how thin I keep. . . .'

Chapter Nine

It was well after picture time when Duror managed to get away from the doctor's. He'd drunk more whisky than he'd done for years. The result was a revulsion against the doctor's reiterated philosophy of endurance; indeed, as he walked slowly but steadily along the pier road back into the village he felt in a mood for murder, rape, or suicide.

At the edge of the harbour he halted and stared down at the water, which he could hear slapping gently against the slimy wall. Another step, and down he'd fall, enveloped in the bag of his own wish for death: perhaps, like the she-cat he'd once drowned, he'd struggle a little, cowardly at the end; but he was no strong swimmer and would soon enough sink, to rise again bloated to sicken the godly tomorrow on their way to kirk with their Bibles in their hands. Then, taking himself by surprise, he began to laugh, louder and louder, more and more harshly, as it occurred to him that perhaps the tide was going out, there was only a foot or so of water, and all that would happen to him would be a leg broken. He would be lugged out like an old boot by some officious hero, and sent home to lie in the house all day, listening to Peggy's whines of sympathy. Still laughing, he glanced along towards the cinema where, years ago, he had seen a comedy about a man who, jilted by his sweetheart because of his torn-trousered poverty, had tried in various ways to commit suicide without success: the fun had been in the failures. He had lain down on a railway track in front of an express; it had switched onto another track a few yards away. He had tried to hang himself: the rope had broken. He had drunk poison: it had turned his hair long and curly. The audience in the picture house had squealed with laughter at his droll disappointments. In the end of course he'd dropped into a fortune and married his repentant sweetheart.

No doubt, thought Duror, a similar comedy could be made

out of his own position: Peggy was fat enough, and he was at the end of the plank of despair.

He headed straight for the hotel bar. A drunk made to greet him with solemn civility, but he thrust him aside. The thought was in his mind to pick a quarrel in there. To feel his fist crashing against someone's face, hateful only for its human shape, would be a relief and compensation, whatever happened afterwards.

Yet inside the door he hesitated, checked by the blast of human enjoyment. Moreover, the fug of tobacco smoke, beer, and breaths nauseated him. He almost turned and went out again. But some had already seen him, and with their polluting interest were now watching to see what he intended to do. What he did therefore was to push roughly past them to the bar.

They were farm labourers, forestry workers, sawyers, timber-fellers, fishermen, and shepherds: all as bronzed with sun as he, and as withdrawn in their thoughts. Some were in his company of the Home Guard. These nodded and wished him good evening. He ignored them.

They all knew about Peggy. That they had often discussed her behind his back was plain from the way they glanced at him, as if they'd like to sympathise but were afraid their powers of speech would be inadequate. His predicament to them was not only sad, grotesque, and terrible; it was also natural, as death by drowning was, or the loss of a hand in a circular saw, or the savaging of lambs by foxes. They were disciples in the religion of endurance. If ever they laughed at the comedy of his fastidiousness forever repelled within the circle of married love, there would be nothing subtle or vindictive or superior in their laughter: it would be a sound as bearable as the hissing of rain to a farmer in the middle of his hay-making, or the roaring of gale to a woman with her man at sea. But farmer and fisherman's wife could look forward, he to another harvest, she to safe return. For Duror there was nothing.

As he stood at the bar, drinking beer, accepting this absolute dearth of hope, and nodding to some commonplaces about the war, he suddenly caught sight of the cone-gatherers. They sat in an alcove. The taller had a glass of beer in his hand and was talking importantly to a man from Ardmore. Beside him crouched the hunchback, not listening to their talk but smiling at their laughter, and now and then stroking his brow with a hand as small as a child's

Duror tried not to look in their direction. He spoke to the bletherer about war. He finished his beer and ordered another glass. He tried to think about the journey home when the smell of drink off him must be noticeable in the car. But he looked again and again.

Soon the hunchback fidgeted sadly and plucked at his brother's elbow. The latter paid no heed to the first tug, but at the second turned, spoke as if to an impatient child, and then resumed his adult conversation. The hunchback smiled and laid his hand on the bag of groceries between his feet.

Duror waited. He seemed to be joining in more enthusiastically to the gossip about the war; but his mind, baulked in its virulence, was prowling in the alcove, sniffing at the affection between the brothers, smelling the fragrance of cones off them, and snarling at their unconscious complicity in his torment.

Then all talk in the pub was interrupted by the boisterous entry of four soldiers. They were English, and one in particular, a big man with a red glistening face, was very hearty and jocular.

'Now then, lads,' he cried, 'make way for four perishing heroes who haven't had a drink for sixteen miles. No M.P.s skulking behind the bar, eh? No ruddy generals in kilts?'

He stood with his back to the bar and addressed the company, like an entertainer at a concert. Some grinned, prepared to enjoy his free jokes. Others suspended their own private conversations, with the imperturbability of men who knew that what they had been talking about anyway was of small importance. A few scowled, resenting his aggressive foreignness.

His mates concentrated on enjoying their beer. They seemed thankful to shift the burden of listening to him onto others.

He told a joke about a sergeant-major and an A.T.S. girl. It was bawdy and full of oaths. Not everybody laughed.

The barman leant across and prodded him in the back.

'No swearing in here, soldier,' he said, 'and no foul language.'

The soldier wasn't abashed. He bellowed with enjoyment at this joke of prudery.

'Beg your pardons, chums,' he cried. 'I forgot I was in the land of heather and blue-noses. No offence. God bless your souls, I'm a married man with two kids; and look, I'm in the King's uniform, to defend the rights of man. I'll be off again in a couple of minutes, lads, for I've got this ruddy war to win; but before I go I'd like to hear you all laughing your heads off. Here's one you'll enjoy. It's as clean as a whippet's tooth. You can tell it to your missuses when you get home. It's about a fighter-pilot, one of these glamour boys, you know, who kept a pet ape. Well, lads, it seems a new chap arrived at this fighter station. When he went into the mess, all the lads were drinking away merrily like Christians, just as we've doing here; except one bloke, he was seated in a corner by himself, like he had a grudge against life. So this new chap wanted to know why, see? He asked somebody and he got the story. It seems this moody bloke was once at a station out east, where he kept a pet ape. Now dozens of times there were false alarms and he and his mates had to rush out dressed in flying-suits and goggles and jump into their planes that were waiting ready to take off. But the signal to take off never came. He got browned off with all this, see, and had the bright idea of dressing up this pet ape of his in flying-suit and goggles, and getting it to scoot out in his place, while he sat and relaxed over a quiet beer.'

He paused to empty his own glass of beer. During the pause

the two cone-gatherers rose and made unobtrusively for the door. Neil carried the bag of groceries. Calum clung to the tail of his jacket.

The soldier saw them. Many had already associated the little hunchback with the monkey in the silly story. Some smiled uneasily at the unfortunate coincidence. One or two laughed. A few were indignant.

The effect on the soldier astonished everyone. He did not, as most expected, laugh still more offensively and use the hunchback as an illustration. Instead, he swung round, set down his glass on the bar, and then, with all humour gone from his face leaving it thick and heavy and stupid, he rushed after the cone-gatherers.

'No offence meant, mates,' he panted.

At the door he gripped Neil's arm.

'I meant nothing by it, Jock,' he said. 'Cross my heart, I swear it.' He touched Calum's hump. 'Christ strike me dead, if I meant anything by it. I never saw you. I should have kept my mouth shut.'

Neil shook off his clutch and said nothing.

Calum smiled. 'It's all right,' he murmured.

Then they pushed open the door and were gone. The soldier hesitated and then went after them. He could be heard shouting that he had meant no offence.

When he came back in he walked straight to the bar, picked up his glass, discovered it was empty, set it down again, wiped his mouth with the back of his hand, and then with a mutter to his companions he left the pub.

In a minute or two they followed him, grinning.

One man stopped them.

'Is there anybody deformed in his family?' he asked.

'How the hell should we know, Jock?' they said. 'Corney tells rum jokes and he likes his beer. You heard him, you saw him. He says he's got a wife and two kids; you heard him. He's in uniform to defend the rights of man; you heard him. Well, that's Corney. Good night, mates.'

'Good night,' said many of them.

In another two or three minutes they heard the lorry start up and rattle away.

In the midst of the babble that broke out one man was heard to cry: 'I hear their mither did away with herself soon after the wee one was born.'

A silence fell.

'Who told you that?' asked someone.

'I can't remember. But I heard it all right. It could be true surely. In Mull it was, or one of the islands. It must have been a shock to her. It seems they were illegitimate. They never knew their father, if they had the same one, which I don't think.'

An old fisherman with bowed back and white moustache spoke with deliberation.

'They are a pair of harmless decent men,' he said. 'I think we should find something else to talk about.'

Most were agreed; the one or two who weren't lacked the effrontery to say so. Orders were shouted at the barmen. There was insistence on standing treat. Men gazed into their friends' eyes with an access of affection not altogether attributable to drink or sentimentality. One too drunk for discretion shook hands with all his acquaintances, as if victory had just been announced.

Duror put down his glass and left.

Chapter Ten

On Sunday morning Lady Runcie-Campbell walked slowly in the absolving sunshine across the policies to visit Mrs. Duror, carrying a bunch of bronze chrysanthemums and pink dahlias specially cut for her by young Harry. She had telephoned that she would call at eleven and did not wish to be even a minute early.

The visit would not be enjoyable. Mrs. Duror, far more obviously than most, was under the jurisdiction of God, but she never suggested that awesome allegiance. By merely enduring, she could have achieved a superiority over any earthly visitor: even a queen in her resigned presence must be humble. Instead, monstrous and feeble, she would fawn and simper and suggest obeisances almost obscene. During the previous visit two or three months ago, it had taken all Lady Runcie-Campbell's self-control, buttressed by good breeding, not to shudder and show disgust; but nothing had been able to prevent her using a tone of voice higher, shriller, and more imperious than any she had ever used before. She had uttered strained pleasantries and platitudinous encouragement in that haughty voice, and had felt horribly ashamed. No quarter of an hour had ever seemed longer or more piteously degrading. When she had left, almost fanatically grateful for slimness and the simple motion of her legs, she had at the same time been full of admiration for Duror who, all during the visit, had sat alertly, never saying the wrong thing in spite of the spawning opportunities, and never betraying by wince or frown or bowing of his head how painful he must have found his poor wife's pathetic garrulous abasement. His marvellous restraint had been in contrast with his mother-in-law's petulance. At least twice the latter had whined that God's ways were hard to understand, for to human eyes it looked as if He punished the innocent and allowed the wicked, such as Hitler, to prosper. Such sayings, even with the qualification of clasped hands and upward snifflings, must always be blasphemous; but in a time of war, with Britain in danger and her enemies triumphing, they were also disloyal, cowardly, and treacherous. Duror's resignation and trust, on the other hand, were in the finest sense patriotic.

Remembering that last visit, therefore, Lady Runcie-Campbell could not look forward with pleasure to this impending one. But there was another reason for her foreboding. She could not deceive herself into believing that her motive was altruistic; it was, she knew, an act of penance on her part, a propitiation; and as such it was inevitably false.

Last night, while praying, she had been overwhelmed again by knowledge of her own unworthiness. All her faults and shortcomings had contributed to it, but especially her contemptuous and instinctive refusal to listen to Roderick's plea that she should give the cone-gatherers a lift home in the car.

To obey Christ by being humble must mean to betray her husband, and also, perhaps, to amuse her equals. Sir Colin was franker, bolder, and more sincere than she: he believed in God, he said, and therefore in heaven; but it was a heaven where there must be rank as on earth. It was beyond even God's ingenuity to achieve an equality that would work. As his wife, and the cherisher of his title, she had to agree with him; but as ambitious Christian, and as her father's daughter, she could not help seeing how barren and impious was that argument.

If she had not altogether inherited her religion from her father, certainly it had been much influenced by him. Accustomed to seeing humanity in its most vicious aspects, he had been uncompromsing, imperturbable, and ironical in his Christianity. For the Church as an institution he had often expressed a distrust all the more effective for being so judicially delivered. Towards Colin, as a typical master of that Church, with his own feudal enclosure in the local kirk, he had been similarly tolerant but distrustful. She would remember all her life his murmuring to her at her wedding-feast, held during a time of hunger-marching, a verse from the grim old ballad which so well represented his own view.

> *'If meat and drink thou never gavest nane,*
> *Every night and all,*
> *The fire will burn thee to the bare bane,*
> *And Christ receive thy saule.'*

He had given her marriage his enigmatic blessing, so that his fondness for her first-born, Roderick, had seemed to many, certainly to Colin himself, perverse and revengeful: the boy, so puny in body and backward in mind, was his proof that the marriage had been a misalliance.

She knew her father's love had been genuine, and also that Roderick had deserved it. Although naturally timid, so that riding a pony was an ordeal, her son had nevertheless always shown a self-forgetfulness in opposing any act of injustice or cruelty; and in his attitude towards people, whether lords or labourers, he had maintained out of infancy a tenderness and sincerity, disappointing to his own father but as refreshing as faith to hers. Now her father was dead, but Roderick was now stronger in body, keener in mind, and still with that simplicity in his soul which so often showed up the twisted doubts in hers.

His father anxiously, in almost every letter, inquired after him, and particularly wanted to be reassured about his manner of speaking to servants and the lower orders generally. In an infant friendliness towards inferiors was quaint and excusable, Sir Colin pointed out; in a boy it was unfortunate; but in a man it would be downright disastrous. He hoped she was doing all she could to educate their son in this, the most important fact of life. Even in a church itself, Colin informed her, there could be none of this fatal throwing away of the privileges and responsibilities of rank. If the minister was socially inferior, he must even with his robes on be treated with that correct degree of condescension which was never offensive but which indubitably was the true preserver of society. It was her duty to see that Roderick acquired it; and she had made, and still was making, efforts to fulfil that duty.

As she walked through the grounds this bright Sabbath morning, on a visit so painful and yet so false, she knew the problem was far more complicated than Colin thought. She wished her children to grow up and possess this beautiful earth as their rightful inheritance, but as the truly meek. Therefore, as she gazed at the vast wood, in which Duror's house stood so peacefully, she felt glad that in the spring its grandeur and loveliness would be cut down by the axe of war. Colin had vowed to plant another as soon as he came home. He would return home then, thanks to God, and in that prospect the trees still unborn, still in their cones, seemed dearer than these silent aloof giants which represented the barren past and the anguished stunted present rather than the green abundant future.

She was smiling as she pushed open the gate at Duror's house and walked up the path to the door.

She was not smiling when she came back, as both Roderick and Sheila noticed at lunch. The flowers on the table displeased her; she ordered the maid to remove them at once; she did not, she snapped, enjoy her food with decay before her eyes. Sheila, who had helped to arrange the flowers, ventured to say she thought them fragrant and fresh. For her interference she was snubbed, and spent the rest of the meal in practising nonchalant impervious smiles. Roderick said nothing: he had planned that afternoon to go to the cone-gatherers' hut, and he was worried that he had not yet asked his mother's permission, and would probably have to go without it.

After lunch Lady Runcie-Campbell retired to the drawing-room where under the portrait of her father in his robes she sat down and tried to read a magazine. Roderick came in quietly and stood by the window looking out onto the lawn.

113

His quietness irritated her.

'Is there anything wrong?' she asked.

He shook his head.

'Well, if you've got nothing to do,' she said, 'why not get on with your studies? I thought you promised Mr. Sorn-Wilson you'd keep at them?'

'I've done some Latin and Maths.,' he murmured.

Suddenly she flung the magazine down.

'Would you please ring the bell for Mrs. Morton?' she asked.

He rang it.

'It's a private matter I want to discuss,' she said. 'I think you ought to be out enjoying the sunshine. This fine spell is sure to end soon.'

He frowned as he lied. 'Will it be all right if I go down to the beach to look at seals?'

'With Sheila?'

'She doesn't want to go.'

'Are you going alone?'

'No. I'm going to ask Harry to come with me.'

His mother considered. There might be a little danger in his going down to the beach, but to forbid him might be to drive him back into his old timidity. To admire seals in one's own waters was of course permissible, even laudable, in her husband's code.

'You'll be careful,' she warned.

'Yes, of course.'

'I suppose it should be all right. Harry's a sensible boy, who knows his place and keeps it admirably. Don't be long though. Be back by four.'

As she was speaking Mrs. Morton knocked on the door.

'Come in,' cried her mistress.

As the housekeeper entered Roderick appealed to her.

'I'm going down to the beach to look at the seals, Mrs. Morton,' he said. 'Harry's coming with me. May we have a cake to take along with us?'

'Surely, Master Roderick,' she replied, smiling. 'As soon as your mother's finished with me I'll look you out the biggest in the pantry. You'll need it, if Harry's going with you.'

'Don't let him be a bother to you, Mrs. Morton,' said his mother irritably.

'He's no bother, my lady,' murmured the housekeeper.

'Thank you, Mrs. Morton,' said Roderick, going to the door.

As he was closing it behind him he heard his mother burst out: 'It's about Duror I want to talk to you, Mrs. Morton. Have you noticed any extraordinary change in him recently?'

He was tempted to linger there and eavesdrop, but hurried out and walked about the lawn, where he could be seen from the drawing-room windows. The temptation continued. It would be easy for him to stroll casually out of view of the windows and sneak up the steps into the hall. There he could pretend to be waiting for Mrs. Morton to come out, but all the time he would be listening to their conversation about Duror, whom he disliked.

He had yielded so far that he was standing in the hall when Mrs. Morton appeared. She was flushed and worried-looking. When she saw him she tried to smile, and came over to lay her hand for a moment upon his shoulder.

They walked downstairs to the kitchen.

'I suppose you'll be going through the wood?' she asked.

'Yes. That's the only way to the beach, isn't it?'

'You'll be careful. Now won't you?'

It seemed to him that she must be warning him against greater dangers than spraining his ankle over a root. Her voice shook as if she was about to weep.

'Of course, Mrs. Morton. I'm afraid I'm always careful.'

She ignored his rueful self-criticising smile.

'Always be careful,' she said. 'There's evil about.'

He wondered what she meant. Was the evil to be feared from Duror?

'Those men who gather cones,' she said. 'You'll keep well back from them.'

'Why?'

She did not answer immediately.

'Because they're not to be trusted, that's why,' she said at length.

He remembered that Duror too had accused the cone-gatherers of being evil. She was Duror's friend.

'I'm not blaming them,' she said. 'They're poor unfortunate men. They've not been lucky. But all the same keep back from them.'

As she handed the cake to him, carefully wrapped in paper, she smiled.

'No harm will come to you, laddie,' she said, 'if God looks after His own. If,' she added, turning away.

'Is Alec all right, Mrs. Morton?' he asked shyly.

She turned back to him with an appearance of briskness; but there were tears in her eyes.

'Oh yes,' she said. 'He's in America, I think, living on the fat of the land. Now off you go, and enjoy yourself.'

As he went he felt sure that she would weep, but why or for whom he could not say. He was old enough to know that every human being had private griefs, which no outsider could ever assuage.

Carrying the cake in the gamebag which his father had given him, and which he meant to offer to the cone-gatherers to collect their cones in, he was soon knocking at the door of the white-washed bothy where Harry lived with old Graham.

Graham came yawning to the door. When he saw who his caller was he immediately added to his customary acerbity a grin of liking and respect. Harry, he said, had gone off half an hour ago with Betty the landgirl to gather hazel nuts and carve their initials on trees. Harry had taken his mouth organ as well as his knife. Betty was wearing a red coat more suitable for Glasgow streets than for thickets of hazel.

Roderick thanked him and made straight for the wood.

He was afraid that he was going alone, and yet he was glad too. Had Harry been with him, he would have been nigglingly inquisitive as to the exact purpose of this visit to the cone-gatherers' hut; and the explanation that it was a kind of pilgrimage would never have satisfied him. Harry did not approve of mysteries. When he had been told about Sir Galahad he had appreciated that shining knight's prowess with a sword and also his rescuing of maidens captured by ogres, but he had been sceptical and indifferent about his quest for the grail of goodness. As for Christian in the *Pilgrim's Progress* he had scoffed at him as dreary and old-fashioned. These were Roderick's heroes, and this visit through the silent sunny wood was in their company.

Therefore there was magic and terror. The wood was enchanted, full of terrifying presences. A knot in a tree glowered like a green face. Low-hanging branches were evil birds swooping with talons ready to rip his face and pluck out his eyes. The sky was now a vast kingfisher's wing, now myriad eyes blue and watchful. Here were clusters of juniper, grey with fungus, jungles of withered willow-herb, taller than himself, piles of dead leaves like graves, rashes of slimy yellow black-spotted toadstools, dark glades entered through gates of sunshine, and sunny spaces where on the green grass nothing moved. Every creature he saw was a prisoner of that enchantment: each was alone, a squirrel on a pine branch, a rabbit in rhododendron undergrowth, a blackbird amidst those dying junipers, an insect with a golden back at his feet, and a deer flitting through far-off pillars of sunshine.

Once, as he was about to cross a ride, and as he was gazing with fascinated eyes down the great aisle towards the loch, he heard from that direction a series of hootings, rising and falling in forlorn undulations. In a minute they were answered by another reiterated cry, shriller and not so melancholy. Harry and Betty, searching for nuts in different copses, were calling to each other.

Here was his last chance of regaining human companion-ship, and so of escaping from the invisible enticements lurking in the wood between him and his goal – the hut. He hesitated, and even had his hand at his mouth to halloo back, to make contact even by sound. But if he were to go down to the beach and join Harry and Betty, and offer them a share of his cake, he would feel that he had failed in something which he could not name, but which seemed important as life itself. The cone-gatherers in their tiny hut did not expect him, and would never know that he had failed to come; but for many years, perhaps always, they would in his imagination sit there waiting for him, and he would never come. They would then never be redeemed; they would never eat his cake of friendship, which would protect them from the spite of Duror; and all the sinister presences of the wood would remain to terrify and defeat him. To save himself as well as the cone-gatherers he must go on.

By the time the hut came in sight he was exhausted, in body and spirit; sweat of exertion and of fear drenched him. Near some yew trees whose branches reached the ground, forming dark caverns, he halted, to look into his bag to make sure that the cake, the symbol of reconciliation, had not been made to vanish by the evil presences he had just defied. Reassured, he stood breathing in the woodsmoke drifting up so peacefully out of the rusted chimney.

If his senses had not been so preternaturally alert, and if from the dirty hut had not irradiated a light illuminating every leaf on all the trees about it, he would never have noticed the lurker under the cypress, entangled in the thin green bony arms that curled out like an octopus's. No sunshine struck there, and even the luminance from the hut seemed to fail. At first he could not tell who it was, although he was sure it was not one of the cone-gatherers. He felt cold, and frightened, and sick at heart. Here at the very hut was the most evil presence of all, and it was visible.

When he realised that the motionless figure under the cypress was Duror, he crept in dismay into a cave of yew. It was his first retreat, and it was cowardly. Yet he could not force himself to complete the pilgrimage and knock on the door. Duror was a barrier he could not pass.

As he crouched in the earthy darkness like an animal, he

wondered what Duror's purpose could be in lurking there. The gamekeeper hated the men in the hut and wished to have them expelled from the wood. Was he now spying on them in the hope that he would find them engaged in some wrong-doing, such as working today, which was Sunday? By their agreement with his mother they were not to work on Sundays. But Duror himself shot deer on Sundays; he did not often go to church, and when he did he sat with his arms folded and a smile of misery on his lips. Why then did he hate the cone-gatherers and wish to drive them away? Was it because they represented goodness, and himself evil? Coached by his grandfather, Roderick knew that the struggle between good and evil never rested: in the world, and in every human being, it went on. The war was an enormous example. Good did not always win. So many times had Christian been overcome and humiliated; so long had Sir Galahad searched and suffered. In the end, aye, in the bitter end, the old judge had said, with a chuckle, good would remain alone in the field, victorious.

The minutes passed. Nothing had changed. The blue smoke still rose from the chimney. Duror had not moved. In his den of yew Roderick grew cramped; and in an even darker, narrower den of disillusionment his mind whimpered.

Half an hour, at insect's pace, crept by. Only a leaf or two had fallen from a tree, as a breeze stirred. Far away, over the loch, a gull had screamed.

Had Duror gone mad? Was this the change his mother had asked Mrs. Morton about? Again Roderick recalled the scene at the deer drive with Duror embracing as if in love the screaming deer and hacking at its throat with his knife. Mrs. Morton, who was Duror's friend, had talked about the perils of the wood; she had mentioned the cone-gatherers, but perhaps in her heart she had been meaning Duror. If he was mad then, was he now waiting with a gun to commit murder?

Peeping through the yew needles, Roderick saw in imagination the door of the hut open, and the cone-gatherers come out, the tall one who slightly limped and always frowned, and the small one who stooped and smiled. Then in the cypress the gun cracked, and the two men lay dead on the grass.

It was while he was imagining Duror come stalking out to gloat over the corpses that the idea took root in the boy's mind that perhaps it was Duror himself who was dead. That idea sprouted. Duror had been strolling through the wood, had felt a pain at his heart, and had clutched at the cypress to keep from falling; there he had died, and the green bony arms were propping him up.

To Roderick, growing in a time of universal war, distant human death was a commonplace: he had listened to many wireless estimates of enemies killed and had loyally been pleased. Only once, when his grandfather died, had death appeared to him as a tyrant, snatching ruthlessly away what he loved, putting darkness and terror in its place, and at random moments, even in the middle of the night when the rest of the house slept, creating fragments of joy only to annihilate them thereafter. Now the thought of Duror standing dead among the branches of the evergreen brought no hope, but rather began to infect the whole visible world with a sense of loss and desolation and fear. Every single leaf was polluted; even a tiny black beetle close to his head represented the vast tyranny. It was as if all the far off deaths he had rejoiced at were now gathering here around the yew trees to be revenged. Yet was not Duror evil, and if evil died did not goodness triumph? Why then were all the birds not singing, and why did the sun not begin to shine again with morning splendour, and why, above all, was the hut now in shadow? Unable to answer those questions, the boy knelt in an unhappiness too profound and violent for tears or prayer; its only outward signs were paleness and the extra prominence of his teeth.

When at last, in the gloaming, Duror moved, it was to the stricken boy like a resurrection, darkening incomprehension and deepening despair. From the arms of the tree Duror stepped forth, and stood for a minute in the clearing in front of the hut. It was a minute of cessation. Incalculable in thought or feeling, gigantic in horror, as if indeed newly come from the dead, Duror merely stood. Then, without any inter-pretable gesture, and without a sound, he turned and vanished among the trees, as if this time forever.

Roderick waited, on his knees, cramped and cold, his eyes closed, his mind stunned by a disappointment intolerable and permanent. He knew that he could never now take the cake and bag to the cone-gatherers, and that, with each darkening minute, the journey back through the wood grew more and more formidable. At the end of it, too, his own house, with his mother and sister, would not longer exist in its old way.

At last, leaving the cake under the yew to be devoured by beetles and ants, he crawled out, sobbing, and made for home.

Chapter Eleven

In the tip of the tall larch they were in a good position to watch the approach of the storm. At the sea end of the loch for the past half hour indigo clouds had been mustering, with rumbles of thunder still distant and half-hearted. More ominous was the river of radiance pouring straight down into the orange mass of the tree. After long excited consultations, the finches had whisked away. The two men were the only living creatures left in the tree tops.

At the very crest, Calum was frightened and exhilarated. He chattered involuntarily, making no sense. Instead of dropping the golden cones safely into his bag he let them dribble out of his hands so that, in the expectancy before the violence of the storm, the tiny stots from one transfigured branch to another could be clearly heard. Several times he reached up and raised his hand, so that it was higher than the tree.

Neil, a little lower down, was fastened by a safety belt. His rheumatism had heralded the rain, so that the climb to the top had been for him a long slow agony which he did not wish to repeat. That was why he did not give the order to go down; he hoped the storm would pass over without striking them. He too was agitated, finding the cones exasperatingly small and his bag insatiable. The belt chafed his waist, and his arms and legs ached. Above all, Calum's meaningless chatters distressed him. He shouted to him several times to stop. Calum only screamed back, not in defiance, but in uncontrollable excitement.

Then that cascade of light streaming into the larch ceased, leaving it dark and cold. Black clouds were now overhead. Thunder snarled. Colour faded from the wood. A sough of wind shook the gloomy host of trees. Over the sea flashed lightning. Yet, far to the east, islands of peace and brightness persisted in the sky.

The first few drops of rain fell, as large as cones.

'We'd better get down,' shouted Neil, and he tugged frantically at the buckle of his belt with his stiff sticky blackened fingers.

Calum slithered down and helped to loose him. He was giggling.

'Whether we go down or not,' said Neil, 'we'll get soaked to the skin. But up here the lightning might be dangerous.'

'I don't like the lightning, Neil.'

'Nobody does. What's been the matter with you? You're not a child. You've been in a storm before.'

'Did you see the light, Neil?'

'How could I miss seeing it? It was in my eyes, blinding me.'

'Was it from heaven, Neil?'

'Heaven?' Neil's shout was astonished and angry. 'What are you talking about?'

Calum pressed close to him eagerly.

'Do you mind what you said yon time, Neil? We were in the shed together, with the horse. You said it was always as bright as that in heaven.'

'In the shed, with the horse? What shed and what horse?'

'It was called Peggy, Neil.'

Neil remembered. 'But that was more than twenty years ago,' he cried.

'Aye, but you said it, Neil. You said heaven was always as bright as that.'

His face wet with rain and tears, Neil clung to the tree and shut his eyes.

'Maybe I did, Calum,' he said.

'And mind what else you said, Neil? You said that was where our mither was. You said that, Neil, in the shed.'

'Maybe I did.'

'I saw her, Neil.'

'What are you talking about, Calum?'

'I saw her up there, Neil.' He pointed to the sky above the tree.

Neil opened his eyes. It was now as dark as twilight. The

rain still plopped down in single large drops. As yet there seemed no enmity or hatred in its falling, only a kind of sadness and pity; but in five minutes, or less, it would come roaring down mercilessly. He would be soaked; his rheumatism would be so aggravated it might cripple him for ever. If he was unable to walk, far less to climb, who would look after Calum with his derided body and his mind as foolish as a child's? Wherever that light had shone from, it had not been from heaven. There was no such place. There was no merciful God. There was nowhere their dead mother could be.

Calum was waiting to have his vision accepted.

Neil shook his head.

'You couldn't see her, Calum.'

'But I did, Neil.'

'You just thought you did. People that are dead can never be seen again.' He tried to control his voice. 'It's not your fault, Calum. I told you lies. I don't think there's any heaven at all. It's just a name to please children. But we'd better start getting down. You go first, Calum. I'm depending on you. Take it easy, whether it rains or not. My legs and arms are stiff.'

Calum nodded, and prepared to start the descent.

'Maybe I did see her, Neil,' he said shyly.

Neil just shook his head.

Then lightning flashed straight at them, followed instantly by a crashing of thunder which seemed to be caused by the tree itself, and all the trees around, splitting apart.

Rain rushed into the tree.

The brothers crept slowly downward. Every time lightning flashed and thunder crashed they thought their tree had been shattered, and clung, helpless as woodlice, waiting to be hurled to the ground with the fragments. The tree itself seemed to be terrified; every branch, every twig, heaved and slithered. At times it seemed to have torn its roots in its terror and to be dangling in the air.

At last they reached the ground. At once Neil flung his bag

of cones down and snatched up his knapsack. He shouted to Calum to do likewise.

'We'd never get to the hut alive,' he gasped. 'We'd get killed among the trees. Forby, it's too far away. We're going to the beach hut.'

'But we're not allowed, Neil.'

Neil clutched his brother and spoke to him as calmly as he could.

'I ken it's not allowed, Calum,' he said. 'I ken we gave our promise to Mr. Tulloch not to get into any more trouble. But look at the rain. We're soaked already. I've got rheumatics, and you ken your chest is weak. If we shelter under a tree it might get struck by lightning and we'd be killed. In three minutes we can reach the beach hut.'

'But we promised, Neil. The lady will be angry again.'

'Do you want me then to be a useless cripple for the rest of my days? What if she is angry? All she can do is to tell us to leave her wood, and I'll be glad to go. I don't want you to do what you think is wrong, Calum; but sometimes we've got to choose between two things, neither of them to our liking. We'll do no harm. We'll leave the place as we find it. Nobody will ever ken we've been in it. What do you say then?'

Calum nodded unhappily.

'I think maybe we should go,' he said.

'All right then. We'd better run for it. But didn't I tell you to drop your cone bag?'

'They'll get all wet, Neil.'

Neil stood gaping; he saw the rain streaming down the green grime on his brother's face; beyond Calum was the wood shrouded in wet.

'They'll get wet,' he heard himself repeating.

'Aye, that's right, Neil. Mind what Mr. Tulloch said, if they get wet they're spoiled.'

It was no use being bitter or angry or sarcastic.

'Is there never to be any sun again then,' cried Neil, 'to dry them?'

Calum looked up at the sky.

'I think so, Neil,' he murmured.

'All right, take them if you want to,' shouted Neil, moving on, 'if it'll put your mind at rest. Keep them dry. They're as precious as diamonds.' He sobbed now to the storm as he ran through it, for he knew that this saving of the cones was his brother's act of atonement for entering the forbidden beach hut. 'They laughed at you in the pub, Calum, and I was angry at you for giving them the chance to laugh. But don't change. Keep being yourself. You're better than all of us.'

Where the beach hut stood was, in fine weather, a delightful spot for a picnic, with a small sandy bay and a sea-meadow of smooth turf. Now in the hissing rain, with the sky black and the lightning frequent, it would have been even more desolate than the wood itself but for the beach hut. This represented not only dryness and warmth, but also humanity.

It was built in imitation of a log cabin, with one gable of brick. On the side facing the loch was a verandah; here, too, was the door. It was locked.

Neil pushed against it furiously.

'She must have locked it for spite,' he cried.

Calum stood shivering beside him. 'We don't need to go in, Neil,' he said. 'We're in shelter here.'

Neil glanced out at the rain so heavy it obscured the loch.

'I'm cold,' he said. 'My clothes are soaked. So are yours. If we get in we can light a fire. Haven't we got a right to keep ourselves alive? Is the lady like the rain, and the thunder and lightning, that we should be forced to flee from her as well? This hut's never used. When the war's over they're going to pull it down and build a new one. What harm will we be doing if we just sit in it for half an hour drying our clothes?'

He left his brother and tried one window; it was fastened. He tried another at the back; it slid up at his first heave.

He rushed round to fetch Calum, and found him crouched on his bag of cones. He had to help him to his feet and then to pick up the bag, which he still refused to leave.

'We can forget the storm now, Calum,' he said.

In another five minutes they were both inside, and Neil had lit a fire with some sticks and coal from a scuttle. For paper he had used some children's comics taken from a box full of them. When it was blazing he had leisure to join his brother in admiring the furnishings.

There were some pink basket chairs with a sofa to match, a table stained with different colours of paint, a carpet, a large hamper, and pictures on the walls.

Looking at this luxury, Neil felt his rheumatism particularly painful.

'This is where we should be quartered,' he said dourly, 'even if we are just labourers. It's war-time, isn't it? Didn't somebody say on the wireless that in war-time everybody's equal? If it wasn't for the war, do you think I'd have agreed to come and do this job, at my age?'

Calum wasn't listening. He was examining the pictures in delight. In every one were trees, weird yet recognisable. They seemed to have been painted by children.

Neil opened the hamper and rummaged among the contents. These were children's toys of every kind: guns, yachts, dolls, pails, spades, balls, bats, and others.

'They're lying here rotting,' he said, 'and many a child in Lendrick would be glad to have them.' He laughed. 'I ken two would have been glad of them at one time. Eh, Calum?'

But Calum's pleasure in the toys could not be adulterated by such regret. When he reached in and picked one up, Neil laughed.

'I was just saying to myself that's the one you'd pick,' he said. 'Trust you.'

It was a small wooden doll, naked, with a comical red-cheeked face; one leg was missing. Calum held it tenderly.

'It's broken,' he murmured.

'They're nearly all broken,' said Neil. He lifted a small rifle, aimed it, and pulled the trigger. There was no report. 'Broken. There wouldn't be any need for those children to take care of

127

them. Anything broken would be replaced at once.' He was about to go on and make some remark about the children being therefore spoiled when he remembered how friendly the boy had been in Lendrick. It had been genuine friendliness too; to deny that would be wrong.

He returned the gun gently.

'Put it back, Calum,' he said.

'Would it be all right if I took it away and put a leg on it?' asked Calum eagerly. 'I would bring it back.'

'No, it would not. It would be stealing. Put it back. In any case, it's just a doll, fit for a wee lassie. Put it back.'

Neil went over to attend to the fire.

'Get your jacket off, Calum,' he said, 'and hold it in front of the fire.'

As he spoke he was cautiously taking his own off. His shoulder joints were very stiff and sore.

'Do you know what I'm going to do?' he asked, as he was helping to take off his brother's jacket. 'I'm going to have a puff at that pipe you bought me in Lendrick.'

Calum was delighted. 'Is it a good pipe, Neil?'

'The best I ever had. It must have cost you a fortune.'

Calum laughed and shook his head. 'I'm not telling,' he said.

Neil was feeling in his pocket for the pipe when other noises outside were added to the drumming of the rain on the roof: a dog's bark, and voices.

As they stared towards the door, there came a scratching on it as of paws, and a whining. A minute later they heard the lady cry out: 'Thank God!' and then a key rattled in the lock. The door was flung open to the accompaniment of the loudest peal of thunder since the start of the storm.

From a safe distance the little dog barked at the trespassers. The lady had only a silken handkerchief over her head; her green tweed costume was black in places with damp. In the midst of the thunder she shouted: 'What is the meaning of this?' Though astonishment, and perhaps dampness, made her voice hoarse, it nevertheless was far more appalling to the two men than any thunder. They could not meet the anger in her face. They gazed at her feet; her stockings were splashed with mud and her shoes had sand on them.

Neil did not know what to do or say. Every second of silent abjectness was a betrayal of himself, and especially of his brother who was innocent. All his vows of never again being ashamed of Calum were being broken. His rheumatism tortured him, as if coals from the stolen fire had been pressed into his shoulders and knees; but he wished that the pain was twenty times greater to punish him as he deserved. He could not lift his head; he tried, so that he could meet the lady's gaze at least once, no matter how scornful and contemptuous it was; but he could not. A lifetime of frightened submissiveness held it down.

Suddenly he realised that Calum was speaking.

'It's not Neil's fault, lady,' he was saying. 'He did it because I was cold and wet.'

'For God's sake,' muttered the lady, and Neil felt rather than saw how she recoiled from Calum, as if from something obnoxious, and took her children with her. For both the boy and girl were present.

The dog had not stopped barking.

Even that insult to Calum could not break the grip shame had of Neil. Still with lowered head, he dragged on his jacket.

'Get out,' cried the lady. 'For God's sake, get out.'

Neil had to help Calum on with his jacket. Like an infant Calum presented the wrong hand, so that they had to try again. The girl giggled, but the boy said nothing.

At last they were ready.

'I'll have to get my cones,' whispered Calum.

'Get them.'

Calum went over and picked up the bag lying beside the hamper of toys.

Neil led the way past the lady, who drew back. He mumbled he was sorry.

Calum repeated the apology.

She stood in the doorway and gazed out at them running away into the rain. The dog barked after them from the edge of the verandah.

'You'll hear more about this,' she said.

In the hut Sheila had run to the fire, with little groans of joy. From the corner to which he had retreated Roderick watched her, with his own face grave and tense.

Their mother came in and shut the door.

'I shall certainly see to it,' she said, 'that they don't stay long in the wood after this. This week will be their last, whatever Mr. Tulloch may say. I never heard of such impertinence.' She had to laugh to express her amazement. 'Your father's right. After this war, the lower orders are going to be frightfully presumptuous.'

'Did you see the holes in the little one's pullover?' asked Sheila.

'I'm afraid I didn't see beyond their astonishing impudence,' replied her mother. She then was aware that Roderick still remained in the corner. 'Roderick, come over to the fire at once. Your jacket's wet through.' She became anxious as she saw how pale, miserable, and pervious to disease he looked. 'You'll be taking another of those wretched colds.'

He did not move.

'What's the matter?' she asked.

His response shocked her. He turned and pressed his brow against the window.

She sprang up and went over to him. 'What's the matter? Are you ill?' She felt his jacket and found him shivering. 'Just as I said,' she cried peevishly. 'You're taking a chill. It was silly of us to go walking in such weather.'

'It was a beautiful day when we set out,' said Sheila sensibly.

'Yes, but we ought to have brought raincoats. All the same, Roderick, there's no sense in sulking here while there's a good fire to warm yourself at.'

'I know what it is,' said Sheila. 'He's angry because we sent those men into the rain.'

'I'm not angry,' he said.

'Well, you're in a huff.'

He was about to reply to that too, but decided it would be safer not to try.

'I don't understand,' said their mother.

Sheila was amused by such incomprehension.

'It's their fire,' she pointed out.

'Their fire? How can it be their fire if it's in our hut, and was made with our coal?'

'They lit it.'

'Yes, they did, which was part of their impudence.'

'Well, I'm glad they did,' said Sheila, 'and so is Monty. One thing you'll have to admit, mother,' she added, sniffing, 'they've left a nice perfume behind them.'

Lady Runcie-Campbell stood beside her son. She had taken off his cap and was holding it in her hand. She noticed the perfume Sheila had mentioned.

'It's off the cones,' said Roderick.

His mother spoke to him eagerly. 'Surely you don't think, Roderick, we should have asked them to share the hut with us?'

He did not answer.

'It's silly,' remarked Sheila, 'but that's what he does think.'

'How could we?' asked their mother, genuinely perplexed. 'It isn't as if there were two rooms. Why, they would have been far more uncomfortable than we.'

'The big one was just about dropping with shame,' said Sheila.

'Yes, I noticed it, and I suppose it was to his credit. Oh, come now, Roderick, this quixotic sense of fair play leads you into the most ridiculous positions. If you must have your huff, at least have it beside the fire where it's warm.'

'I'm almost dry already,' said Sheila, 'and so is Monty.'

'Men in their job must be accustomed to rain,' said her

mother. 'They'll come to no harm. But you might, Roderick, darling. Now be a dear and come over to the fire. All right, you think I was unjust in sending them out into the storm; please don't punish me by taking a cold and being ill. Please, Roderick.'

He turned and went over to the fire. There were tears in his eyes, as both his mother and sister noticed. The latter, though interested, offered no comment, much to her mother's relief. He himself said nothing, but taking off his jacket held it in front of the fire.

His mother stood looking anxiously down at him. To take cold so easily was dangerous, and might lead to lifelong feebleness or even early death; which made this complication of over-sensitive conscience all the more exasperating.

Reconsidering the matter, now that her natural anger was past, she still saw the cone-gatherers' intrusion as dishonest and insolent; therefore her son's concern on their behalf was in some disquieting way unhealthy. She remembered what her father had once said, that scruples could burn a heart out, if that heart was not fortified with a robust and intelligent appraisal of humanity.

She remembered Duror so savagely callous to his wife.

She determined later to have a long talk with her son on this subject of pity.

Chapter Twelve

As Mr. Tulloch walked through the wood to visit the cone-gatherers, he stopped to look at a beech split almost to the ground by yesterday's lightning. The freshness of the tortured wood was for him the most powerful of all the fragrances this sunny windy morning. He lingered beside the tremendous tree, pitying it. Anyone sheltering under it during the storm would have been squashed like a wood-louse under a thumb; and anyone clinging to its upper branches would have been sizzled like a flea in a fire. Before he moved on, he plucked up a handful of old leaves still damp from yesterday's deluge, and scattered them in the air. One or two fell upon him, but he did not immediately brush them off. This was his gesture of grief.

Last night, in the conversation by telephone, Neil had told him where they would be working that day; if they were not there, they would be in the hut, being too ill to work, although the hut itself, flooded by the rain, was no fit place for an invalid. Neil at first had been almost incoherent; he had had to be calmed before he could explain that he and Calum wished to be taken away from the wood, because of some encounter they had had with Lady Runcie-Campbell. The forester had promised to come and investigate. That morning, as a first step in the investigation, he had telephoned Lady Runcie-Campbell, asking for an interview. She had granted it for the afternoon: his men, she had said briefly, had offended her, but she had not yet made up her mind what she ought to do about it. Their offence, it seemed, had consisted of taking shelter in her beach hut during the storm. In spite of his respectful, almost encouraging expectancy, she had not been able to make it sound as heinous as she wished. He had consulted his own wife; she had promptly declared that in such a storm a body might run into a lion's den for shelter. Smiling, he had carefully kept his mind empty of decision.

When he caught sight of Neil ahead of him, he halted and watched from behind a slender spruce long ago wind-blown, with its roots in the air. From that distance, judged only by his gait, Neil appeared like an old man. He was gathering 'beech seed, which he had been instructed to do whenever bad weather kept him from climbing. He would cautiously go down on his haunches, wait, apparently to gather strength and endurance against the pain of that posture, and then would begin to pick up the seed-cases or mast, squeeze each one with his fingers to find if it were fertile, and drop it if it were not. The watching forester knew most of them would not be, unless this luckily was the tree's year of fertility: otherwise as many as ninety out of a hundred would be barren. To fingers crippled with rheumatism it would not be easy to examine them with the necessary patience. When that area had been searched, Neil hobbled on his haunches to another. Thus he would go on until break-time. Such fidelity to so simple but indispensable a task was to the forester as noble and beautiful a sight as was to be seen in that wood so rich in magnificent trees. To praise it would be to belittle it, so inadequate were words; but to fail to appreciate it or to refuse to defend it, would be to admit the inadequacy of life itself.

He stepped out from behind the hanging roots, and without hurry approached the intent seed-gatherer.

Neil looked up, saw him, stared a moment, and then went on with his inspection of the beech nut. That one was fertile. He held it out to his employer.

'That's the first good one in the last half hour, Mr. Tulloch,' he said.

'Well, it's a slow business, Neil,' replied the forester, smiling, 'but look at the result.' Walking forward he touched the huge grey trunk.

Behind him Neil began to sob. He did not turn to look, but kept stroking the tree.

'Don't fret over it, Neil,' he said.

'It's not for me,' sobbed Neil. 'It's for Calum.' And he began to pour out an account of the expulsion from the beach hut, all mixed up with the story of the insult in the hotel bar. The forester had heard about that episode from one of his workers, but he had been given to believe that the soldier had apologised, and that afterwards the sympathy of nearly everybody in the pub had been with the brothers.

'I'm responsible for him, Mr. Tulloch,' said Neil. 'If you were to ask me to whom I'm to give account for the way I've looked after him, I couldn't tell you; but I'm responsible just the same.'

'No man on earth has ever looked after his brother so well,' replied Tulloch. 'We all know that. You can give a good account, no matter to whom.'

He turned round and saw, with a shock he did not show, how stooped and contorted Neil was then, by rheumatism and despair: it was as if, in some terrible penance, he was striving to become in shape like his brother.

'Why is it, Mr. Tulloch,' he asked, 'that the innocent have always to be sacrificed?'

'Is that really true, Neil?'

'Aye, it's true. In this war, they tell me, babies are being burnt to death in their cradles.'

The forester was silent; his own brother had been killed at the time of Dunkirk.

'I suppose it's so that other babies will be able to grow up and live like free men,' he said. 'But I see what you mean; in a way, aye, the innocent have to be sacrificed.'

'We were driven out like slaves, Mr. Tulloch. Her dog was to be saved from the storm, but not my brother.'

'I think maybe she was taken by surprise, Neil. She didn't expect to find you there. After all, you did get in by the window. Maybe she got a bit of a shock.'

'Did she think we were monkeys that would bite her?'

'I think she was in the wrong, Neil, but I would like to be fair to her. She's a good woman really; but she's got a code to live by.'

Neil shook his head dourly.

'My brother's the shape God made him,' he said. 'What right has she, great lady though she is, to despise him?'

'No right at all, Neil. But don't think about it any more. I'm seeing her this afternoon, and I'm going to tell her I'm taking you back to Ardmore.'

'But what about the cones?'

'If she's willing to let me send two others in your place, good enough; if not, we'll just have to go elsewhere.'

The two whom he had in mind to send were conscientious objectors; he intended to tell her so, to find out if they too were ineligible. He saw her confronted by a vast multitude of people, as thick as his own conifers at Ardmore: even though she had her hands outstretched, she must repulse them all, because of her code. She seemed to him to be a victim, rather than a persecutor. In nature knapweed grew beside wild roses, scrub oak near gigantic redwoods: birds and bees visited all indiscriminately.

Neil asked him if he would get into trouble with his superiors. The truth was, he might: the District Officer, if she complained, would naturally take her side and wish to have the brothers reprimanded or even dismissed. But he did not think she would complain.

'Never mind that, Neil,' he said. 'Where is Calum?'

'He's gathering larch along there.'

'He's none the worse then of his drooking?'

'He's just got a bit of a cough.'

'You haven't come off so well though, Neil. I notice your rheumatics are bad.'

'Not too bad, Mr. Tulloch. They've been worse before and they got better.'

'That's the spirit. Well,' the forester looked at his watch, 'it's just on break-time. Where are your piece-bags?'

'Beside the larch.'

'If you've no objections, I'll eat along with you. I brought a sandwich and a flask of tea. Mary was baking last night. She insisted I take along a sample for you. Bramble tarts. Do you like them?'

Neil nodded: all his gratitude was in the stiff little gesture.

They walked towards the larch tree.

'What bothered me most, Neil,' said the forester, 'was the thought that your beds were wet. I wasn't comfortable in my own, though it was dry enough. I knew the hut was no palace, but I was sure it was weatherproof.'

Neil held his head high. Inside his gathering-bag his fist tightened on his tiny yield of fertile seeds; if he squeezed too hard, he would destroy them.

'I told you a lie last night,' he said. 'The hut was dry. There was a puddle on the stove, but the beds weren't wet. It was a lie.'

The forester was silent.

'It worried me, Neil,' he murmured.

'I knew it would. That was why I said it. I wanted revenge.' Neil paused; his fist was still round the seeds. 'She was beyond me, so I told you a lie that would hurt you. You have been a good friend to us, the best we have ever had that I can remember, and I wanted to take my spite out on you. I deserve no mercy.'

The forester smiled. 'We all say things in anger that we regret afterwards.'

'Then none of us deserves mercy.'

The forester made no reply. There was a pause.

Neil's fist slackened on the seeds; he withdrew it from the bag.

'If it would help,' he said, 'we could stay till the end of the week.'

'But you don't want to, Neil.'

'We would do it.'

'Thanks. Well, it might help. I could get Raeburn and Yuill to transfer their gear on Saturday, so that they could start gathering on Monday. But what if the lady tells me she's sorry, what if she apologises, would you be willing to stay then?'

'I mean no disrespect to you, Mr. Tulloch,' said Neil, 'but it would not be an apology at all if she said it to you.'

'You mean, she ought to say it to you?'

Neil nodded.

The forester reflected, but said nothing.

Then they reached the larch tree with the knapsacks and a bag of cones lying at its foot. As the forester ran his fingers through the sticky golden cones, Neil shouted up to Calum, who quickly came down to join them, shy but pleased.

'Hello, Calum,' said the forester, noting how like a collier the climber was from the tree. If they were as black-faced yesterday in the beach hut, with their jackets so torn, perhaps there was justification for the lady's astonishment; but none of course for her callousness.

They found a sunny hollow sheltered from the breeze, and in it ate their sandwiches. Tits and chaffinches hopped near to beg, and even a few seagulls ventured from the loch in amongst the trees which they distrusted so much.

The forester talked about his boyhood on his father's croft; with his young brother, since killed in the war, he had climbed cliffs for kittiwakes' eggs, brought in the cows for milking, gathered seaweed to spread on the field, and all summer worked at peats. The brothers listened in a silence deeper than respect or interest. Their own memories were stirred, filling Calum with delight and Neil with profound cleansing sorrow. The lady could have no place in these recollections: she had then been a girl at an expensive school, acquiring polish, accent, and poise suited to her station. Between her and the sharny-toed brier-ragged heather-nibbling boys had been no kinship: just as now there was none, she in her many-roomed mansion perplexed by duty, they in a sunny hollow in her wood, throwing scraps of bread to her birds.

Chapter Thirteen

In none of her many rooms that morning could Lady Runcie-Campbell find decision and rest; the one where she sought them most was Roderick's.

As soon as they had returned to the house after the storm, she had insisted he take a bath and go to bed. Later, sniffling herself from an incipient cold, she had carried up to him some hot soup. He had had almost to be bullied into taking it, and was so lack-lustre and dilatory she had pulled the spoon out of his hand and fed him, accusing him in a childish pique of being childish. Though she had taken his temperature and found it high, she had known it was not fever which had deprived him of his vitality and optimism: he was, she realised, bewitched; and by her. Shame over her treatment of the cone-gatherers had numbed in him the zest and courage which for the past two years she had watched growing slowly in him, like some rare, beautiful, and fragile flower. Yet no matter how she looked at it, whether from the point of view of conscientious parent or responsible landowner or practical Christian, she could not see how in the circumstances she had done wrong.

This morning, after breakfast, she went up to him again, prepared to have that long-deferred quarrel on the subject of pity. He would be hurt by what she would have to say, but this mawkish debilitating stuff in his mind must be cut out.

She found him astonishingly changed. No longer supine with his head dampening the pillow and his eyes dead on the ceiling, he was sitting up, with a smile secret but eager. His breakfast tray was on a table by his bed; he had eaten everything. Earlier he had been so wan and dejected that she had gone straight downstairs, still in her dressing-gown, and telephoned for the doctor. Now the latter seemed unnecessary. It did not seem likely that food could have achieved so great a change, especially in a boy whose asceticism had so often affronted and irritated his father. The cause then must surely be spiritual. For her own sake, as much as for his, she must find out what it was.

At first, dissembling her relief at his recovery, she remained brisk, matter-of-fact, and cool.

'I've sent for the doctor,' she said.

He smiled and nodded. 'Sheila told me. There wasn't any need. I'm fine, mother.'

'You do look better, thank heaven,' she said. 'But it'll do no harm to have you looked at. Last night you had quite a fever. This morning even you looked so lethargic. Now you're as bright as ever. What's come over you?'

From his smile she was sure he was thinking that the doctor with his appliances would never find out.

'Don't be selfish,' she said, smiling. 'If you've found the secret of cheerfulness you can't keep it to yourself. It's especially precious these days. It wasn't some potion that Mrs. Morton put in your porridge?'

He smiled and shook his head.

She stood by the window, clutching the curtains and gazing out at the wood.

'It's sunny again,' she said, 'but breezy. I'm afraid the fine spell's over. We can prepare for winter now, I suppose.' She could not keep from sighing: the war itself was a long bitter winter, with spring not even promised. She thought she might never see her husband and brother again, alive.

'Do you think it will rain?' asked Roderick anxiously. She glanced up at the massive clouds.

'Not today. Tomorrow perhaps.' She looked again at the wood: soon it would be cold, dreary, and repelling; and in the spring, when it would begin again to shine and be hospitable, it had to be cut down. There were few sights on earth more desolating than a decimated wood, especially one familiar and beloved. But melancholy was defeatist.

'I came up to talk to you about those men in the wood,' she said, her voice stern.

He glanced at her in surprise, but without huffishness.

'I see, however, you seem to have thought it over.'

'Yes,' he admitted.

'With a different conclusion, I hope?'

The smile went from his face; he looked sad but tranquil.

'You still think I did wrong?' she cried.

'I don't want to answer, mother,' he said.

'I can see that. But if I ask a question I want an answer.'

'We were wrong then.'

'We? No, Roderick, you do not get out of it in that way. *I* was wrong, you mean. If it had been left to you, your mother and your sister would have had to shelter under trees or in a filthy cave while those ruffians enjoyed the shelter and warmth of our hut.'

He was shaking his head.

'There was room for us all, mother,' he said, with a gentleness that almost insulted her into angry frustrated tears.

'How dare you pronounce judgment upon me?' she cried. 'Let me tell you, Roderick, your sister has a far more intelligent and mature attitude towards people below us in the social scale. I agree we ought never to be arrogant and overbearing; common decency itself, apart from any higher consideration, would forbid that. But that is not to say we must regard everybody as our equal. Such hypocrisy seems to me as abhorrent as arrogance. Mr. Sorn-Wilson has several times warned me you were shaping to be such a hypocrite; but of course I've noticed it myself. Your father often asks about it in his letters. These cone-gatherers, for instance. Obviously, in any way you like to look at them, they are our inferiors; they would be the first to admit it themselves; it is self-evident. It is our duty to find an attitude to them, and to all like them, which recognises that inferiority, but not offensively. The maintenance of society on a civilised basis depends upon us. One can become irresponsible and slovenly in personal relationships; yes, and cowardly too. You wished me to give them a lift in our car? Didn't it occur to you that the offer might have seemed to them patronising condescension? Surely such an attitude must humiliate them more than one of frank intelligent superiority?'

She paused, waiting for his callow hesitant refutations, to pounce on them and tear them savagely to pieces: thus the tigress waiting by the pool for the shy ineffectual beautiful deer.

His answer took her unawares.

'I don't know, mother,' he said.

'Don't you?' she cried. 'You have no right any longer to such ignorance, Roderick. You are not an infant now, to whom the world is a fairy-tale. You are growing up in a world at war. How often has your father impressed on you the supreme importance of asserting your inherited position in that world? How often have I? Every single person of our class has, by precept and example. Yes, Roderick, ignorance can be both cowardly and treacherous. Do you not know then whether I did right or wrong by ordering your precious cone-gatherers out into the rain?'

'They are not my cone-gatherers,' he said sharply.

'Oh, I think they are, Roderick. They are your toys.'

Though quiet he was obviously angry.

'They are not mine,' he repeated.

She misunderstood his anger. 'Well, that's something anyway,' she said, with a forced laugh. She knew she ought now to end the conversation before she did harm. But she had not yet found the secret of his cheerfulness. Already his anger was past, and he was smiling again.

'It is possible, I suppose,' she said, 'to renounce one's privileges, rank, and money.'

'Bhudda did it,' he said.

His calmness, in uttering what seemed to her a grotesque irrelevance, caused her at first to stare and then laugh sarcastically.

'How long ago was that?' she asked.

'Thousands of years.'

'And ever since he has been squatting, in hundreds of absurd colossal statues, with a cynical smile.'

His own smile was so far from cynicism she felt greatly moved. She could not bear it, and had to gaze out of the window.

'I've made up my mind what to do about those two men,' she said. 'I'm going to do what your father would do. I'm going to send them away.'

'Not today?'

'The sooner the better. Their employer is coming here this afternoon, and I shall ask him to withdraw them. For me anyway the wood will feel healthier and look lovelier with them gone.'

All he said was: 'May I get up?'

'Not till the doctor's seen you.'

'I feel all right, mother.'

Paradoxically his apparent selfishness, his so casual dismissal of the cone-gatherers, brought uppermost in her mind her own guilt. Love for him sweetened it.

'Thank God you do, darling,' she said, going over to him. 'And no thanks to me for coming here to thwart you and take away your confidence. Keep cheerful, please keep cheerful.' She closed her eyes, with her cheek against his hair. 'We are just not rich enough, darling,' she murmured. 'There's a kind of innocence we can't afford. That's it, that's it exactly.'

Then, with her tears flowing, she rose and left the room.

Roderick, smiling, knelt in his bed to gaze out of the window at the wood.

The doctor was an energetic grey-haired man, whose own robustness was an advertisement for his profession. He practised in Inverard, a small town thirty miles away, so that his journey to Lendrick House and back would take over two hours. The request for his services by the local aristocracy was of course a potent testimonial, and he was besides sufficiently sincere to take as much pride and pleasure in alleviating the pains of a baronet's son as of a ploughman's; but he had also a native dourness which prevented him from feeling flattered at being asked to travel sixty miles along winding mountain roads to confirm a mother's diagnosis that there was nothing the matter with her son.

As gentleman and physician, he had to hide his dissatisfaction: the disguise he chose was over-confidence.

'Absolutely nothing the matter, Lady Runcie-Campbell,' he said, as she accompanied him downstairs. 'In fact, the lad's as fit as I've ever seen him.'

'If you had seen him last night, doctor, you wouldn't have said that. He was so feeble and listless.'

'Storms do that to some people,' he said. 'They seem to empty them of strength.'

'It was more than that. His recovery struck me this morning as nothing short of miraculous.'

He smiled indulgently at this typically maternal exaggeration. On the point of remarking that medical science didn't accept such miracles, he decided it would be tactless. The lady was reputed to be religious, which in his experience was extraordinary amongst the gentry. He thought that she herself was more in need of medical attention. She seemed thinner, and her beautiful face, once her fortune, so it had been maliciously said, was now considerably spent; her nose, for instance, was reddened with too frequent silken wiping. Her hair, reminding him of the autumnal scenes he had motored through, had the ashes of winter in it. Without doubt the war was no respecter of persons. The baronet and the farm-labourer were both mortal; their wives suffered the same sad forebodings, and would weep the same salt tears.

'I've been thinking of sending him to school again, doctor,' she said. 'In a fortnight's time his sister is returning to hers, and I thought it might be a good time to try him again. There's so much he misses through not being at school. For one thing,' she added, with a laugh he didn't quite understand, 'he wouldn't be able to go off by himself, and brood, and hatch up absurd ideas. Last Sunday, for instance, he put us all into a panic by being away for hours. When I asked him where he had been, he told me, in all sincerity; 'On a pilgrimage.' Now, doctor, do you go on a pilgrimage to seals?'

The doctor smiled. 'Well, a boy's imagination is often very intense,' he said cautiously.

'Do you consider he's physically fit to return to school?' she asked.

The doctor gazed out at the wide lawn, with the great wood beyond: these represented the garden of this large house, and it of course was home for the people who lived in it. Perhaps, he thought, his own six-roomed villa with its quarter acre was cosier, securer, and more fertile in such human values as parental love and filial trust. One of the most heart-warming sights in his own life was that of his two boys' return each day from the local Academy, in their red blazers and caps.

'Physically, yes,' he murmured. 'But it may be that the improvement in his health was caused by his being here at home. Not every lad is suited to the rough-and-tumble of public school life, I suppose. My advice of course must be based on theory. I never was at a public school myself. The Scots tradition of education has always linked the school with home.'

She said nothing, but he could see she was not pleased at his insinuation that by sending their children to public schools the Scots gentry were aping a foreign tradition.

'He would be among his equals,' she said at last, and surprised him by the peculiar spurt of emphasis she put into the last word. 'I shall think it over. It is his father's wish, naturally.'

He did not ask if it was also the boy's wish.

About lunch-time she telephoned Duror's house. His co-operation might be necessary in ensuring that the cone-gatherers left as she had decided, but she felt reluctant to see or speak to him. His performance during her visit to his wife still perturbed her: it was indeed a part of the harassing and darkening of her mind: first, the War, and her husband's and brother's safety; then Roderick's fabulous innocence; then these cone-gatherers, one so deformed and so inhuman as if to test her own humanity; and now this sinister transformation in Duror, itself an episode from a macabre fairy-tale, suddenly in the wood the straight stalwart immaculate ash tree turning to a squat warty bush swarming with worms. It might be, she thought, that just as in the war so many lives and properties had to be destroyed to make hope struggle afresh in the wilderness, so the wood itself had to be cleared away, a necessary sacrifice. Over the raw stumps and the resurgence of weeds would be seen, summer and winter, the wide austere loch. Every turning towards it would for a long time be like a revelation.

Mrs. Lochie answered the telephone. She sounded more dismal and lachrymose than ever; indeed, she had hardly spoken three words before she broke into polite little sobs.

Lady Runcie-Campbell was indignant. It must be, she decided, a plebeian weakness, to grieve in public and whine for sympathy; people of her class suffered too, but privately and with dignity.

'What is the matter, Mrs. Lochie?' she demanded. 'All I want you to do is to tell Duror I want to see him at half-past two. Is he at home?'

'Yes, my lady. Will you speak to him, please?' That was a shriek of beseeching, rather than humble inquiry.

'No, it's not necessary. Just you tell him. Half-past two, in the office here. Is that clear?'

'Yes, my lady.'

She was about to put down the telephone when it occurred to her that the weeping must really be an appeal for help and comfort. She was the mistress of this estate: if respect and honour were due to her on that account, they must be earned; the accidental possession of greater material wealth was not sufficient. Indeed, by heeding such an appeal, and by responding to it even in the midst of her own troubles, she would best demonstrate what she had failed to describe to Roderick.

She softened her voice. 'You seem upset, Mrs. Lochie. Is it because of your poor daughter?'

'It's always that, my lady. But it's John now.'

'John?' For a moment Lady Runcie-Campbell forgot this was Duror's first name.

'Aye. He was always clean-mouthed. I'll say that for him. But this morning he came in with a doll.'

'A doll? Good heavens, did you say a doll?'

'Yes, my lady. I don't want to speak about it, my lady, especially to you. I hope I ken my place, and it's not for me to foul the ears of my betters. What he said this morning before me and my poor lassie was meant to be no doubt, in the good Lord's plan of things, for our punishment and our betterment; but I would never have thought such foulness could lie in a man's mind so many years without ever showing. It showed today, God help us. I ken, my lady, I shouldn't be saying all this to you. I'm likely keeping you from your lunch, and I can hear my ain potatoes boiling over in the kitchen. I'll be sure to give him your message, my lady, but it'll be like talking to a wild beast through its bars.'

Lady Runcie-Campbell had let her run on for want of something pertinent to say to stop her. She knew how Mrs. Lochie exaggerated, and how she had always miscalled her son-in-law; but even as she made these reservations, into her mind kept coming some understanding of the horror that might be in Duror's.

'Where did he get this doll?' she asked.

'I couldn't tell you that, my lady. It's not got a stitch on.'

'All right then, Mrs. Lochie, don't worry. I'll find out all about it when I see him this afternoon. In the meantime, you go and see to your potatoes. Depend on me. If there's anything to be done, I'll see that it is done. However, I don't think there's any reason for you to be alarmed. Probably what's wrong with him is simply that he's mentally exhausted. It's a common enough complaint these days. Goodbye then for the meantime. I shall keep in touch with you.'

As she put down the telephone the smile that she had involuntarily been manufacturing to give support to her tone of encouragement, faded.

'It is no business of mine,' she murmured. 'Why should I become involved?'

The answer came in her father's voice. Years ago, twelve years to be exact, when she was pregnant with Sheila, her father had been judge in a sordid murder trial. The verdict had been guilty, and he had had to put on the black cap and sentence the murderer to death. Though living here by the wood, which was in its summer splendour, and though avoiding all newspapers at the time and all talk about the trial, she had felt a dreadful but inescapable kinship with the poor brute doomed to be hanged; and the child forming in her was condemned to the same relationship. Afterwards, months later, when she had confided in her father, in an apparently facetious but really desperate complaint, he had asked her how could she avoid that kinship since, when passing sentence, he had known the miserable creature in the dock to be his brother in God.

By being born therefore, or even conceived, one became involved.

Chapter Fourteen

After lunch the forester helped Neil and Calum to carry their long ladder down to a rocky promontory where pine trees grew. He had already reconnoitred the place, and had ascertained that the cones were not only plentiful but could also be got without too much exertion; but what chiefly caused him to send the cone-gatherers to work there was his belief that of all the bonny corners in the wood this was the bonniest. Walking over the short heather and the smooth turf, from one great gnarled red-branched tree to another, he had felt, with some cones in his hand and the glitter of the loch in his eyes, that the purpose of life was good and would be fulfilled. He had lingered there longer than he ought. In other forests time was so hoarded that men had been dismissed for lengthening their breaks by five minutes; he himself in loyalty to his instructions would reprimand for such thieving. With such miserliness necessary in the interests of one's duty, it was an inestimable liberty here on this promontory to holiday for half an hour and feel at one's disposal a whole skyful of time.

Therefore he helped to carry the ladder there, and for an hour climbed trees to throw twigs down to the heather where Neil could pluck off the cones. In an adjacent tree Calum filled his bag, and looked so happy there, so oblivious, so eager, and indeed so indigenous, that to the forester he seemed time's favourite, never to be abandoned to dullness or frustration or despair.

When it was time for the forester to go up to the big house, he bent down at the loch's edge and, dipping his handkerchief in the clear water, wiped the grime of the trees off his face. Seeing his reflection, he grinned in appreciation at the jokes made about his face: its flatness, high cheekbones, narrow eyes, and yellowish tan, had from childhood ensured that in every volley of abuse to come his way was some reference to the Chinese. Then it had lacerated his pride, although he had never shown it; now it amused him. His wife could see no humour in it; in revenge she ridiculed the appearance of all the jokers, finding in each of them a resemblance to some other nation, Africans or Japanese or Eskimos or, what was the worst abuse these days, Germans. It increased his amusement that so small a place as Ardmore should represent so universal a humanity.

He took his leave of the brothers. Neil's arm he gripped for a moment.

'I won't quarrel with the lady, Neil,' he said. 'You wouldn't want that, and neither would I. All I'll do is tell her you're returning to Ardmore on Saturday.'

'What if she tries to get us the sack altogether?' asked Neil.

'She won't do that, Neil. She's not a vindictive woman. In any case, I'd have a say in that.'

'But she might want us to go before Saturday.'

'If she insists on that, then I'll come straight back here and let you know. We'll make different arrangements in that case. But don't worry, you'll be here till Saturday. I'll be out myself with the lorry. In the meantime keep here and gather pine cones. You don't have to climb yourself if you don't feel like it. Calum can break off small branches as I was doing, and you can strip them on the ground. This is a bonny spot, Neil. I'm sure, after working here for a day or two, you'll leave on Saturday without any feelings of bitterness. As for Calum – ' he paused, smiling, and glanced up at the tree where the little man was as busy as a squirrel.

Neil proudly finished the sentence for him.

'He's got no bitterness in him,' he said, 'for the lady or anybody else. Not even for the gamekeeper.'

'Has he troubled you since the deer drive?'

'No, he's kept his distance. But he frightens Calum.'

'Well, after Saturday he'll be well away from him. Cheerio, Neil. Take things easy till your rheumatics get better.'

Neil took a step or two after him.

'Thank you, Mr. Tulloch,' he called. 'Thank you.'

Tulloch waved thanks aside, and then widening the gesture turned it into a farewell to Calum, who snatched off his cap and brandished it vigorously, like a man repelling wasps or cheering a goal scored at shinty.

'Cheerio, Calum,' he shouted.

'Cheerio, Mr. Tulloch, cheerio,' sang the little man.

Laughing, the forester turned and made up through the wood towards the house.

He was within sight of it, indeed near enough to distinguish its mistress between the pillars of the portico, when he was hailed eagerly by name. From behind some bushes Roderick came hurrying. It seemed to him somehow that the boy's was a penitential eagerness, and his first words strengthened that impression.

'Where are your cone-gatherers working today, Mr. Tulloch?' cried the boy.

Tulloch stopped: he had only a minute or two to spare if he was not going to be late for the interview, and surely that green speck against the tawny walls of the house betokened impatience.

'They're gathering pine cones on the Scour Point,' he answered.

'Will they be there all day?'

'Till finishing-time.'

The forester smiled, but stooping to pluck a blade of grass to chew found his fingers clumsy. He had to do what he hated: oppose this boy's sincere repentance and wish to atone.

'I don't want them disturbed,' he murmured, still crouching, with his eyes on the distant house. 'They're still upset, after what happened yesterday.'

'I'm sure they must be.'

'They want to be left alone till Saturday. They're going home then.'

'Are they leaving the wood?' The boy's voice was sad. 'I thought they would be.'

'I believe you're their friend.'

'Oh yes.'

'Please cause them no more trouble then. If you were to seek them out today, or tomorrow, just to tell them you're sorry for what happened or even to say goodbye, your mother might be angry with them. You can understand that.'

Roderick nodded. Suddenly a disappointment overwhelmed him, that seemed to the forester quite disproportionate: his eagerness went out like a light, leaving his face with its large eyes and protuberant teeth haunted and afraid; even his hands on their thin wrists seemed to wilt.

'Did you have your mind set on going to wish them well?' asked the forester.

The boy nodded.

Tulloch rose to his feet. 'Your mother may be angry,' he said, 'and they themselves might not understand your purpose; but you have my blessing.'

The disappointment fled, and relief equally disproportionate took its place.

'Thank you, Mr. Tulloch. I have my own reason for wishing to speak to them.'

Tulloch was walking away towards the house.

'They might not understand,' he repeated.

'They will, I'm sure they will.' Then he came running after the forester. 'Mr. Tulloch, please.'

'Well?' Tulloch had to wait.

'I've got a book here.' He dragged it out of his pocket. 'It's a book on trees. I've been trying to identify as many as I can. Are those big ones noblesse silver or common silver? I can't be sure from the description.'

'All those,' said Tulloch, staring slowly towards the plantation of tall trees, 'are common silvers. They are beautiful trees. But I'm afraid I'll have to hurry now. Your mother's waiting for me. I'm sorry I haven't time to discuss trees with you; there's no subject pleasanter to me.'

Again he hurried away.

'The cones are very large, aren't they?'

'Yes, some are six inches long.'

'It wouldn't take long to fill a bag with those. Not like larch or pine. Eucalyptus cones are the tiniest of all, aren't they?'

'Well, they're pretty small.'

'And yet they come from such large trees.'

Grinning, the forester had to break off this shouted conversation, which must have been heard at the house. He gave a last wave, and made straight across the lawn for the front steps.

Lady Runcie-Campbell sat on a chair that had not been chosen for comfort; with its upright back and carved top it looked like a throne or judgment seat. Her hands were clasped on her lap, and her feet in their solid brogues were firmly on the stone. To the approaching forester, light-hearted after his encounter with her son, she seemed to be impersonating some goddess in disdainful contemplation of human frailties. Yet as he came nearer, and saw her face unflinching in the sunshine, he realised that, if she were condemning those frailties, she was not omitting her own.

'I hope you don't mind our talking out here, Mr. Tulloch,' she said. 'I have a cold, and I have a belief that the quickest cure is fresh air and sunlight.'

'A sound belief, my lady,' he said.

He halted on the second top step, and leaned against a stone urn. It was a position that accorded her honour, without damage to his own self-respect.

'Was that my son Roderick you were talking to?' she asked.

'Yes, my lady. He was asking me about trees.'

'Did you notice if he had on heavy shoes? He really ought not to be out. The grass must still be damp after yesterday's deluge.'

The forester noted how she had been about to say rain, and had deliberately changed it for the much stronger word.

'I did notice,' he said. 'He had on a very sensible pair of shoes, with thick soles and tackets.'

'Thank you. I warned him not to go out of sight of the house. I had the doctor in seeing him this morning.'

Then round the corner of the house came her daughter Sheila on a bicycle, with the dog Monty yapping disconsolately behind.

'He wants carried in the basket,' cried Sheila as she passed. 'He's too fat.'

They watched the girl and her dog disappear again behind the house.

'Have you any children, Mr. Tulloch?' asked Lady Runcie-Campbell.

'Two, my lady; like youself, a boy and a girl. The boy's five, the girl's just thirteen months.'

She showed surprise.

'I thought of you somehow as clear of such entanglements,' she said, laughing. 'A mountain pine, with only the storms of nature to contend with.'

'My wife thinks the wee lad's such a storm whiles.'

'I have no doubt she does.' For a moment or two she paused, evidently thinking about her own son. 'Your men will have to go, Mr. Tulloch,' she said suddenly, and looked very tired.

'I understand that, my lady. I was hoping, maybe, you'd let them stay till Saturday. It would be more convenient to have them shifted then.'

She lifted her hand and let it fall: permission was granted; Neil and Calum could enjoy the liberty of the pines till Saturday.

'Thank you, my lady.'

'Where are they working today?' she asked, without much interest.

'On Scour Point, gathering pine cones.'

Still apparently not interested, she began to smile. 'I think it is the most beautiful place on the estate,' she murmured.

'I think so too.'

He waited but she said no more on that subject.

'There's something else, my lady,' he said.

'Yes?'

She expected, he thought, a justification of his men's sheltering in her beach hut.

'May I replace them with two others?'

She carefully showed no relief. 'Yes, I think so. The cones are necessary, I suppose.'

'Thank you, my lady. The two I have in mind as most suitable are conscientious objectors.'

'I see.'

He paused. 'You don't object to them on that account?'

Her hands on her lap tightened painfully in their clasp, and then relaxed.

He remained silent. By doing so, he said more eloquently than by any form of words that these men, she must remember, had a deformity of the mind just as Calum had one of the body. They were human, they were in God's shape, but they lived in a hut at Ardmore which still had the inscription, in faded paint: 'This is the den of the yellow-bellies.' He had wanted to have it scrubbed off, but they had asked him to leave it.

'Ought I to?' she asked.

'Most folk do,' he said, 'to begin with. My own men did; my own wife.'

'Did you, Mr. Tulloch?'

It was hardly possible to miss the mockery in her voice.

'I did not,' he said, calmly and firmly.

'Really. You shame us all. I suppose people who have men in danger cannot be expected to look with approval upon these men.'

He refused to remind her that his brother, whom he had loved, had been killed.

'Are they cowards?'

'I don't think I'd send them to climb trees if they were.'

She glanced towards the wood. 'Is it not child's play? When I was a little girl I loved to climb trees. My daughter seems to have inherited the liking.'

But not your son, he thought.

'You have a magnificent wood, my lady,' he said. 'Many of the trees are over a hundred feet in height. I love trees. I would not send men I distrusted to gather their seed.'

While she was meditating, with apparent tranquillity, this challenge, round the corner of the house walked Duror, with his gun over his shoulder. No dogs accompanied him: the effect was as startling as if in that bright sunshine he lacked a shadow.

To Lady Runcie-Campbell he had not come merely from the rhododendron thickets behind the house, where every leaf, and every insect on every leaf, had its ordained shape and shadow. He was from some gruesome other world where a child's toy became an obscene symbol, and potatoes boiled over as a housewife watched horrors rearing out of the dark icy pools of her mind. A moment ago she had been irritated by the forester's facile Oriental grin and by his assumption of messianic forgiveness: now she was grateful he was present. He would not be needed to protect her from Duror, from whom she anticipated no violence either of word or action; but he might prevent her from stumbling into Duror's other world.

She noticed the gamekeeper was again unkempt, with the neck of his shirt grubby. His tie was askew with the knot low, as if, choking, he had wrenched it loose. Two buttons of his waistcoat were unfastened; his boots were thick with mud. When he took off his cap, she frowned as if displeased; yet she was feeling a strange, remote, sterile pity: his hair was so much whiter than she had remembered. When he spoke, too, his voice was like an old man's, harsh, yearning, querimonious. She was reminded, grotesquely, of Sheila's dog cheated out of the ride in the bicycle basket.

'I'm sorry I'm late, my lady,' he said. 'Ever since the storm yesterday my wife's been badly upset; she's still a bit hysterical. Her hand shakes so much' – he held out his own, and could not still its shaking – 'she has to be fed.'

She wondered if he had fed her.

'I'm very sorry to hear that, Duror,' she murmured.

Tulloch prepared to leave. 'If you will excuse me, my lady,' he said, 'I'd better be going. My car's at the foot of the drive.'

'No, no,' she said quickly. 'Please wait another minute or two. What Duror and I have to discuss concerns you, or rather your two men.'

'It surely does,' muttered Duror, and he took from his pocket a doll that she immediately recognised, though she had not seen it for years. It had belonged to Sheila, and during its reign had been an especial favourite. Now when she saw it, naked, without its gay frilly clothes, squirming one-legged in Duror's huge lustful fist, it seemed to her that her daughter's innocence was somehow being publicly outraged. Faint swellings represented a bosom, and its buttocks seemed, in their saucy chubbiness, unutterable, shameful.

'Where did you get that, Duror?' she asked, her voice faint.

'In his hut, in his bed.'

'Whose hut? For heaven's sake, don't make a filthy mystery out of it. Please give it to me.'

He was unwilling to hand it over.

'Give it to me,' she repeated sternly.

When she had it she did not know what to do with it. She held it as if it was visibly soiling her hand.

'May I have it?' asked the forester quietly. 'My little girl would be delighted with it.'

She wondered that he could see it so innocently.

'I'm afraid it's just rubbish now,' she said.

'I don't think so.'

'Well, you're welcome to it.' She handed it to him.

In his hand it was innocent again. She breathed in relief.

'All it needs,' he murmured, 'is a new leg; and that's what Calum took it for, to fashion a new leg for it.'

'Did he tell you so?' she asked.

'No. But I know him. He's fond of carving. He carves squirrels and rabbits out of wood. My wee girl has a squirrel carved by him that she has to have hanging over her cot before she'll go to sleep.'

She smiled at that picture of guarded innocence. It reminded her of her own children: a fluffy teddy called Bruin had been Sheila's guardian; a knight in gilded armour Roderick's.

Then, her smile blasted, she turned towards Duror. Leaning forward, as if sick, he had begun to utter quietly, hoarsely, and with an undercurrent of pleading, the most loathsome accusations against the little cone-gatherer. During that half-minute as she listened against her will horror caused her right hand to jerk about on her lap like a dying rabbit's paw; she could not raise it high to order him to stop. Nor could she find strong speech, only an ineffectual drivel of no's. In Duror's repetitious incoherence the word seed kept recurring.

She sprang to her feet. 'For heaven's sake, Duror,' she cried, 'hold your tongue. Have you gone mad? Do you realise whom you're talking to?' She stamped her foot on the stone as he persisted. 'I order you to be quiet,' she said imperiously.

He was at last silent, his head bowed, his eyes on the stone steps, his cap in his hand.

She was trembling. When she glanced at Tulloch, she found herself hating him because he was so self-possessed, so human, and so male; and because he still held the doll in his hand.

'I think you should go home, Duror,' she said. 'Don't argue. Go home.'

'I have work to do, my lady,' he muttered.

'Then for heaven's sake go and do it.'

Nodding all the time, he retreated backwards a few steps, and then slunk away along the side of the house towards the wood. He had to step aside to let Sheila whizz by on her bicycle. In the basket Monty yapped triumphantly.

Lady Runcie-Campbell shouted to her daughter. The latter, disconcerted by the urgency of the command, braked so abruptly she nearly fell.

'Come here at once,' cried her mother.

Slowly the girl cycled towards the steps. Her face was pink with indignation.

'What's the matter, mother?' she asked coolly.

'Never you mind. I want you to go into the house.'

Sheila was astonished and aggrieved. 'Why, mother? I wasn't doing any harm. Monty enjoys it. And if I did nearly run into Duror, it was his own fault; he wasn't looking where he was going.'

'I want no impertinence. Please go into the house. Leave your bicycle here.'

Huffishly, Sheila obeyed. Then she decided that to be in a huff was to lose an opportunity. Smiling, and with her head held high, like one unjustly persecuted but not daunted, she ascended the steps and entered the house.

Tulloch, still self-possessed, and still holding the doll, remained leaning against the urn. Lady Runcie-Campbell did not sit down again on her chair; she stood with her hand resting on its carved top.

There was a short silence between them.

'The man's ill,' he said at length.

'Which one?' she asked hoarsely.

'What he said about Calum were lies,' he said.

'Can you prove that? Duror may be ill, as you say, but why in heaven's name should he manufacture such abominable lies?'

'He seems always to have had a spite against Calum.'

'In heaven's name, why?'

He wondered how many times she had used that phrase so querulously pious, so indicative of faith exhausted. Then he concentrated on her question: Why had Duror taken a spite against Calum? This was not the first time he had considered the gamekeeper's animosity. It could be the whole man's disgust at the deformed man, unreasonable and instinctive: he had seen, for instance, crows mobbing one that had a broken wing. Or it could be that Duror resented their intrusion into the wood: again in nature animals had their own hunting grounds and chased off trespassers. Or it could be that the dislike was simply inexplicable: once he had known a horse that showed its teeth in anger every time it saw a certain man;

and that man had certainly never treated it cruelly. Of course Duror and Calum were human; and at that very moment, in different parts of the earth, men were blowing one another to pieces without personal bias or hatred, in pursuance of their respective ideals. Why then seek an explanation of one childish grudge?

The forester shook his head.

'Is he not an unhappy man?' he asked.

'Duror? Yes, I suppose he is, but unhappiness is no excuse for vicious slander.'

'No excuse, but perhaps an explanation.'

'You will certainly have your men removed on Saturday,' she said.

He nodded. 'I was thinking maybe I should do it earlier, but I don't think the lorry will be free before then.'

'Saturday at the very latest. Good afternoon, Mr. Tulloch.' She made to go into the house, but turned at the door. 'It must have occurred to you that your man stole the doll,' she said.

'I'm sure he meant to return it once he had mended it.'

She smiled cynically. 'You know, I suppose, that Duror's wife has been a helpless cripple for years?'

'Yes, my lady.'

'Have you ever seen her, Mr. Tulloch?'

'No, my lady.'

She came back a step or two with a peculiar smile; it was as if she wished to confound him. But all she said was: 'Good afternoon,' and then she hurried into the house.

He lingered on the steps for another minute, wondering whether he should go down to the point and warn Neil and Calum he might be out tomorrow to take them home. He decided he had better not, as they might wait all day in hope, and he would not be able to come.

Yet, even when his decision was made, and he was walking down the avenue towards his car, he went slowly and twice paused, in doubt.

Chapter Fifteen

Sheila was seated nonchalantly on a sofa, looking at the photographs in a magazine. Monty lay at her feet, gazing up at her with his head nodding and his tongue protruding in agreement with her air of persecution bravely borne.

Lady Runcie-Campbell walked shyly over to her daughter.

'I'm sorry, dear,' she said.

Sheila turned and smiled with a sweetness that indicated apology was acceptable, but hardly sufficient. Then she resumed her martyred inspection of the pictures.

It was not possible, of course, to tell her the truth: to say, standing in that lovely peaceful room within their home, that she had been brought in to save her from pollution; that danger of worse than mutilation from bombs had, outside on the sunny sparkling grass of the lawn, threatened her. But if the truth was not possible, to lie would be to cast the shadow of the foulness upon her; while to say nothing, to offer no explanation, would be to damage the trust between them.

'Was that my doll the man had in his hand?' asked Sheila, casually.

Her mother was startled.

'Why, yes, as a matter of fact it was,' she answered. 'Did you recognise it?'

'Yes.'

'Yet it must have been years since you played with it.'

'I remember it. I think I remember all my dolls.'

'What did you call it?'

'Clementine.'

'Are you sure? I thought Clementine was a little fat-faced fair-haired creature.'

'That was Evangeline.'

'Oh. How did she lose her leg?'

Sheila smiled. 'Perhaps Monty chewed it off.'

161

Hearing his name, Monty acknowledged it with a few conceited barks.

'I think she was before Monty's time, dear.'

'I suppose it just came off. Was Duror drunk, mother?'

The slyness as much as the impropriety of the question shocked Lady Runcie-Campbell. Here truly was involvement.

'What a thing to ask!' she cried.

'He looked queer.'

'He isn't well.'

Sheila hummed a little.

'Was he and the other man quarrelling?' she asked.

'Sheila, I'm afraid you've got a vulgar mind.'

The girl smiled as if she took that as a compliment. She bent down to admire at closer range the photograph of six aeroplanes in flight.

'May I go out now?' she asked.

It was not simply a request, it was a move in the game. She waited with ruthless politeness for an answer.

For the first time Lady Runcie-Campbell forced herself to consider whether or not she believed Duror's dreadful accusation. On the promontory, a place dear to her courting days, the mysterious little hunchback was climbing the pine trees to gather their seed. Inconsequentially then, causing her to turn away from Sheila, whose head she had been touching, she remembered how long ago, when she had been as young as Sheila, she had visited Edinburgh Zoo with some other girls a little older and more knowledgeable. They had gone into the monkey house, despite her objections: the very heat and smell at the entrance had nauseated her. From one cage she had hurried, horrified; and the horror had not been diminished by the subsequent conspiratorial giggles of her companions. She had been a member of the conspiracy, without the password; now she had it. Yet the hunchback might be innocent.

As she stood at the window, gazing out at the loveliness and amplitude of her land, she felt her whole being contract in frustration and resentment, that she should thus be embroiled and degraded in such a predicament as this because of common men like Duror and the cone-gatherer and the forester. Her husband would justly have accused her of foolishness and disloyalty. She heard him say: 'What d'you expect, Elizabeth? They're still brutes under the skin, y'know. It's taken centuries of breeding to produce our kind. For God's sake don't get us mixed. After the war they'll be trying to drag us down to their level. It's up to us to see they don't manage it.'

She was interrupted by a loud knock on the door. Mrs. Morton came in quickly, her hands still white with flour; her hair too was smeared with it, giving her a weird momentary resemblance to Duror. Like him, too, she was under some stress.

'Young Harry's in the kitchen, my lady,' she said, 'with a story that Master Roderick's climbed a tree and can't get down again.'

Sheila burst out laughing. 'Just like him,' she scoffed 'He always gets dizzy.'

'Keep quiet, Sheila,' said her mother, who imagined her son perched ignominiously a few feet from the ground. 'Why didn't Harry assist him down instead of coming here to alarm us all?'

'It's one of the very big trees at the end of the park: a silver fir.'

From Sheila came a pooh of incredulity.

Lady Runcie-Campbell glanced out of the window. From there she could not see the silver firs. Was this, she thought, the time of crisis? Had the events of the past few days been leading to this?

'Tell Harry I want to see him,' she said.

Mrs. Morton hurried away.

'I'm sure he won't be as high as grandfather,' chuckled Sheila, pointing to the portrait of the Judge.

'I hope so,' said her mother.

'What was he climbing for anyway? There aren't any nests at this time of the year.'

'There are cones.'

As Sheila was frowning over this mention of cones, Harry

163

entered, pushed by Mrs. Morton. He was ill at ease before his mistress in the luxury of the house. Monty the dog, indeed, was offended by his shy presence, and scampered over the carpet to growl at him.

'What's this nonsense you've been telling Mrs. Morton?' asked Lady Runcie-Campbell.

His freckled face, already glum and anxious, now looked guilty. He was bringing the bad news, therefore he was to blame.

'It's Master Roderick, my lady,' he stammered. 'He's stuck up one of the big silver trees.'

'How high up?'

'Near the top, my lady.'

'Near the top,' she said. 'Don't be an idiot. How could he possibly be as high as that?'

'I don't know, my lady.'

'Were you involved in this? Was it some idiotic caper you and he were up to?'

'Oh no, my lady. I was working in the garden. Graham and me were wheeling some rubbish down to the dump in the wood when we heard a shout. For a while we couldn't tell where it was coming from. Then I saw him, high up in a tree.'

'And where is Graham now?'

'He's at the tree, my lady.'

'Didn't he climb up and bring my son down?'

'He said he was too old, my lady.'

'Why didn't you, then?'

Harry blushed with shame and stared at the carpet. On it Monty snarled up at him.

'I've never climbed as high as that before, my lady.'

'You were afraid?'

Harry nodded. 'Yes, my lady.'

His mistress, despite her anxiety, was elated: her own son had not been afraid.

'Good heavens,' she cried, 'am I surrounded by cowards, too?' She made for the door. 'Mrs. Morton, would you please telephone the farm and ask Mr. Baird to come at once, and to bring with him anyone that's available; and ropes too. Harry, you run to the garden and fetch Mr. Hendry; bring with you the longest ladder you have. But first point out to me the tree.'

'Will I telephone for Duror too?' asked Mrs. Morton.

'No, no. We don't want him here.'

Mrs. Morton showed surprise and displeasure at this slighting of Duror's services. With tight lips she went to telephone.

Lady Runcie-Campbell, Sheila, Monty, and Harry hurried out, down the steps, and onto the lawn. Harry pointed. In that direction the trees were the tallest. Their tops seemed inaccessible.

'I can't believe it,' said Sheila.

'Suppose this ridiculous thing is true,' said her mother to Harry, 'why in heaven's name if he got up can't he get down again?'

'Maybe he's lost his nerve, my lady.'

It was a timid, earnest, sympathetic, respectful suggestion; its reward was a blow on the head.

'How dare you tell me to my face my son's a coward!' whispered Lady Runcie-Campbell.

Harry dared not put up his hand to his head, nor move back a step.

Sheila was shocked. She gasped and glared indignantly at her mother. When Monty, encouraged, made to snap at Harry's legs, she bent and slapped the dog hard.

'Don't stand there like a fool,' said Lady Runcie-Campbell. 'Go and fetch Mr. Hendry, and the ladder.'

'Yes, my lady.' Instantly he raced away.

Monty pursued him.

'Come back, Monty,' shouted Sheila. 'Come back.'

Peeved, the dog trotted back; it looked up at Lady Runcie-Campbell as if asking her to take note that, if he had failed to nip Harry's ankles, the fault was not his.

He soon had reason to think he was pardoned. Not only

Sheila, but her mother too, began to run across the lawn, as if for his diversion. He let himself be diverted; he frisked on ahead; he pretended he had caught a rat and worried it to death, with ferocious snarls; he rushed back to exhort the two humans to go faster; he let Sheila know he had forgiven those unmerited slaps; and all the way to the tree he remained blissfully and pompously in the belief that the haste and excitement were for his benefit.

They saw Graham under the tree, but not Roderick in it. The latter was hidden by the foliage; the former, when he caught sight of his superiors, gave the trunk a few kicks. He had his cap off and his sleeves rolled up to show scratches caused by an abortive attempt to climb the tree. He would not tell them he had retreated after twenty feet.

'Is this the tree?' panted his mistress. Her hair was tousled by exertion and on her cheek was a tiny scratch.

'Yes, my lady, this is it.'

She gazed up its great perpendicular trunk. For about fifty or sixty feet there was little foliage, only the broken-off remnants of branches as close together as the rungs of a ladder. Where the foliage did begin it seemed impenetrable.

Gazing up, and imagining her son at the swaying top, turned her giddy.

'I don't see him,' she said.

'No, my lady, not from here. You can from there, though, if he's not shifted.'

Graham led the way to a little knoll. Monty, accepting this new recruit to the game of chasing, nipped his leg. He swore softly, and his next heel's lift cracked against the dog's chin. It yelped at such unfairness, while he pretended to have noticed nothing, so intent was he to point out where Roderick, ninety feet up, clung to the trunk.

'How in heaven's name did he ever get up there?' murmured Lady Runcie-Campbell, proud and terrified.

'Usually he's too frightened to go very high,' whispered Sheila. 'I always beat him at climbing.'

'I've not shouted to him, my lady,' said Graham. 'I thought I'd better wait till you came. He'll be encouraged by you.'

'I hope so, Graham.'

Before she could shout she had to silence Monty, who refused to agree that the game was suspended, and was suggesting it be resumed at once. Reproved so fiercely, he slunk away in a pet.

Lady Runcie-Campbell tried to make her voice reassuring and confident.

'Listen, Roderick,' she cried. 'This is your mother. There's no need to be afraid. Just hold on for a few minutes more. Help is coming.'

She paused to give him a chance to reply. He did not take it.

'I tried,' said Graham, 'but I'm too old.'

'What's that he's got round his shoulders?' she asked.

'I've noticed it, my lady. It's a bag. I think he was meaning to collect the cones, like those men from Ardmore.'

'Yes. I think so.' Then it occurred to her where salvation lay: at Scour Point, gathering cones, were men who better than anyone else could help her son down; and they were morally obliged to do it, as it was their example which had enticed him into this danger.

'Graham,' she said urgently, 'you know Scour Point, where the pines are?'

'Surely, my lady.' In the summer he'd fished for saithe there off the rocks.

'Go there as fast as you can, and fetch the men from Ardmore. Quickly, Graham.'

She had spoken with a sense of sacrifice: her son was to be saved by an obscene misshapen labourer; his virginal body was to be handled by hands, or paws rather, accustomed to bestial practices; his demoralisation was to be seen by eyes that had gloated over unimaginable vileness.

'I hope to God,' she said, 'we have him down by the time you come back; but go as fast as you can, and bring them.'

167

'At the gallop, my lady,' he said solemnly, for, though he was willing to run all the way, he was not at all sure his heart, lungs, and legs could stand it. It was likely he would collapse somewhere, maybe in the middle of a burn, and would die, the subject not of lamentations but of revilements because he was taking too long. If his mistress was willing to take the risk, he thought sardonically, why should he grumble?

He galloped off.

Monty watched, and saw insincerity in that exaggerated hurry: he refused, therefore, to follow.

Chapter Sixteen

The quickest way to the Point lay through a field in which the home farm cows often grazed. Graham clambered over the fence, cursing at the barbed wire and the stiffness of his bones which made him unable to lift his leg high enough to avoid catching his trousers. Cramp resulted, as well as torn cloth. Nevertheless he hirpled as fast as a hero, and was amongst the cattle, smacking them out of the way, when he became aware that one was brawnier than the rest, and had a ring in its nose. In fact, it was the home farm bull, white as a daisy, but far less unassuming. It began to bellow and paw the ground, obviously resenting his familiarity with its seraglio. For a moment Graham was inclined to argue: his thigh was still cramped, and he was on a desperate mission for the damned thing's owner: why then should he wrack his spine and rip the backside off him scuttling over the nearest fence, thirty yards away? The bull approached at a jaunty trot, and Graham set off for the fence. As he struggled over it, part at least of his prognostication was proved: his seat caught in a barb, both flesh and cloth, so that when he descended on the other side he had a wound which might turn gangrenous owing to rust, and which could never be demonstrated when he paraded for his medal. So enraged was he, he stood roaring at the bull and shaking his fist. It roared back, and hinted powerfully it was considering steeplechasing the fence: in that case he himself would have to run up a tree. A fine world, he shouted scornfully, with everybody up a tree, waiting for everybody else to come and help them down.

He had now to traverse a great Sargasso of withered leaves. Every step was a slither, and took him over the boots; one step was particularly unlucky, it landed him waist-deep in an ice-cold concealed pool. A few yards off stood a dead Chili pine, with the ground beneath littered with its fragments, like ordure. As Graham splashed out, damning all creation, more pieces dropped off and rattled to earth. Shaking himself, he uttered every scrap of oath he knew. Some wood-pigeons flew off, clapping their wings smartly in reproof. When he moved on again, he passed under the pine stricken by disease so far from its native land; it was a tree, however, and he did not then feel well-disposed to trees; so he kicked savagely at its relics in his path.

By the time he reached the promontory he was convinced he was suffering in a cause already won; he was like a soldier wounded after the signing of victory. Young Roderick would be safely descended, revived on chicken broth, cossetted in pink cotton wool, and snug in a bed with six hot-water bottles. Lady Runcie-Campbell would be showering out the praise to them all, even to young Harry; for him there would be none, for of all things in the world praise and gratitude were the most perishable; when he arrived back, more likely there would be blame for having taken so long. His jagged behind, sodden boots, chilled and shamed manhood, and his time-consumed lungs, might win derision, but damn-all else. If anyone laughed, he vowed, even if it was the lady herself, he would claim a free man's privilege to say what he thought: not one tree in the wood would turn brown and die: the whole damned lot would shrivel under his blast.

As if for perversity's sake, the cone-men were working on the pine tree at the very edge of the loch. An angry man's spit from the top of the tree would easily reach the water. Luckily one of them was on the ground. Luckily too this one was a decent sober man, not given to vain and foolish joking. There were men, Graham knew, who, despite the gravity of his message, would nevertheless have to waste minutes in showing off their humour at the expense of his own sweaty, soaked, bedraggled, and gasping condition; which would have necessitated his retaliating, with the loss of more time. This tall cone-gatherer would listen, appreciate, and go.

When Graham reached him, however, he felt so exhausted he could not immediately explain; he had to sit on the ground, peching like a seal. The cone-gatherer, also seated, nodded a good-afternoon, and kept on picking cones off a fallen branch. Above in the tree the other, the hunchback, shouted down: 'Hallo!' Graham responded with weary wave.

He gave a glance over the loch. Two facts struck him about it: it was flat, and there were no trees. He thought he should have been a sailor.

'Give up your cones,' he said. 'There's other fruit to gather.' He was so pleased with the phrase he was reluctant to elucidate it. Still, the man he was talking to looked dumbfounded.

'You've to come with me,' he said, getting to his feet, 'at the gallop.'

'Did Mr. Tulloch send you?' asked Neil.

'No. It was the mistress herself. Get your brother down. Leave your bags, leave everything. The boy's got himself stuck at the top of a big silver fir tree, and you've to go and fetch him down.'

Neil had himself risen, in courtesy. Now with trembling deliberation he sat down again, and went on with his plucking of cones.

Graham kept patient: not every man was as keen-eared as himself. He seized Neil's shoulder and shouted into his ear.

'You've to come with me and fetch the young master down from a tree. He's climbed up, and he's not able to climb down again. It can easily happen. I once put my head through railings, and they'd to send for a plumber with a hacksaw to get me out.'

Still Neil plucked the cones.

Graham persevered: not every man was as bright-witted as himself. These cone-men, too, came from Ardmore, where even the midges were ignorant.

'There's a boy up a tree,' he roared. 'You, and your brother, have to come and fetch him down. The mistress sent me for you. Now what could be simpler than that?'

Neil shook his head. 'I can hear you,' he said, in agitation. 'I am not deaf. We will not go.'

Graham clapped both hands to his head. 'God Almighty,' he cried, 'all you've to do is to climb a tree and help to bring the boy down. You've climbed dozens of trees as high as yon. I've seen you do it. Your brother up there could climb to the moon if there was a tree high enough.'

'We are not her servants,' said Neil.

On another occasion Graham would have admired such irrelevancy: it was a conversational ruse he often adopted. Here it was abhorrent.

'Would you save a life?' he cried. 'Would you sit there and let the lad fall and break his neck?'

'There are other men besides us, if we are men in her eyes. I tell you,' went on Neil, with passion, crushing a cone in his fist, 'she cannot one day treat us as lower than dogs, and next day order us to do her bidding. We will starve first. If she wishes our help, let her come and ask for it.'

'The mistress! Are you daft? Don't you know she owns all this estate, or at least her man does, and everybody knows she's the brains and the heart of the partnership? You can't expect her to come like a byremaid and say, "please!"'

'I expect nothing of her. Let her expect nothing of us.'

Graham gave a jump of rage; yet he was impressed: such thrawness he had never encountered before in a sober man.

'Listen to me,' he said. 'Save the boy, and you can name your price. I have no authority for saying that, mind you, but the boy's the heir and she loves him, and if you were to save him she'd show you gratitude like a queen.'

'I love my brother.'

Graham shot up both hands to clutch God out of His sky for having created such stupidity. Then he saw; he went down on one knee beside Neil.

'Was she angry with him at the deer drive?' he asked. 'Is that it, eh? Was she displeased with your brother? All right, I saw it with my own eyes, and sharper eyes than Erchie Graham's were never fashioned. They sent your brother on a deer drive, and it was a cruelty. I saw it. I admit it. You have a right to your grievance, and a Scotsman, if he's worth his porridge, nurses his grievance till it grows to be a matter for compensation. But why punish the boy, who's as innocent as any herring in the loch there? He's a good lad, with no conceit in him. Nobody has a bad word for him, not even me. Maybe he's a bit soft for his position, but is that a reason why he should be allowed to fall a hundred feet and be broken? We should spread pillows as wide as the sea to let him land easy. If it was his father now, maybe we could leave a space here and there of the good hard ground, just as a gamble; but for the boy, pillows and prayers.'

To this eloquence, which Graham knew was exceptional, Neil returned one curt shake of his head.

'To abstain,' said Graham gloomily, 'will be murder, if the boy falls.'

'We could have perished in the storm, for all she cared. Was that not murder?'

'There's more in this,' said Graham, 'than meets the eye, even of Erchie Graham.' He rose stiffly. 'I came here at personal inconvenience, as you can see. For the boy's sake I would walk into that loch, up to the chin; further would help nobody, for I can't swim. Neither can I climb trees. If it wasn't that I'm sure he's already rescued, I'd make an effort to carry you both back on my shoulders.'

'If she wants our help, let her come and ask for it.'

'There are surer ways of winning favour than taking such a message back,' said Graham. 'But I'll take it back. For the last time, are you coming?'

'No.'

'It was your example he was following. Mind that. He saw you climbing for cones, so he thought he would climb for them, as boys do; and he's got stuck. Would it not be neighbourly to give him a lift down?'

Neil said nothing, but it was evident to Graham that his refusal, though causing him anguish, was final.

'If it was a cat up the tree would you rescue it?' he demanded.

'I wish the lad no harm,' said Neil, 'but a man can surrender only so far.'

'I don't understand it,' grumbled Graham, 'but then, most things have always been mysteries to me. For instance, to begin with, why were we ever born at all? Where's the purpose in it? But I'll need to go back and report. What about your brother? Is he of the same opinion as yourself?' As he asked, he knew the answer was the poor fellow in the pine tree had no opinions at all, any more than a squirrel or a seagull had.

'Calum is in my care. I am answerable for him.'

'I take it,' muttered Graham, as he began to trudge away, 'in a world that's at war we can't expect sanity from every man we meet in a wood.'

The next man he met in the wood was Duror. As he was wading with as much caution as tiredness allowed through the deep leaves, he caught sight of the gamekeeper under the dead Chili pine; and though Duror seemed to be as still as the tree itself, Graham assumed he had been sent to hasten the arrival of the cone-gatherers. He shouted to him therefore that it was no use, they were determined not to come.

Duror's head had been bowed. Now he looked up and saw the old man staggering towards him across the wilderness of decay. He kept silent till Graham was panting beside him.

'What is it?' he muttered. 'Where are you going?'

Graham was astonished. 'Don't you know, Mr. Duror?' he cried. 'I thought the very worms under the leaves would have heard by this time.' And he kicked at the leaves.

'What are you talking about?'

Glad of the excuse to loiter and rest, Graham explained about Roderick and his own unsuccessful errand to the cone-gatherers.

'I thought,' he ended, 'it was just the wee bent one had fairies in his brain; but the big one's got them too; and, God help us, no wonder in the old stories fairies had faces like fish and hearts of gall.'

As he spoke a piece of the tree broke off and dropped at his feet. Startled by it, he next moment was clutched by Duror's powerful fist, biting his chest like a gigantic spider. His protest dribbled away to a series of gasps: Duror's face was so compulsively fascinating that pain, indignity, and even fear, were momentarily forgotten. He could not have described that expression; but when, a minute later, Duror was stalking away towards the Point, it was as if the rotting tree itself had moved.

Rubbing his chest, Graham shouted after him: 'Maybe you'd better wait till we hear what the mistress says, Mr. Duror.'

Duror did not heed.

'If they'll not come,' shouted Graham, 'you can't drag them by force. They're not deer, remember. You can't just cuddle them and cut their throats. Even if their wits are all asquint, they're still men, with the right to say yes or no.'

Duror never stopped or turned or spoke.

'In any case, Mr. Duror, likely the boy's down now.'

Then Duror was gone.

'To hell with you,' muttered Graham, and he gave the dead tree a kick. 'You always did think yourself a lord among men. Maybe what happened to your wife was a punishment for your pride, though Christ forgive me for saying what many have thought. But I'd better get back to a tree that's alive.'

He had assured himself so often that Roderick would be down, that when he plodded into sight of the silver fir and saw people round it he felt dismayed. If they were still waiting for him, his arriving without the cone-men would cause as much commotion as if he'd come without clothes. Even the bloody poodle would yap at him. He had sweated out his guts, had run the risk of pneumonia, and had likely ruined a good pair of boots; yet he would be upbraided as if he'd just gone off to some mossy sheltered nook, smoked his pipe, and returned with a lie. Here he was with the baffling hard-earned truth, and he would be barked at and badgered like a rat at a threshing. Perhaps, after all, he thought, it was a good job he'd met Duror by the dead tree: Duror's attempt would at least keep hope alive.

He had been plodding; now he broke into a gallop, and puffed and peched and reeled so well he was astonished to realise they were not shams. Bursting amongst them, he collapsed at the foot of the fir. When he opened his eyes it was the lady's brogues he saw. He was already hearing her voice.

'Where are they?' she was crying. 'Are they coming?'

'No, my lady,' he replied, 'I'm sorry to say they're not coming.' It would have been easier on his nerves to talk thus, to her shoes; but politeness, and honour, were injured. He rose with groans, holding on to a ladder that lay against the tree. A glance round showed him faces like hungry wolves: they were hungry for good news, and were savage that he was not providing it. Baird from the home farm was there, with Manson the ploughman and Betty the landgirl; Hendry the gardener, his boss; Sheila who was sobbing and the dog which was bored; and the mistress. Harry was not to be seen: he was looking round for him when Lady Runcie-Campbell seized him in a grip that, for all its fragrance and jewellery, was as fierce as Duror's.

'Did you explain it to them?' she cried.

The imputation was that he had bungled the message, with his labourer's obtuseness. When he recalled the eloquence and emotion expended yonder by the pine tree, he almost smiled in a pity in no way personal, but universal.

'I did, my lady,' he said. 'I told them the boy's life was in danger.'

'And they actually refused after that?'

'Not they, my lady. To be fair, the wee one was never in the conversation. He was gathering his cones. The big one was on the ground. I spoke to him.'

The picture she had of the tall cone-gatherer was of him

slinking past her in the beach hut out into the rain and the lightning.

'What possible reason could he give for refusing?'

'I'll tell you what he said, my lady, though I don't understand what he meant by it. He said: "A man can surrender only so far." It seems to me they've both lived in loneliness so long that they're strange in the mind.' Again he almost smiled: who so lonely as he, and who so wise?

She retired into thought for a few moments, leaving him free to learn that Harry was up the tree keeping Roderick company; that Manson the ploughman had been up too; that Roderick, who'd been sick, kept moaning for the cone-gatherers. It seemed he had faith only in them. The pathos of the situation was not lost on Graham. He felt that there by the giant tree tremendous issues were involved; and at the very heart stood himself.

With a confidence borrowed from the vastness of the moment, he approached the lady although her beauty and haughtiness were then at their height. The rest had shrunk back a little from her terribleness, but he went so close that he heard her breathing.

'My lady,' he whispered, so that only she could near, 'begging your pardon, but he said he would come if you were to go yourself and ask him.'

She seemed about to strike.

If the blow came, he would forgive and treasure it. 'I told him, my lady, that was an unseemly thing for the like of him to say.'

She glanced up into the tree.

Then he remembered Duror. His own stupidity astounded him; he was, after all, what he looked, a common labourer. In contrite bitterness he told her. The effect was far different from what he expected.

She put her clenched fists to her cheeks.

'My God,' she muttered. Then she added, almost as if she was afraid to ask it: 'Did he have his gun?'

177

Graham frowned. Could he say definitely Duror had it? One took it for granted a gamekeeper carried his gun. In any case, what did it matter? He tried to imagine Duror against the rotting tree, and walking away over the withered leaves.

'I think so, my lady,' he said. 'Yes, he had it. He hadn't his dogs.'

Again she glanced up into the tree. She put her hand on it, as if pleading with it.

'Roderick,' she cried, 'listen to me. I'm going to fetch the cone-gatherers myself.' She could not keep a sob out of her voice. 'Hold on. Don't lose heart.'

He did not answer.

'Harry,' she then shouted.

'Yes, my lady,' came Harry voice, faraway, small, and scared.

'Will he be all right for another few minutes?'

'I think so.'

'You must be sure.'

'Could somebody come up and help me? My arms are getting tired.'

Baird immediately volunteered on behalf of his ploughman.

'Bob here will go up again, my lady, and give Harry a hand.'

'Will you, Manson?'

'I'll do my best, my lady.' Manson's face was badly scratched; his right eye too was bloodshot where a sharp branch had jabbed it. 'There's not much room for three of us, but I'll try.'

'Thank you. Just see that he does not fall. You'll not regret it, I promise you. Graham, will you come with me?'

'Gladly, my lady,' he said.

She understood. 'No, I was forgetting, Graham. You must be tired. Stay here and rest. Mr. Baird, will you come, please?'

'Certainly, my lady.'

As soon as she saw Manson begin his ascent she made for the Point, with Baird following at what he judged to be a respectful distance.

As she ran, and stumbled, climbed fences, jumped over streams, scrambled up banks, and plunged deep into leaves, Lady Runcie-Campbell tried to make her anger against the cone-gatherers grow. Their insolence, independence and their even more outrageous attempt at revenge, resulting in the prolonged danger to her son, were surely just reasons for hating and despising them; for wishing Duror well in his intention to chastise them into decency and obedience; and for vowing, when all this was over, to obliterate the forester's false yellow smile of comprehension and forgiveness by complaining to his superiors so strongly that they must either dismiss him or degrade him. As a mother, as a landowner, as a Christian even, surely she was justified? Yet not for a second of that dreadful journey to the Point did she convince herself. Whatever she ought to feel, anger seemed wrong and unavailing. She kept remembering Roderick's strange chatter that morning about Bhudda; Harry after she'd struck him, and also before he had, trembling with shyness and trepidation, offered to climb the tree; Duror with the naked doll in his fist and the obscene accusations so lusciously on his lips; old Graham at the fir tree stinking so rankly of sweat and whispering so compassionately into her ear; and always, dominating every other memory, the two cone-gatherers leaving the beach hut. Fear, anxiety, love, sorrow, regret, and hope, were in her mind, but not anger.

From the silver fir to the Point took ten minutes; during them she seemed to travel to the furthest limits of her being, there to be baulked by not finding what she had hoped to find, and without which she could never return.

Behind her, always at that proper distance, ran Baird, a big red-eared solemn man, who kept thinking what a good thing it was he had, after all, taken Manson with him to the tree. The lady had promised to reward Bob; but it was a recognised rule of the world that if a subordinate was rewarded, his master must be rewarded also, to maintain stations, and of course more handsomely according to his higher degree. In the war, for instance, there were different medals for privates and officers, although they fought in the same battles.

From a bank of whins and bracken she looked down on the promontory. Never had the loch been so potently beautiful: it was as vast, bright, and detailed as in a dream; and there seemed to be a wonderful interpretation, if it could only be known. A warship steamed down the loch. So intimate a part of the dream was it, she seemed, during those few moments of suspense upon the bank, to know all its crew and what was to be each man's fate in the sea towards which it was bound. There, too, dream-like, were the pines, her favourite trees, making against sea and sky what had always struck her as Scottish gestures, recalling the eerie tormented tragic grandeur of the old native ballads. Gulls, as prodigal of time and sky as she must be parsimonious, flew and shrieked high over them.

She could not see any men; they must be hidden by the trees. But as she began to go down the bank, tearing her clothes on the whins and splintering the bracken, she heard the report of a gun, followed by a scream, and then by the quickened wails of the gulls.

As she raced among the pines, making for that gunshot, she prayed that Duror in his madness had not hurt the cone-gatherers, not for their sakes, nor for his, nor for his wife's, but for her son's.

She saw Duror before she saw them. He was walking away among the pine trees with so infinite a desolation in his every step that it was this memory of him, rather than that of the little hunchback dangling from the tree, or that of his brother climbing so frenziedly up into it, which was to torment her sleep for months.

She forced herself to go over to the tree. It was the strap of his bag which had caught on a branch. He hung therefore in twisted fashion, and kept swinging. His arms were loose and dangled in macabre gestures of supplication. Though he smiled, he was dead. From his bag dropped a cone, and then another. There might have been more, but other drops, also singly, but faster and faster, distracted her: these were of blood.

With moans and yelps of lamentation like an animal his brother was struggling along that branch to try and reach him.

As she watched, with Baird as horrified as she, another gunshot rang out. She glanced at him and saw that it had not occurred to him so soon what it meant. She knew that somewhere, on her beloved promontory, Duror, with his face shattered and bloody, lay dead.

Then, while she stood there emptied by horror, she heard far away a voice she loved screaming in excitement: 'Mother, he's down. It's all right. He's safe. Harry got him down.'

Baird thought she had not heard. Not looking at the cone-gatherer still trying to reach his dead brother, and not daring to approach too close to her, he took a step forward and told her what Sheila was still screaming. What she did then shocked him, even there amidst those shocking sights.

First she said: 'Help him, Baird.' Then she went down on her knees, near the blood and the spilt cones. She could not pray, but she could weep; and as she wept pity, and purified hope, and joy, welled up in her heart.

Glossary

Considering that *The Cone-Gatherers* is set in Scotland and that it was written by someone who had lived there for most of his life, the novel contains relatively little Scottish dialect. Certainly the novel's Scottishness is no barrier to its comprehension by non-Scots. Nevertheless Robin Jenkins maintains that he can speak the Glasgow dialect 'like any bus-driver', and it is only natural that the reader will come across some words of Scottish origin which are unfamiliar. The meaning of many of the following will be obvious from the context but they are listed here out of interest and for ease of reference.

ain	own
aye	yes, indeed
bletherer	babbler
blethering	talking nonsense
bonniest	prettiest
bonny	good-looking, pretty
braw	brave
byke	nest
cushat-doves	wood-pigeon, ring dove
dram	drink, normally spirits
drooking	soaking
flyted	quarrelled
forby	besides
glaikit	foolish
grue	shiver, shudder, make the flesh creep
hirpled	hobble, walk or run as if lame
ken	know
kirk	church
lassie	(young) girl
loch	Scottish lake
oxter	armpit
peching	panting

poke	bag
policies	pleasure-grounds around a mansion
saftie	simpleton
saithe	coal-fish
scunners	disgusts, exasperates
scunnersome	annoying, exasperating
sharny-toed	'with mud on their boots'; *sharn* is literally dung.
sleekit	crafty
snash	abusive language
stots	bounces
tackets	hobnails
thole	endure
thrawn	usually perverse or disobedient, hence *thrawness* (page 172) but sometimes meaning 'torn two ways'
tocher	dowry, often property
wean	contraction of *wee ane* – small person, child
wee	small
whiles	sometimes
yonder	over there, often when pointing at something in sight.

Notes

The notes in this section are intended to serve the needs of overseas students as well as those of British-born users.

Chapter 1

1 *It was a good tree . . . comfortable as chairs*: see Introduction, page xxiv.

 indigenous: native to, or more loosely, at home. See also Introduction, page xi.

2 *puissance*: power or strength.

 abdication: legal term meaning 'resignation of sovereignty' or 'surrender of ownership'.

 ineluctable: inescapable; see also Introduction, pages xi and xvi.

3 *This was the terrifying mystery*: see Introduction, page xi.

 the boy and girl who lived in the big house: Lady Runcie-Campbell's children, Roderick and Sheila.

 Yonder: see Glossary.

4 *Ken*: see Glossary.

 It just wouldn't do . . . grand folk once used: Neil is particularly bitter and resentful of the way he and his brother are treated by the aristocracy.

6 *other rabbits would attack it because it was crippled*: this is, after all, nature's way and has been explained as a means of keeping the species strong and healthy, the survival of the fittest. Notice how Duror behaves in exactly the same way.

 quandary: a choice between favourable alternatives, not knowing which way to turn.

7 *thrawn*: see Glossary.

8 *Sir Colin*: Lady Runcie-Campbell's husband, the baronet.

 bothy: one-roomed accommodation for farm labourers, often used to mean a hut or cottage.

9 *feebleminded hunchback grovelling over the rabbit*: Notice how harsh and exaggerated language is used to express Duror's hatred of Calum.

purgatory: now used loosely to mean simply suffering, but originally denoting a place where souls departed this life were cleansed by suffering and prepared for Heaven. It is therefore a somewhat ironic image for Duror, a self-confessed atheist.

So passionate had been his visualising of that scene: This flight of fancy, virtually a hallucination, is the first sign that Duror is intermittently losing control of his mental faculties.

10 *like the whining prostrations of a heathen*: Since the predominant image of Calum is as a meek, humble, Christ-like figure, this simile is highly ironic and shows how Duror's hatred has warped his judgement.

diabolical: devilish, similarly untrue. If anyone is infected by the devil, it must surely be Duror.

obnoxious: offensive.

11 *tribulation*: great suffering and unhappiness.

When he did kneel, on one knee: Duror kneels on one knee to deliver the blow, not on two, which is a posture suggesting humility.

13 *fratricide*: the killing a brother. Notice that at this stage Duror contemplates killing both brothers.

Chapter 2

14 *and wished he had waited in the wood a half-hour longer*: Duror wishes to be left alone with his preoccupations and rejects the friendly company of the talkative Dr Matheson.

inanities: silly or empty-headed remarks. Much of what the doctor has to say is, of course, quite the reverse.

15 *monarch of the woods*: sole and absolute ruler.

pine: waste away (for want of food).

scunnersome: see Glossary.

16 *sleekit*: see Glossary.

as stripped of emotion as a winter tree: another use of the tree image; see Introduction, page xxvii.

vicissitudes: changing moods which occur naturally.

palmy: flourishing, fruitful.

17 *Mars had claimed his nymphs and paid them well.* Mars, the God of War, had created work for his nymphs, young women, in munitions factories.

stoicism: firmness and courage in the endurance of adversity.

thrawn: see Glossary.

What she was for doing to Hitler: the things she said she would like to do to Hitler.

Home Guard: a part-time defence corps created during the war for men whose jobs were regarded as essential or who were too old for military service.

19 *deranged*: disturbed the normal workings of, unhinged.

20 *insinuation*: a remark which attempts to curry favour by indirect suggestion or persuasion.

whins and briers: both thorny shrubs.

inveterate petulance: obstinate peevishness and impatience.

21 *wheedling*: softly persuasive.

coquettish: flirtatious.

bonniest: see Glossary.

22 *Stalingrad*: The battle of Stalingrad marked the beginning of the German decline and was one of the major turning points of the Second World War. Although the Germans occupied the city in August 1942, the Russians held a crucial hill and subsequently reversed the tide, freeing the city by January 1943 and capturing and killing an estimated 330,000 German troops.

23 *lassie*: see Glossary.

24 *forby*: see Glossary.

Aye: see Glossary.

wean: see Glossary.

Chapter 3

30 *policies*: see Glossary.

iridescent: glittering with the colours of the rainbow.

contrition: repentance.

a time of innocence before evil and unhappiness were born: Duror's hatred is now too far gone to be redeemed by the beauty of the morning and its innocent game of cricket.

31 *benison*: blessing.

33 *Home Guard*: see note to page 17.

when all the young cock sparrows have been shot off the tree: when the young recruits have been killed.

with knobs on: humorous idiomatic expression meaning 'definitely' or 'certainly'.

34 *tyranny of Monty*: humorous exaggeration; Monty is a short-legged terrier and much smaller than Duror's gun-dogs, but even pets seem to be aware of class distinction.

36 *tittle-tattle*: petty gossip.

whiles: see Glossary.

37 *gean-tree*: wild cherry tree.

38 *dour*: see Introduction, page xvi.

39 *wee*: see Glossary.

Chapter 4

41 *humdrum*: dull and undistinguished.

42 *gawky*: an unflattering word meaning awkward and ungainly. It is clear from his description of Sir Colin that Duror does not have as high an opinion of him as of Lady Runcie-Campbell.

This war with its dreadful separations: see Introduction, page xxiii.

44 *that incommunicable phantom, his son*: the son that he can now never have.

45 *Betty the landgirl*: the land army consisted of women who undertook to do farm work during the war.

47 *fervent*: ardent, earnest.

48 *callow*: naïve.

conscientious objectors: persons who, for reasons of conscience, were opposed to armed conflict and refused military service in the Second World War. Like many 'conshies', as they were disapprovingly called in real life, they were initially despised by the villagers of Lendrick but eventually became accepted.

patrician: originally a Roman noble and now more generally a noble or an aristocrat.

50 *Are we being unfair* . . .: Even after having asked Duror's advice, which she values highly, Lady Runcie-Campbell is taunted by a final pang of conscience about Calum's participation in the deer drive.

51 *assignation*: arrangement to meet.

Chapter 5

52 *another good tree by the lochside* . . .: recalls the happiness of the opening sentence of the novel; disaster has not yet struck.

tocher: see Glossary.

Gaelic: It is described as the language of Neil's ancestors because it was once much more widespread than nowadays, when it is spoken by fewer than 100,000 people exclusively in the Scottish Highlands.

54 *cushat doves*: see Glossary.

59 *He was like a tree still straight, still showing green leaves*: In this episode which foreshadows what will happen to Roderick when he gets the urge to climb, the tree image is once again used to illustrate Duror's condition.

60 *transitory*: fleeting, short-lived.

61 *he did not shout after him that they would be at the lilypond*: Indecision in Neil's mind increases the reader's curiosity to find out whether they will respond to the summons to take part in the deer drive or not.

Chapter 6

62 *official khaki*: the uniform of the land army.
   racked: strained.

66 *Tipperary*: popular marching song during the war, not inappropriate for the work in hand – 'It's a long way to Tipperary, it's a long way to go'.

68 *saftie*: see Glossary.
   flyted: see Glossary.
   delf wife: a street-trader often selling pottery.

71 *glaikit*: see Glossary.
   bole: trunk of a tree.

74 *oxter*: see Glossary.

77 *patrician*: see note to page 48.
   grandiloquent precept: a principle of conduct, rather pompously expressed.
   I find no fault in them: see Introduction, page xxv.

Chapter 7

80 *beneficent*: kindly.

81 *snash*: see Glossary.
   placating: conciliatory.
   obduracy: hardness of heart; notice how similar this word is to Duror's name.

82 *Wellingtonia*: giant sequoia, the world's bulkiest tree. Found in California in 1952 it is now common in Europe and, fortunately for Neil, has thick, spongy bark.

83 *grue*: see Glossary.

84 *cantankerous*: quarrelsome.
   poke: see Glossary.

85 *hobnobbing with the gentry*: 'hobnobbing' originally meant to drink with and therefore to be on friendly terms with; see Introduction, page xxii.

86 *extra rations*: rationing, the restriction of necessities to a limited weekly supply issued only on production of a

ration book, commenced in 1940 with butter, bacon and sugar. It subsequently covered most groceries, meat, sweets and soap and ended on 3 July 1954 when meat and bacon were finally taken off the ration list. Clothes were also rationed from 1941 to 1949.

86 *bothy*: see note to page 8.

87 *byke*: see Glossary.

Greenock: town on the south bank of the Clyde.

87–8 *tholing the cacophony from*: enduring the noise from.

88 *conscientious objectors*: see note to page 48.

daftie: simpleton.

89 *scrimshankers*: shirkers.

Chapter 8

93 *quixotic*: resembling Don Quixote's exaggerated idealism in Cervantes' novel of that name.

prig: conceited or affected person.

mawkish: falsely sentimental.

obsequious: unduly servile.

94 *the little one is an evil person*: Duror's first public accusation of Calum apart from his conversation with Effie.

95 *whin bushes*: see note to page 20.

96 *panacea*: remedy for all diseases.

97 *blethering*: see Glossary.

98 *saps*: juice, liquids.

mak siccar: make certain.

100 *Keep your shirt on*: don't get angry – an unconscious pun in the circumstances?

101 *scunners me*: see Glossary.

102 *thole*: see Glossary.

Hercules relieved Atlas of the world: Hercules was a hero of classical mythology who had to perform twelve labours in order to atone for the murder of his wife and children. The eleventh labour entailed holding up the heavens on his shoulders while Atlas went in search of the golden apples of the Hesperides.

103 *dram*: see Glossary.

Chapter 9

104 *kirk*: see Glossary.
106 *bletherer*: see Glossary.
   baulked in its virulence: its violence (temporarily) checked.
   M.P.s: members of the military police.
107 *A.T.S. girl*: Auxiliary Territorial Service, now the Women's Royal Army Corps.

Chapter 10

110 *platitudinous*: containing platitudes – obvious, commonplace remarks.
111 *altruistic*: benevolent, caring for others.
   propitiation: conciliation.
112 *self-forgetfulness in opposing any act of injustice or cruelty*: a quality he has in common with Calum and which makes Roderick befriend him.
116 *Alec*: Mrs Morton's son, see page 35.
   acerbity: sharpness of tone.
117 Pilgrim's Progress: see Introduction, page viii.
118 *from the dirty hut ... irradiated a light ...*: a particularly vivid, descriptive passage contrasting the light shining from the stable-like hut with the sinister gloom around, in the darkest part of which lurks Duror.
119 *Had Duror gone mad?*: even to a fourteen-year-old Duror's eccentric behaviour suggests insanity.
120 *like a resurrection*: not Christ's resurrection which brings hope but the resurrection of evil which conquers Roderick's charity.

Chapter 11

122 *stots*: see Glossary.

    sough: rushing or murmuring sound of the wind.

127 *in war-time everybody's equal*: hardly, in view of what is about to happen.

128 *From a safe distance the little dog barked*: like most terriers, the bark is worse than the bite.

131 *quixotic*: see note to page 93.

Chapter 12

133 *This was his gesture of grief*: as in the symbolical scattering of earth in the funeral ceremony.

    heinous: criminal and offensive.

    in such a storm a body might run into a lion's den for shelter: another Biblical parallel, reminiscent of the story of Daniel in the lions' den.

135 *Why is it . . . that the innocent have always to be sacrificed?*: This exchange between Neil and Mr Tulloch anticipates and explains the events of the final chapter.

136 *drooking*: see Glossary.

138 *sharny-toed*: see Glossary.

Chapter 13

139 *incipient*: in its early stages.

    accusing him in a childish pique of being childish: Resentment on the part of Roderick breeds resentment in his mother. Notice that they are both described as childish.

    Shame over her treatment of the cone-gatherers: In following her code – ruthlessly maintaining her social superiority – Lady Runcie-Campbell has harmed her dearest child's health. She is now seen to suffer since her values, and her absent husband's wishes, are in direct conflict with Roderick's happiness.

140 *decimated*: largely destroyed.

141 *Mr Sorn-Wilson*: Roderick's private tutor.

142 *Bhudda*: a particularly pertinent reference in view of the debate about class and privilege. Buddha (563–483 BC), meaning 'the Enlightened One', was the son of a wealthy tribal chieftain in south Nepal. He gave up his wealth to lead a life of meditation and self-discipline in the search for enlightenment. It is clear from Roderick's composure throughout his mother's visit that he has conceived a plan, and once again the reader's curiosity is maintained by the author not revealing it until the penultimate chapter.

144 *the war was no respecter of persons*: the war affected all classes of society.

146 *sinister transformation in Duror, itself an episode from a macabre fairy-tale*: In recognising and drawing attention to the unaccountable and almost unbelievable changes in Duror's state of mind and health, as seen through another major character, the writer makes them seem more convincing.

lachrymose: tearful.

an appeal for help and comfort: Notice that it is only Lady Runcie-Campbell's consciousness of her position that makes her respond to this appeal. There is no question of her showing pity for the misfortune and suffering of a subordinate.

147 *ain*: see Glossary.

148 *By being born . . . , or even conceived, one became involved*: This anecdote from Lady Runcie-Campbell's past reinforces the notion of the brotherhood of man in which class barriers are artificial and ultimately irrelevant.

Chapter 14

151 *shinty*: a Scottish variation of hurling played in teams of twelve.

153 *if she were condemning those frailties, she was not omitting her own*: Lady Runcie-Campbell is as aware of her own faults as those of other people.

tackets: see Glossary.

156 *messianic*: literally, 'of the Messiah', hence Christian.

Duror's other world: the world of insanity, where judgement and vision are distorted.

querimonious: full of complaints.

159 *Why had Duror taken a spite against Calum?* See Introduction, page xviii.

160 *he . . . twice paused, in doubt*: Mr Tulloch is aware of just how vulnerable the cone-gatherers now are with Duror in his present mood. Mr Tulloch's doubts heighten the reader's sense of danger and impending tragedy.

Chapter 15

165 *Peeved, the dog trotted back . . . the fault was not his*: Monty provides a humorous canine commentary on a series of emotional encounters (see also pages 154 and 161).

167 *slunk away in a pet*: in a bad mood from not being made enough of.

saithe: see Glossary.

168 *the subject not of lamentations but of revilements*: Note the humorous exaggeration of Old Graham's self-pity, heightened by use of words like 'lamentations' and 'revilements' instead of 'regret' and 'abuse' for example.

Chapter 16

169 *hirpled*: see Glossary.

seraglio; members of its harem, cows in this context.

A fine world . . . with everybody up a tree: Old Graham has a knack of making otherwise serious and potentially tragic situations seem funny.

Sargasso: a species of floating weed, often found in great masses, as in the Sargasso Sea in the North Atlantic between the Azores and the Canaries.

171 *peching*: see Glossary.

He gave a glance over the loch: The reader might feel that, with Roderick about to fall 100 feet from a tree, this is no time to indulge in thoughts about hypothetical, alternative careers. It is another means of heightening the tension.

not every man was as keen-eared . . . not every man was as bright-witted: Note the humour and irony of these observations.

172 *byremaid*: cowgirl.

thrawness: see Glossary.

173 *but for the boy, pillows and prayers*: Notice that Old Graham's generosity of spirit towards Roderick (which incidentally he makes much of, considering he is only executing orders) does not extend to the baronet.

175 *Even if their wits are all asquint*: Although Old Graham shows the cone-gatherers all the loyalty to be expected of a fellow workman, he is mistaken in this suggestion. It is true that Neil has allowed his grudge to get the better of his judgement, and not for the first time, but Neil's wits are not nearly as 'asquint' as Duror's. Old Graham attributes Duror's behaviour to pride rather than insanity.

bloody poodle a term of derision for Monty, Sheila's terrier.

176 *threshing*: the process of separating the grain from the straw either by beating or mechanical means.

180 *Never had the loch been so potently beautiful*: Notice how the description recalls the opening passage of the novel; the story has come full circle.

parsimonious: sparing.

not for their sakes . . . but for her son's: Notice that in spite of her apparent stirrings of conscience about her treatment of the cone-gatherers on the previous page, when Lady Runcie-Campbell hears the shot and suspects that the cone-gatherers have been hurt, her first thoughts are not pity or sympathy for them but for her son.

supplication: humble pleading; a harrowing image – perhaps recalling Christ's appeal from the cross, 'My God, my God, why hast thou forsaken me?'

Study questions

1 Trace the references to death in Chapter 1. What is their combined effect on the reader?

2 Why is Dr Matheson unable to cure Duror's sickness? Look carefully at Chapters 2 and 8 when considering your answer.

3 Do you feel any sympathy for Duror and, if you do, why? Does your sympathy increase or decrease as the story develops?

4 Look closely at the descriptive language in the opening chapters. What are the effects of these descriptions and how are they achieved?

5 'Deer drives can be revealers of personality' (page 68). In what way do the events of the drive reveal the different personalities of those involved?

6 Chapter 6 depicting the drive is the longest in the novel and the drive could be said to be its turning-point. Consider whether this is an appropriate description by investigating the effects of the drive on the minds and preoccupations of the participants.

7 After the violence and suffering of the deer drive, the visit to Lendrick provides a brief period of relaxation for the cone-gatherers. What does this episode show the reader about their relationship with each other and their position in society?

8 What is your opinion of the way Lady Runcie-Campbell behaves towards the cone-gatherers? If you find fault with her conduct, suggest how she should have acted.

9 Why is it appropriate, in view of the different layers of meaning in the novel, that it should take place in the autumn?

10 Why are tension and suspense important to this novel? How are these effects achieved?

11 Consider some, or all, of the following minor characters:

Betty and Harry, Old Graham, Effie Morton, Dr Matheson, Mrs Lochie and Peggy, Captain Forgan, Mr Tulloch, Corney the soldier, the doctor from Inverard. What are their functions in the plot and in the overall structure of the novel?

12 Roderick is described as having 'a look of dedication, to what the forester could only guess' (page 79). In the light of later events in the novel what do you think is the object of Roderick's dedication?

13 Consider the time scale of the novel and the pace with which the story unfolds. Pay particular attention to the chapter endings.

14 'The perfect exemplar of uniqueness was Christ Himself' (page 49). Apart from uniqueness, what other characteristics does Calum have in common with Christ and how are they demonstrated?

15 Iain Crichton Smith has called this novel 'a fable of eternal significance'. Do you agree with him? In what ways, if any, might the story be eternally significant?

16 Consider the women characters of the novel. Do you find them as convincing as the men?

17 How significant is the novel's Scottishness?

For creative or extended writing

18 Could this story take place in another country? Rewrite an episode from the novel set in one of the following locations:

   a a logging camp in British Columbia;

   b an equatorial rain forest;

   c a Forestry Commission plantation in England.

   The main characters may differ slightly, especially in name, but should be recognisable from their personalities.

19 Imagine that Lady Runcie-Campbell writes a letter to her

absent husband relating the events of the novel. Write the letter.

20 Imagine that Duror does not succeed in killing himself in the final chapter but that he eventually recovers. Write the statement he makes to the police after he is apprehended, giving an explanation for his actions.

21 Imagine that at Duror's trial sentence is deferred pending medical reports. Write the dialogue of the interview between him and the psychiatrist.

22 Write the psychiatrist's report.

23 John Steinbeck's long short story *Of Mice and Men* is often compared with *The Cone-Gatherers* because of the apparent similarity of plot and character. Compare the characters of Calum and Neil with their counterparts in *Of Mice and Men*, Lenny and George.

24 *Of Mice and Men* has formed the basis for a play and an opera. Do you think *The Cone-Gatherers* could be adapted for any of the following: a radio play, a stage play, a film, an opera? If so, describe the qualities which make it suitable for such adaptation.

25 Write the script or libretto of an episode of your choice from the adaptation.